The Siege of Dragonhome

By John Peel

Dragonhome Books
New York

This book is a work of fiction. Any resemblances to actual events, places or persons is entirely coincidental.

Dragonhome Books, New York
ISBN # 9780692779569

For Nicole Lane

Prologue

"The war is over! The war is over!"

Baraktha glanced up from where he was seated. He was engaged in polishing the head of his thrusting spear. He liked to joke that nobody wanted to be impaled on a dirty spear, but the fact was that he was a methodical, tidy man and he took pride in keeping himself clean and orderly. In a war zone it wasn't always possible, of course, and most of his companions hardly bothered. Some, in fact, attracted more flies than the horse turds that seemed to be everywhere you wanted to walk. But Baraktha didn't care what other people did or didn't do; he had his own standards and he kept to them.

Seated beside him, polishing her own spear, was his companion in arms – and bed – Shara. Thankfully, she was another of the few who looked after herself. She was a little on the skinny side, and her hair needed a good wash instead of the quick drenchings it usually got, but she was a good person, caring and passionate. There was no one he'd rather fight besides – and, sometimes, with.

She glanced up as the messenger moved along the line of soldiers, calling out his message. "Reckon it's true?" she asked him.

He shrugged. "The Captain wouldn't let him go on so if it weren't," he pointed out. "I don't suppose it matters much to us, though." He looked back down at his spear. "Best get on with our duties, I reckon."

Shara nodded and went on cleaning her weapon. The messenger moved on, but none of the soldiers moved. After a short while, the company leader came from the command tents a short distance off. He glared at the men and women sitting around.

"All right, you lazy bunch of misfits," he growled. "Pay attention, now. Didn't you hear that the war's over?"

"It's *always* over,' one of the men complained. "Then we end up fighting a different bunch of enemies, is all. Nothing ever changes."

"Well, it has this time," their leader snapped. "The war is *over*. Done. Finished."

Baraktha sighed. "Does that mean we get our pay and go home, then?" he asked.

"Well, no, not exactly."

"Then it *isn't* over," Baraktha said. He knew better than to get his hopes up. This war had been running for decades; the only thing that ever changed was who their allies were and who the enemy were. "Who are we going to fight next?"

"Not that it matters to any of us," Shara added. "You say fight, we fight. Who is it this time? Vester? Stormgard?"

"None of them," the leader said. "We're not fighting any of the other Kingdoms anymore."

"Really?" another of the women asked. "So, who are we fighting, then? The Far Islands? The Sea Raiders?"

Another soldier laughed. "Maybe each other?"

"Yeah, I know where I'd like to stick my spear," another man joked.

"Knock it off, you comedians," the leader growled. "The war's over, and you're not supposed to fight one another."

"Fighting's all we know," one of the soldiers objected. "I can't do anything else."

"Yeah," Shara agreed. "I've been a soldier since I was twelve. If the war's over, what do we do?"

"The war's over, but the fighting isn't." The leader looked around, clearly annoyed with them.

Baraktha sighed again. "Look, we've never expected a lot of sense from the army, but we do expect at least *some* sense. If the war's over, how come the fighting isn't?"

"Because we're not fighting some outside enemy," the leader replied. "This time it's one of our own we have to face. Any of you jokers ever heard of a place called Dragonhome?"

"I have," Baraktha said, surprised. "I've got a sister lives out that way. It's a broken-down old castle on the edge of a chain of mountains. Some mad lord lives there, if I recall correctly."

The leader smirked. "Well, it's not broken down any more. It's been rebuilt and there's an army camped out there right now. They're in revolt against King Aleksar."

"Hang on," one of the men asked. "King *who*? Our king is Juska."

"*Was* Juska," the leader replied. "He died a short while ago. Aleksar's your king now."

"Oh, aye?" The man shrugged. "Juska, Aleksar, Lord of Dragonhome... Don't make no difference to me. Whoever's on the throne sends us off to war to fight for their honor or something."

The leader glared at him. "You're supposed to have loyalty to your king."

"And I will, right enough – on the day *he* shows a bit of the same back to me. Right, lads?" There was a vague chorus of agreement with this sentiment, but most of the soldiers didn't get involved. It simply didn't matter to them.

"Getting back to the point of what any of this means to us," Baraktha said. "Are we to take it that this King Aleksar has cancelled our current war in order to send us off to fight against this upstart Lord of Dragonhome?"

The squad leader rolled his eyes. "Finally," he said. "Somebody is starting to get the point. Gods, you're the dumbest bunch of mud-hogs I've ever been cursed to suffer."

"Maybe," a voice called out. "But any one of us could still kill you before you could move. So I'd be a little more polite if I were you."

The leader looked a little worried, but mostly annoyed. "Talk like that could get you executed," he warned. "Threatening a superior officer..."

"Oh, yeah?" The man stood up. He held up one hand, which immediately burst into flames. "I'm a Fire Caster, and a powerful one. You want to try executing me before I fry you?"

The leader swallowed nervously. "You'd better think about what you're saying."

"Or what?" the man asked. "You know and we know, the only way anybody ever leaves the army is in a box. If there's enough of their body left for burial, that is. So what are you going to threaten me with that isn't already going to happen to me, hey?"

These kind of sentiments were thrown about all day on the front lines, mostly without meaning. But Baraktha wasn't sure this time it would end so peacefully. "Warra," he said. "Knock it off. What's the point of threatening our squad leader? He can't help it if he doesn't have a Talent like the rest of us."

"Because I'm sick and tired of being ordered about in wars we have no say in, fighting for kings we'll never meet, and only until we get killed. At least I'd *enjoy* killing the leader here, which is more than I get out of burning down any soldiers of Morstan, or whoever it is we're currently at war with."

"It ain't his fault," another of the men called out. "He's just a flunky like the rest of us. If it weren't him giving us orders, it'd be some other monkey."

"So?" Warra shrugged. "We've got *this* monkey here, now. We could always make him dance." Casually, he formed and tossed a fireball, making the squad leader jump to avoid getting burnt. "He's kind of nimble on his feet."

"Knock it off, Warra," Shara said wearily. "You'll just end up in trouble this way. And while I have no problem with you being in trouble, you could spoil things for the rest of us."

Baraktha nodded. "Besides, I wouldn't mind going to Dragonhome – I could call in and see my sister again on the way. I haven't seen her in almost a decade. She was always kind of nice to me." To be honest, he could barely recall her face, but the idea of seeing family again after all this time was appealing. He wondered if she'd remember him at all – she was just a baby when he left.

After a moment, Warra shrugged. "It don't matter much to me who we fight," he decided. "I guess I'll go along, too." He grinned. "Is your sister cute?"

"She's off limits to the likes of you," Baraktha told him. "Maybe even to the likes of me. They're not too fond of Talents where we're going."

"They'd better *get* fond of us," Warra stated. "We've been fighting their war for them for long enough – it's time we got a bit of appreciation, if you know what I mean." He started talking with a few of his cronies, his complaining forgotten for the moment.

Shara nudged Baraktha and took him off toward the tent they shared. "This might not be the best idea any king's ever had," she muttered.

"What do you mean?"

"Taking battle-hardened Talents away from the front line here and turning them against some rebel lord..." She shook her head. "It seems to me like he's asking for trouble. Talents have never fought inside a kingdom before..." She looked at him hard. "And what happens after *this* fight? If this King Aleksar tries to send us all back to fight Morstan again... will they go? Warra's right in one way, you know – there's no normals could stop a Talent army if it decided to do what it wants instead of what it's told. Taking us to Dragonhome might turn out to be the worst mistake Aleksar could make."

"I'm sure these thoughts must have occurred to the King," Baraktha replied. "Which brings up the question – why is it so important to him to put down this rebellion? What's going on in Dragonhome that could be such a menace?"

Shara shook her head again. "I don't know. But I suspect that we're going to find out soon." She hesitated. "Baraktha... once this is over... do *you* want to come back here to another war?"

He took her hand. "I can't despise a war too much that brought us together, love," he said slowly. "But – well, if there's a chance of getting out of this insanity, I think I'll be ready to take it."

"If we try and run, they'll just send the Seekers after us," Shara said. "And kill us if they catch us."

"If just one or two of us flee, maybe," he agreed. "But if we *all* do? I don't think they have enough Seekers to catch us all. After this fight... Well, we'll all be almost home again. I think everyone in the company might feel the way we do. Anyway, if we serve the king well in this battle, maybe he'll *allow* us to go home finally. A new king – maybe new ideas."

Shasta laughed bitterly. "None of the old kings have ever done anything good for us Talents, love. Why should this new one be any better?"

Baraktha considered her point. "Well, we'll be in the heart of the kingdom with an army – maybe we can *make* him treat us better..."

"Aye, maybe we can at that," she said, thoughtfully. "At any rate, this is an opportunity for us all. It'll be up to us to do our best with it."

"Right." Baraktha gave her a cheery grin. "Well, we'll fix this upstart Lord of Dragonhome first – and then we'll see what's to be done about the king..."

Chapter 1

Melayne looked around the room at her friends and allies. "We're in deep trouble," she announced.

Devra – inevitably – sighed and looked down at the floor. "So... everything's normal, then?" she commented.

"I wish it were." Melayne had been hoping for a period of respite, time to properly greet her newly-recovered brother and her friends; time to get to know her latest allies; time to play with the dragons.

And, especially, time to go back to the Far Islands and hold and love her children again. She'd barely seen her silent son yet, and she really missed her daughter, Cassary. Not to mention her own dragon, Tura, who had been badly wounded... But she was forced to steel herself and hold those desires in check. There was simply too much to do right now to give in to selfishness.

She and her husband, Lord Sander, were back in his ancestral home of Dragonhome. That was one good thing that had come out of this. She was reconciled with her younger brother, Sarrow. He was seated at the table with her now, the almost-forgotten smile back on his face. She had recovered and lost her older brother, Kander. The endless wars had driven him mad, making him think he had been the Burning God. In the end, he had been consumed by the flames of his own Talent, but he was finally at peace.

Which was more than she was. She had somehow won the fight, but the future was horribly uncertain. She looked at the other faces, all turned to her, waiting for her to explain. There was Sander – his eyes full of love and trust, and the strength she needed to draw on. Beside him, his son, Corran.

He had recently discovered his own Talent – that of being Unseen – and was having a lot of fun exploring it.

Then there were her own friends who were Talents. Devra, first and foremost. She had the gift of Finding, and the most argumentative nature of anyone Melayne had ever met. But she was fiercely loyal and – despite her grumbling – Melayne's most fervent supporter. Beside her was her best friend, Corri. Corri was fair where Devra was dark, and cheerful and sunny. Nothing seemed to bother the Flyer, especially since she'd started romancing Margone.

He was a bit of a puzzle to Melayne. He had trained most of his life to be a dragonslayer, but she had managed to convince him that dragons were not to be loathed, feared or killed. He had now developed quite an attachment to her reptilian charges. But it was difficult to see what he was going to make of his life – except that it would likely be firmly linked to Corri's. He had no Talent, but he seemed to be fitting in fairly well with those who did.

And then there was Poth. Here, though, she was completely out of her depth. Poth was... strange. Well, more than strange, almost crazy. The problem was that Poth had a similar gift to that of Melayne's husband. Sander could touch anyone and see something of their future. It would be something that *would* happen, and he had too often seen the death of whoever he touched. That had happened with his first wife, Corran's mother. It was Sander's greatest fear whenever he touched *her*, Melayne knew – though he had not seen anything like that yet. It could happen at any time to him, though, and it cast an air of gloom over his life.

Poth's gift was slightly different. She didn't need to touch anyone – she saw in her own mind what *could* happen. If person A made a certain decision, then Poth could see the outcome of it. If they made a slightly different decision, then Poth would see something different happening. What it meant, though, was that Poth was mentally living in a number of mutually exclusive futures at the same time. It resulted in her being rather unstable.

It didn't help, either, that she had a serious crush on Sander. She had seen a possible future where he and she were together and she was blissfully happy. But Poth knew that it could never happen as long as Sander had Melayne. Which meant that the elfin blonde woman had a very good motivation for wishing Melayne dead...

Despite this, Melayne rather liked and somehow trusted the other woman. Her own Talent was that of Communication. She could speak to animals, and recently she had discovered that her Talent also extended to people. When she spoke with them, they had to tell her the truth. So she was certain that Poth would do her no harm... probably. There was always the possibility that the Seer might find a way around Melayne's ability.

It didn't make her situation any easier to deal with. And Poth had warned her of what was happening about her that would have serious repercussions for them all.

"Poth," she said, gently, "please tell everyone here what you told me."

Poth blinked, and turned her shocking, pale blue eyes on Melayne. "Which part?"

Right. Not the part where she wanted to bed Sander, obviously, though it was clear from where her eyes had been focused that this was uppermost in her mind. "About King Aleksar."

"King?" Devra leaned forward. "Wasn't he just a jumped-up lord when we saw him?"

"Things change," Poth said, with a mysterious smile. "Trust me, I *know*. Aleksar didn't like being just a lord, and he saw a chance to better himself. The old king is dead – long live the king!" She blinked, and then came back to herself. "So, Aleksar is now King of Farrowholme. But he's smart as well as ambitious and vicious. He knows that he's safe on the throne only as long as he kills Melayne. So he's making plans to that effect."

Margone looked puzzled. "Why does he feel he's got to kill Melayne?"

"Use your brains, idiot," Devra growled. "You've hung about with Melayne long enough by now to know that she's got this huge streak of time-for-me-to-set-the-world-right in her. From what we saw of Aleksar, he was a whiney, spoiled jackass who thinks that being born into a noble family gives him the right to look down his nose at everyone else and to exploit them as much as he can. Now that he's King, he's going to abuse his power something rotten. And he knows Melayne won't stand for that, so he's elected to make a pre-emptive strike and get her first. Actually, it's quite smart of him." She gave Melayne a big grin. "And let's not forget that you had his pet hawk rip his hand to shreds. He's not the type to forgive something like that."

"Not quite the way I'd have phrased it," Sander said drily, "but essentially correct, I fear." He looked at his wife. "It's you or him, and he knows it."

Melayne sighed. "Why does everyone think I'm planning to cause him trouble? I just want to be left alone."

"You're not *planning* to cause him trouble," Devra replied. "You don't *plan* much of anything. The problem is that your nature won't allow you to just sit by and do nothing when you see somebody abusing their power or authority – and, believe me, I'm certain Aleksar will do both."

"Well, not in those words," Corri piped up, "but Devra's pretty much correct, Melayne. You *know* you'll have to stop him. *He* knows you'll have to stop him. So, what else can he do?"

Corran nodded. "The Five Kingdoms are still sending all of their Talents off to fight that stupid war they designed just to kill off the Talents. You can't let them keep on doing that, can you?"

Melayne could see the pain in his eyes. "No," she agreed. "No, I can't. Those wars drove my brother insane, and they've led to the death of too many people. They have to be stopped."

"They *have* stopped," Poth said brightly. When everyone turned their surprised faces toward her, she added: "King Aleksar sent envoys to the other four Kings. He convinced them that you're a danger to them all – a Talent gathering other Talents in a fortified castle. He told them that if you lead a successful rebellion against him, then *they* will be next. Of course, he's quite right, they would be. So they agreed to stop the war and allow Aleksar to withdraw all of his Talents."

"To what end?" Melayne asked, amazed.

"To send them all against *us*," Poth explained. "There's going to be Farrowholme's entire Talent army on its way here to kill the lot of us."

There was absolute silence for a minute. Then Devra sighed. "Well, that news just made my day complete."

Corri snorted. "Look on the bright side for once," she said. "Melayne just stopped a war without doing anything at all. How neat is that?"

"The war hasn't stopped," Devra growled. "It's just changing its location. Instead of being far, far away, it's going to be in our backyard and aimed at killing *us*. That's not exactly what I'd call an improvement."

Margone gave a half-smile. "Yes, but think of all the traveling that's saved us. We don't have to go there to stop it – it's coming to us."

Devra gave a theatrical sigh. "There are days when I think I'm the only sane person left alive. We're going to be attacked, you morons, by an overwhelming force. This isn't the time to be looking on the bright side of *anything*."

"I can't think of a better time," Melayne said, gently. "If we start focusing on the possibility that we'll all get killed it won't help us at all."

"But Devra is right," Sander said. "We are in for trouble."

"We're always in for trouble," Corri complained. "I sometimes think that's Melayne's true Talent – finding trouble, and putting us right in the middle of it." She shrugged. "But what else can she do? She's always right, and we don't have any real say in these events. Aleksar is fighting for his nasty way of life and to keep the power he doesn't deserve."

"We could plan on leaving Dragonhome," Devra said. "Now, before the army gets here."

"This is my home," Sander said simply. "I had to abandon it once – I do not intend to leave it again." He looked around the table. "Of course, that doesn't bind any of you others to staying here, does it? You're all free to go at any time, with my thanks for all you've done to help us so far."

"Well, *I'm* not leaving," Melayne replied. "You're my husband, and I stay with you."

"And I'm staying, too," Corran added. "I'm going to be Lord here one day, so I have to deserve it."

"And I won't leave when Melayne needs me," Corri said.

"And I won't leave if you don't," Margone told her, gripping her hand. They smiled at each other, making Devra roll her eyes.

"And I can't go since you need at least one sensible voice among the lot of you," she growled.

Poth gave a wide grin. "And I have nowhere else to go, anyway," she said. "So I guess we're all staying."

"Then we'd better start making plans," Sarrow said. "It looks like it was a good thing that I made all those repairs to the castle."

"It does," Sander agreed. "And I thank you for that."

"But it brings up another point," Melayne said. "Those Lords that joined with you in rebellion – most of them you used your Talent on, and Persuaded them to help. We have to change that. They have to decide of their own free will whether they'll join us or not."

"And what about the dragons?" asked Margone. "That new one, Hagon, seems pretty set on leaving here – and taking Brek and Ganeth with him."

"Ganeth won't leave me," Corran said firmly. "At least – I don't think she will."

"She may not have much choice," Melayne told him, gently. "She and Hagon are now mates, and they'll be having baby dragons soon. A war zone isn't likely to be the safest place for them to start a family." She looked at her friends and family. "And, on that subject – *my* family is still back on the Far Islands. I had to leave my babies there to come on this quest. I can't bear to be separated from them for much longer."

"But as you said yourself," Sander pointed out, "a war zone isn't the safest place for a family. They might be safer where they are."

"Well," said Poth, slowly, "that may not exactly be the best choice…"

"Another vision?" Devra growled.

Poth nodded. "Yes, and this one's really quite wild." She gave Melayne a sympathetic glance. "The people you've entrusted your children to… They don't want to give them back."

Melayne felt giddy. "*What?*"

"Don't get me wrong," Poth said hastily. "They mean no harm to the children – quite the contrary, they dote on them. And *that's* why they don't want to give them back. They're hoping to make one of your babies their heir."

"They want to *adopt* my babies?" Melayne asked. She was having a very hard time processing this information.

"They'd be happy with just one," Poth said, helpfully.

"They can't have my babies!" Melayne yelled. Sander put out a hand to restrain her as she was about to jump to her feet. "They can't!" she snarled at him.

"We know they can't," he said, gently. "But we have to think about this."

"There's no thinking to be done," Melayne replied. "They're *my* babies, and nobody else gets them."

"They're *our* babies," he corrected her. "And one of them I haven't even seen yet. Of course they belong with us. But Darmen and Perria are our friends and they've been very good to us. We have to try and see things from their perspective."

"To the Seven Hells with their perspective!" Melayne yelled. "They're our babies! Taking our children is not what I would call a friendly act."

"They haven't taken anyone yet," he said. "They are *planning* to, is all."

"That's all?" Melayne yelled.

"Poth, explain," Sander ordered.

Poth nodded. "The Lord and Lady of Far Holme need an heir. They're too old for children. They had rather hoped you and Sander would be their heirs, but now you've got Dragonhome back, and they're smart enough to understand you're not likely to give it up again. So they are working on ways to solve their problem; adopting one or other of your children would answer their needs very well."

"They can't have them!" Melayne growled again.

"So what we need to do is to come up with another solution to their problem," Sander explained, gently. "Poth, what are our options here?"

Poth shrugged. "I'm having no trouble seeing what *is*," she apologized. "But I can see almost nothing of the future right now." She glanced at the narrow window that let scant light in from the outside world. "It's the dragons – I can't see any futures in which dragons are involved. And *all* your futures at this point have dragons in them. You'd do better using your own Sight – it's not affected by all of these beasts about us."

Sander paused at that. He could see anyone's future simply by touching that person with his bare hand. But he always paid a price because he often Saw things they'd rather not know – like their death... But it was true, his power was unaffected by the presence of the dragons. "I'd rather keep that for a last resort," he admitted.

"I understand," Poth said. She sighed. "I can only offer advice, Melayne – and you know I'm not always the most rational person around here, so I wouldn't advise you listening to me."

Melayne had calmed down a bit. For a moment her panic for her children had overwhelmed her and she couldn't think straight. She took a deep breath. "Right. So we have a bunch of problems to solve. First, there's Aleksar and his Talent army. That's probably the most urgent. Second, there's my babies and getting them back." She glanced at her husband. "Third, I suppose we'd better figure out some solution for Darmen and Perria's problem of an heir. Fourth, we have the dragons. We have to find out if they're staying, or going, or breeding or whatever." She glanced around the table. "Did I forget anything?"

"Yes," Corran said. "What's for dinner? I'm starving."

Chapter 2

Devra left the meeting feeling the anger inside herself. She was always angry, it seemed, and it was sometimes difficult for her to sort out and understand the exact reasons for her feelings. If she was honest with herself, quite often she didn't really *want* to understand why she felt the way she did.

Part of it, of course, was that Melayne was just so damned *naïve*! Devra always attempted to offer the smart path, and Melayne just as consistently ignored it. It wasn't that Melayne didn't value her opinions – on the contrary, she actively sought out Devra's advice – but that her own nature led Melayne to frequently do the exact opposite of the smart thing. There was no way around that, really – and, somehow, Melayne's way *did* seem to work out in the end... It shouldn't, but it did.

Another part of her anger, frankly, was that she was losing Corri to that reformed dragon hunter, Margone. She and Corri had been a team since they'd both been taken by the King's Seekers into the army. When they had been freed by Melayne, Devra and Corri had taken the rest of the Talents to safety – always working together. It was as if they were two halves of one personality, really – Corri was bright and cheerful while Devra was dark and brooding. Devra had become used to having Corri at her elbow.

And now she was off with Margone.

Devra didn't begrudge her friend her romance – not really. She was glad that Corri had found someone, honestly. But did it have to take her away from Devra so much? Couldn't Corri apportion her time better? Devra snorted – Corri was always one for throwing herself whole-heartedly into everything she did, so it was hardly surprising she was plunging into romance so deeply, was it? And if the romance proved to be solid and serious? That would leave Devra with nobody...

Devra had been walking through the castle's passageways without really thinking of where she was going. She just wanted to be alone, and to have time to think and to be angry. She stopped suddenly, as she realized that she was no longer alone. Leaning on a door jamb, an idiotic grin on her lips, was that crazy seer, Poth. "What are you doing here?" Devra growled.

"Waiting for you," Poth replied, waving her hand vaguely in the air. "I thought we might have an... interesting talk."

"How did you know –" Devra broke off the stupid question. She was a *seer* – it would have been easy for her to discover Devra's path, even if Devra didn't know it. "What do we have to talk about?" she asked, changing the subject. "I don't even trust you."

"Because I'm crazy, or because I'm honest?" Poth asked. "Can't do much about the former, but I suppose I could change the latter, if you like. Do you want me to lie to you?"

"I don't even want you to *talk* to me!" Devra growled.

"Oh, Devra," Poth chided her, with that infuriating grin still plastered on her face. "That's not polite."

"Nobody's ever accused me of being polite."

Poth giggled. "I've no doubt that's true. Ooh, you *do* have such a seething mess of emotions all curled up in your belly, don't you?"

"My emotions are none of your concern," Devra snapped.

"Maybe not, but when they're so obvious, so raging, it's kind of hard to ignore them."

"Try your best," Devra suggested. She started to brush past the other woman, but Poth reached out a hand and touched Devra lightly on the shoulder. Somehow – though it was very gentle – it made Devra stop and turn.

"Am I the first?" Poth asked, and there was a curious far-away look in her eyes.

"The first *what*?" Devra demanded.

"To see the *real* you," Poth said. "Is it possible that none of your friends have ever seen it?"

"I don't have many friends, and you're certainly not one of them."

Poth laughed in delight. "That's only because you can't see the future like I can. I think we're going to become very good friends."

"You're delusional," Devra snapped.

"True," the seer agreed, not at all offended. "But not *completely* delusional. I see things that others miss – and not just future things, either. Sometimes I can see present things very clearly, too. For example..."

Devra felt like kicking herself in the backside, but she bit. "For example, what?"

"I can see that you love Melayne." Poth hung her head on one side and grinned.

"We *all* love Melayne," Devra said, feeling the anger building again. Why was she even talking to this crazy? "It's why we stand by her, even when she's not being sensible."

"Oh, Devra!" Poth clapped her hands in delight and started to do a sort of hopping dance. "Oh, that's a *clever* way to dodge the issue, isn't it?"

"What are you talking about?" Devra's face was flushed, and the anger was growing. She wanted to slap that silly grin right off the other girl's face.

"You don't love Melayne; you *love* Melayne."

It was as if the whole world had come to a halt. Devra's mind was blank, unable to focus on anything but looking at that idiot grin.

"Love, love, love," Poth chanted, skipping. "You want to hold her hand. You want to kiss her face. You want to touch –"

"Enough!" Devra managed to yell. For some reason, though, she was afraid of being overheard, and she looked around guiltily.

"Nobody here but us idiots," Poth said, somehow catching her thoughts. "I made sure I picked a private spot for our little chat."

"You're crazy!" Devra said. "I don't..."

"Love?" Poth prompted her, which annoyed her afresh.

"I don't love Melayne. Not like that."

"Well, you're right about one thing," Poth said. "I *am* crazy. But not about this. Every look you give her, every time you argue with her, every time you pass near her – it's right there." She considered. "I'm honestly surprised that nobody else has seen it before. Well, not Melayne – she's all too focused on so much, I'm not surprised *she* missed it. And Corri – well, she's kind of kissy-kissy cozy with Margone, so she's wearing blinkers right now. And not Sander, of course! He only thinks about Melayne and me. He likes my behind." She turned around. "He thinks I have a cute behind. Do you think so?"

"I think I'd like to give it a good, hard kick," Devra growled.

"Ah! You *do* like it! Anyway, where was I? Oh, yes, and Sarrow and Corran are a bit young to be thinking about things like that, so *they* wouldn't see it." She grinned brightly. "Well, maybe I *am* the only one likely to spot it, then. But I'm right, aren't I? You *do* love her. Come on, be honest with yourself."

Devra wanted to kick her, slap her, punch her, tell her she was a lying fool... But, instead, she stopped and thought. For some reason she couldn't understand, her anger was dissolving. She should be furious with this dimwit, but, instead, she somehow felt herself nodding slowly. "Yes. Alright. I *do* love her." It was something she'd kept to herself, kept buried. It was the fuel to her anger – the wanting, and the knowing it would never happen. She considered what Poth had said, and found it was all true. When she let down her mental barriers, the anger evaporated, and the understanding was left behind. The thoughts of kissing Melayne, touching her, stroking her hair, exploring her –

She jerked back to reality. There was still an ember of anger inside herself and she worked to rebuild it. "It doesn't matter what I feel or want – *she* doesn't feel it or want it, does she?"

Poth shook her head. "No. Never even occurred to her. Probably a good thing, really – it could get awfully embarrassing if she knew you were looking at her like *that*... No, she's completely intent on Sander, and there's no room in her heart for another love. You're out of luck, totally."

"Then why did you bring the subject up at all?" Devra cried. "Just to embarrass and annoy me?"

"Deliberately annoy you?" Poth laughed. "Even I'm not *that* crazy. No, no, no. I brought it up because I thought we might be able to help one another."

"Don't take this the wrong way," Devra began, and then shook her head. "No, take it any way you like. Look, you're *crazy*. I'd have to be crazier to listen to anything you said, wouldn't I?"

Poth appeared to take this point very seriously. She cocked her head to one side and stared at the ceiling. "No," she finally decided. 'Not crazy – but desperate, perhaps." She grinned at Devra. "*Are* you desperate?"

"I doubt I'd ever be desperate enough to need your help."

"Well, who can tell?" Poth brightened up again. "Oh, that's right – *I* can!" She did a little more of her skippy-step dance. "Come on, admit it to yourself – you'd do almost anything if it meant ending up with Melayne, wouldn't you?"

Devra tried to avoid thinking about it, but it was almost irresistible – to have Melayne, finally, as her own... She wrenched her thoughts back. "I don't think that would include listening to you."

"But you're not *entirely* sure," the other girl said, grinning. "Go on – listen to what I have to say. If you don't like it, you can always ignore me, can't you? Yes," she added, catching Devra's thoughts, "you could even punch me out. So what harm can it possibly do to listen to me?"

"I'm going to regret this, I know," Devra decided. "But – go ahead."

"Let me ask you a question first," Poth replied. "Your Talent is Finding. Finding almost anything, right?"

"You know it is."

"So… have you ever tried using it to Find your one true love?"

Somehow this crazy person had hit upon the heart of Devra's dilemma. She *should* be able to use her Talent to do just that. And she had been terribly tempted to do so. But… She sighed. "Honestly – I've wanted to do that so many times… But I'm afraid of the answer. I know it will show me Melayne, and I know just as certainly that I can't have her."

"So why use your Talent just to confirm that you'll be wretchedly unhappy for the rest of your miserable life, right?" Poth sounded way too cheerful.

"Something like that, yes."

"Maybe," the other girl suggested, "you should be asking your Talent something else instead?"

"Like what?"

"Well, *you* want Melayne, and *I* want Sander. But while they're together, neither of us can get what we want. So maybe what we should be doing is finding a way to break them up?"

"What?" Devra felt angry… and, under that, just a small bit of hope. 'No, Melayne's my friend – I won't even think of trying to break her heart like that."

"Oh, come on – *think* about it. Thoughts can't hurt her, can they? Only deeds can hurt. Besides, if we *could* break them up, it would only be in order to make them – and ourselves –

happier in the end."

"We don't know that." Despite herself, Devra was thinking about it... Without Sander, might it be possible that Melayne would finally notice her..?

"Oh, come on – I know." Poth giggled again. "If we can come up with a plan to break Sander and Melayne apart, then I'd be able to predict if it would work, and what the results would be. And we'd only have to go ahead with the plan if it meant that both of us would get what we wanted from it..."

To have Melayne... Devra wrenched her thoughts back into focus again. "We'd have to break their hearts first, and I couldn't do that to Melayne, ever," she said firmly.

"Not even to save her life?" Poth asked, craftily.

"What do you mean?" Devra demanded. "Melayne's not in any danger, is she?"

"Melayne's *always* in danger," Poth replied. "It's a result of all the choices she makes. She can't help being who she is, and she'll never leave well enough alone. Her heart bleeds for all the innocent sufferers in this world, and she's compelled to do something about them." She shook her head, as if trying to shake cobwebs from her thoughts. "But that's not what I meant." She stared earnestly at Devra. "I *like* Melayne – I truly do. I even admire her for what she's trying to do, and I want to help her. I wouldn't ever lie to her. And I *hope* I wouldn't ever harm her. But the problem is, I'm a bit crazy – have you noticed that?"

"I think we've all guessed that little secret."

Poth giggled. "Now I don't *think* I'm crazy enough to want to kill Melayne so I can have Sander. And I don't *want* to do it. But it's always possible that I might be wrong, and, one day – squish." She made like she was crushing a spider.

Devra was furious, and grabbed Poth by the throat, flattening her against the wall. "Don't you ever even *think* of hurting Melayne!"

"I'm not considering it," Poth gurgled. "But..."

"But what?"

"I can't promise that I *won't* consider it someday."

"I swear to you, if *anything* happens to Melayne, I will tear you to pieces one body part at a time," Devra vowed.

"I'm sure you would," Poth agreed, struggling to breathe. "So I'd have to be crazy to do it, wouldn't I? And I *am* crazy... That's the problem." She waved her hands. "Will you let me breathe now?"

Devra considered it. "Maybe the best thing I can do right now is to choke you to death," she said. "It would prevent you from even possibly harming Melayne."

"But it would mean you'd never get her, either," Poth said.

That was true. Devra eased her grip, and Poth took several deep lungsful. "I'm warning you –"

"You don't have to warn me." Poth rubbed her throat. "Believe me, I got the message." She tapped her head. "But things change. If you help me to break up Melayne and Sander, then I'd have no need to hurt her, would I? You'd save her life and make both of us feel better. If I *did* kill her, I promise you I would regret it for as long as I lived."

"Which would be very little longer than Melayne, I promise you."

"Yes, I'm sure of that," Poth said, glumly. Then she brightened up. "Unless I could See a way to kill her so that even you wouldn't suspect me..."

"Uh... *telling* me that means that even if she's eaten by a dragon or something, I'd still suspect you were behind it somehow."

Poth shrugged. "I told you I was a bit mental. I should have foreseen that... Oh well." She grinned. "So – will you think about it?"

"No," Devra said, firmly. "I'm not going to plot against the person I love."

"You sound so certain," Poth said. "But don't forget I can see what you'll do..."

For some reason, Devra felt guilty, even if she hadn't done anything, and wasn't, really, even *thinking* of doing anything... "No," she said, firmly. "You can only see what I *might* do."

"True enough," Poth agreed brightly. "And I can see that you really, really might do this..."

Devra tried to examine herself. Was it possible? Would she consider betraying her best friend? She really hoped she wouldn't.

Not even if it meant that they would end up together...

Chapter 3

There was so much that Melayne still needed to know, but, for the moment, the most important was the status of the dragons. She missed her own special girl, Tura, who was still in the Far Islands, recovering from being attacked by the dragonslayers. She wanted to see her, to know Tura was fine. But, in the meantime, she needed to talk with Ganeth and Brek, Tura's siblings – and, more importantly, with the two new dragons, Kata and her huge brother, Hagon.

This pair were new and unpredictable, especially Hagon. He and Ganeth were now a bond-pair, and Ganeth was with eggs. Quite how this would affect things Melayne had no real idea. And Poth's Sight didn't work as far as dragons were concerned, so she couldn't clarify anything. Which left Melayne only conversation...

Margone insisted on accompanying her. He'd been trained since childhood as a dragonslayer; she'd helped him to see that dragons weren't the monsters he'd always been told, but she could tell that he still didn't quite trust them, though he was now on good terms with the ones he'd known a while. But he was still extremely suspicious of Hagon – possibly rightly so. Hagon had expressed a desire to kill all humans, and had only been prevented from doing so by Ganeth. Melayne couldn't really blame the older dragon, as his only experiences in the past with humans was with slayers. But if human-dragon relationships were to change, Hagon would have to learn to forget the past.

If he could.

Since Margone was accompanying her, that meant Corri came along also. She had fallen hard for the ex-slayer, and it didn't take Poth's Talent to predict a wedding in the near future.

Emerging into the large courtyard, Melayne could hardly fail to see Hagon; the large dragon was curled up in the center of the yard, his eyes following all movement around him. And it *was* around him – the humans trying to clear up the mess from the recent fighting had to take the long way around the lazing dragon. Ganeth was perched on a section of wall above and behind him; there was no sign of Brek and Kata – they were probably off hunting. Dragons tended to eat only every few days, but when they did eat, they needed a lot of food.

Melayne marched up to Hagon's head, flanked by Corri and Margone. The dragon seemed to be mostly amused by their presence, which was a good thing; it would have been harder to speak with him if he was annoyed. He had promised Ganeth that he would behave, but Melayne wasn't sure how reliable that promise might turn out to be if he got mad.

"We need to talk," she said to him.

"Then talk," he suggested. Before she had met Hagon, Melayne had believed that only she could understand dragon speech, unless a dragon bonded with a particular human; in that case, only the bonded human could communicate with only their own dragon. Somehow, though, Hagon could speak to any human. Perhaps it was because he was the most mature dragon, and had developed the gift. She didn't know, and Hagon didn't care.

"I need to know what your intentions are," she informed him. "Life is complicated enough right now for us all –"

"All you *humans*," Hagon replied. "Life is very simple for dragons."

"Maybe so," Melayne agreed. "But I have a lot of responsibilities, and I want to know how you are going to affect them."

Hagon laughed. "I wish to have as little as possible to

do with humans," he stated. "If you vermin leave me and mine alone, I will leave you and yours alone. Is that simple enough for you?"

"It's a little too simple." Melayne sighed; he wasn't going to make this easy for her, that much was clear. "Everyone who is with me knows that dragons are not our enemies – that, in fact, a number of them are our friends. Ganeth and Brek, for example. My people will not harm you."

"Harm *me*?" Hagon reared up and glared down at her from a height. "Child, *none* of you can harm me. Any who tries I will slaughter. Am I making myself clear?"

Before Melayne could answer, Margone stepped forward. "None of us, boastful one?" he asked. "I trained as a slayer, before I came to see that all dragons are not evil monsters." He eyed Hagon disdainfully. "That doesn't mean that *some* dragons are not. And I know your weaknesses, and how to slay you. We're not all powerless."

Hagon made a rusty kind of noise that Melayne took for laughter. "You are small and weak, and I could crush you in a second. Do not try to pretend to be what you are not."

Abruptly, Margone whipped out his sword and then held it against the dragon's chest. Somehow, he had slipped it between two of the armored plates. "Right about *here*," he said, gently, "is your main artery to the brain – such as you have. One thrust, and you will bleed out."

Hagon paused for a second. "Not before I crushed you to death," he said, but he sounded slightly less certain of himself.

"True enough," Margone agreed, not wavering an inch. "So – we could kill each other, or we could respect each other and talk. Your choice." He stared impassively up at the dragon.

After a moment, Hagon said: "Perhaps talking is not so bad…"

"Smart move." Margone sheathed his sword and smiled gently at Melayne. "That's your cue."

Corri laughed and clutched his arm. "That's my man," she said, proudly.

Hagon looked down at her. "You have made a wise choice," he informed her. "He's almost as brave as he is stupid. Definitely one of the more interesting humans." He stared at Melayne again. "Perhaps my judgment of humans was a trifle... hasty."

"We're not so bad when you get to know us," Melayne assured him. She felt a surge of relief – Margone's bold act seemed to have won Hagon's respect. "But I'm afraid that doesn't apply to every human you will meet. There are some extremely aggressive and irrational ones on their way to attack us."

"Us?"

"Well, at the moment, only we humans," Melayne admitted. "But if they manage to destroy us, they will be certain to turn against you dragons next."

"So you are saying that it is in our own interest for the dragons to ally with you?" Hagon lowered his head so that his eyes looked directly at her.

"Well, at the very least, for you *not* to attack us. But, yes, your help would be most welcome."

His twisted his neck to look up at Ganeth, who was quietly watching events. "My mate seems to be very fond of you," he admitted. "She urges me along that same pathway." Melayne waited to see where he was going with this line of thought. However, he spun his head to stare at the mountains in the distance. "Have you visited those peaks?" he asked her.

Puzzled, Melayne shook her head. "No. I know that they are where my husband's grandfather discovered the five eggs that became Ganeth and her hatch-mates," she said.

"We dragons are very territorial creatures," Hagon stated. "Do you know why there are five kingdoms?"

"It has always been that way," Melayne said, puzzled. "Stormgard, Farrowholme, Vester, Morstan and Pellow."

Hagon laughed again. "You humans, always thinking that the world revolves around you, when all of the time it centers around dragons. There are five kingdoms because there are five great dragon nests in this part of the world." He stared at the hills. "*That* is one of them. Since dragons first flew, that has been the one great nest. Until humans decided that we were monsters, and should be exterminated."

Melayne was surprised, and then a thought struck her. "And in Stormgard – where was the dragon nest there?"

"Close to the sea, on a high peak overlooking a fertile plain."

Suddenly it all started to make sense... "I was born there," she said, softly. "There was a dead dragon buried in the lands my parents used to farm..."

"It was a place of much power," Hagon said.

Melayne stared at her hands. "And it is why *I* have such a strong Talent," she said. "Dragon scales possess power that can be transferred to humans."

The great dragon's head abruptly moved closer to her, and she could feel its' warm breath, like steam all over her skin. Hagon sniffed several times. "Yes," he rumbled, gently. "There is a mild scent of dragon about you, human." He chuckled. "In your blood, not because you don't wash enough."

A joke? The dragon was joking with her now? That was encouraging. "What does it all mean, then?"

"That you're a sort of distant relative, I suppose," Hagon admitted. "And all that you call Talents must be." He leaned down to sniff Margone. "Yes, *he's* just stinking of pure human – no dragon in him at all." He sniffed Corri. "Ah, that's more like it – cousin." He gave a great, rumbling sigh. "Everything has changed," he mused. "Perhaps life is not as simple as I imagined it to be." He looked up at the mountains again. "There is my ancestral home," he said. "It belonged once to dragons, and it must do so again." He looked at Melayne and Corri. "And you – somehow you are a part of us.

That makes you my people – reluctant as I am to admit it, there is dragon in you." The great eyes turned toward Melayne again. "You humans are so irritating."

Melayne laughed. "That's true enough." She had to allow him to work this out on his own, though she finally had hope...

"But it would appear that we have common interests, common blood and a common cause," the dragon said, slowly. "Against my better judgment, I agree to aid you. And that goes for all who are with me. In return –" he looked up to the peaks again. "In return, we get the great nest back again, ours forever."

"Agreed." Melayne nodded firmly. She'd inform the other humans about this agreement later, but it seemed to her to only be right and fair.

The dragons were coming home...

"There is one other matter," Hagon said.

Melayne was puzzled; he sounded somehow almost embarrassed. She had no idea why that should be, or what he had in mind. "Yes?"

'I have been speaking to my mate," Hagon said, indicating Ganeth with a nod of his head. "She informs me that she has bonded with your child."

"Corran, yes," Melayne agreed. Perhaps technically he was only her adopted child, but Melayne couldn't have loved him more if she had been his mother.

"She seems to believe that this bond is something very special, something that even her being my mate cannot sever."

"And I can assure you that Corran in his turn feels exactly the same way," Melayne informed him.

Hagon bobbed his head. "I wish to understand this bond," he said. He *definitely* sounded embarrassed now. "She claims that it is special and wonderful and somehow fulfilling." He glared at her, as if daring her to laugh at him. "So I therefore wish to experience it myself. I require a human."

"What?" Melayne was really amazed now. "Uh... any human?"

"Certainly not!" Hagon drew himself up to his greatest height. "*I* will select the person." His long claw reached out and pointed at Margone. "I choose him."

"Me?" Margone was almost squeaking.

"You."

"Why me?" Margone asked. "I was trained to *slay* dragons, not *bond* with them.'

"I choose you *because* you can slay dragons!" Hagon roared. "I would never take a weak and cowardly human. I will bond only with the best."

Corri laughed so hard she almost fell over. "Oh, this has got to be the best joke, ever," she managed to say.

Hagon still seemed self-conscious. "Do you accept?" he growled. Melayne held her breath – so much might depend on Margone's reply...

"Why not?" Margone said. "If I'm to change from being a dragonslayer, then I might as well go all of the way."

"Good." Hagon stared down at Melayne again. "So – how do we go about this?"

Melayne shook her head firmly. "Oh, no, I'm not getting involved in this. The two of you are going to have to work it out together." She hooked her arm through Corri's – she looked like she needed support. "We're leaving you to it."

As they walked off together, Melayne realized that her world was changing irrevocably. She could only pray that it was for the best.

Chapter 4

King Aleksar's right hand hurt. It always hurt, ever since that damned hawk had ripped into it at Melayne's command. He could barely twitch his fingers, much less use the hand. He'd been one of the country's greatest swordsmen until that point. Oh, he was using his left hand now, and he could still swing a sword and fight, but he was no longer the best – and *that* hurt more than the aches and pains that wracked his ruined hand from time to time.

Still, he was now the king, and – ironically! – he owed that to Melayne also. She had so terrified the old king, Juska, that the fool had been easy to kill. The army – led by the newly-promoted General Krant – was behind Aleksar, and the nobles were all falling over themselves to swear allegiance to the new monarch. But there was so much to do. He'd set the most important action into motion, recalling the Talent army from the war and directing it to attack and destroy Dragonhome. Set a Talent to kill a Talent…

Next things next; Juska had to be buried. And that was presenting something of a problem. He turned to his advisor, Lord Nephir. "What should I do with Juska?" he asked.

Nephir – well, Aleksar wouldn't call him a *friend*, exactly; more of a fellow-traveler – shrugged. "He's dead. What does it matter? Throw the body in some unmarked pit."

"I agree that it's no more than he deserves," Aleksar admitted. "However, it *would* set a bad precedent. I would hate to think that the same thing might happen to me after my death."

"Oh, I'm sure that you'll have a long and notable reign, sire," Nephir replied. "You would undoubtedly be greatly mourned when you finally pass away. And your children would ensure you would have a most fitting and glorious funeral."

"That's as may be," the king agreed. "But *some* people were quite devoted to that idiot Juska. They might be unhappy if there isn't some sort of ceremony involved in disposing of him. And it might look as though I'm simply a usurper if I treat his rotting corpse badly."

"Oh, I'm sure *nobody* would think that," Nephir protested. "Still, sire, you do have a point... Perhaps some sort of compromise might be in order? Say, a quiet but dignified burial somewhere, a tiny memorial raised to his memory? Where those who actually miss the old reprobate could go to feel sorry for him? And quickly, so it doesn't detract from the glory of your coronation?"

Aleksar nodded. "That sounds about right," he agreed. "Very well, I'll leave the details to you. Get him planted with the minimum of fuss, but with a veneer of respectability." Nephir bowed. "And you did bring up the second most important point I have to consider at the moment – children. I need to have some, and quickly, so there will be stability for my line. And to do that, I'm going to need a wife."

"Quite right, sire," the courtier agreed. "Someone noble, beautiful, dutiful and... shall we say – pliant?"

"Yes, you can indeed say that," Aleksar agreed. "I don't want some harridan, or someone who thinks for herself. Somebody who does what she's told, and who is capable of having children. And, as you say, a noble. Draw up a list for me to look over, will you?"

"Of course, sire. Ah, I *do* have a cousin who might suit all of your requirements. The Lady Murine."

"Then by all means ad her name to the list. And see that all of the women on it are invited to the coronation. It'll give me a chance to look them all over at the feast and to start my selection."

"A splendid idea, sire," Nephir agreed. "I'll get right to work on all that you command."

"Good." He waved his left hand dismissively. Nephir bowed and fawned his way to the exit. Aleksar then turned his attention back to the most important consideration on his mind. He removed the glove that he wore on his right hand and studied the vivid scars across the back of his ruined hand. *Melayne's doing...* Making her pay for her actions was his main intent.

The day of her accounting was approaching...

Nephir hurried from the palace back to the grand house he owned in the town square. He hammered on the door until one of the servants opened it and allowed him entry.

"Is the Lady Murine home?" he growled at the man.

"Yes, sir. She is in her chambers. Shall I have a maid fetch her?"

"No – I'll go up to her. See we are not disturbed." He didn't wait for an acknowledgment, but took the main staircase two steps at a time. Two generations back, his family had been traders, and had built this mansion from the profits. His grandfather had been wise enough to loan the then-current king money, and had been made a noble for his actions. Since then, the family had focused on both trading and rising in the court. Now here he was, probably the third most important man in the country, after the king and General Krant. Third seemed a little too low.

He didn't bother knocking on Murine's door. Her startled handmaid looked up, and Nephir gestured at the door. "Close it behind you. And if I find your ear to it, I'll nail the damned thing in place." The maid glanced at her mistress for instructions, and Murine nodded. The poor girl fled, closing the door behind her. Nephir heard her hurried steps trot off down the hallway.

"You might knock before entering a lady's private room," Murine admonished him. "You never know what she might be up to."

"I never know what *you're* up to anyway," Nephir said.

Murine laughed. "One of these days you'll see something that will offend your sensibilities, cousin. You *do* have sensibilities, don't you?"

"Stop being so damned unpleasant," he said. "It's time for you to get to work. Aleksar is looking for a wife. He's throwing a big banquet at his coronation, and he's going to start eyeing up prospective candidates. You'd better get into training."

Murine grinned, and shook her long, full blonde curls. "Oh, don't worry, cousin – I shall dazzle and bewitch him."

"You'll do nothing of the sort!" Nephir glared at her. "He's decided he wants a nice, docile, obedient wife who'll fawn over his every word and bear him lots of healthy children."

"Oh." Murine pretended to be upset. "*That* will take some acting ability. I only hope I can be stupid and subservient enough."

"I'm sure that's not beyond your talents." He stared hard at her. "Whoever he chooses has to be above reproach. Are you above reproach?"

Murine shrugged her pretty shoulders. "As far as he'll ever know."

Nephir knew his cousin. "There isn't any man in your life, is there?"

"Not to speak of."

He groaned. "Is he likely to cause problems?"

"Well, he swears that he's in love with me and is utterly devoted to me." She looked apologetic. "I'm afraid to say he probably means it."

"Damn." He glared at her again. "Are *you* in love with him?"

"Don't be silly, cousin," she drawled. "You should know me better than that by now. It's just that he's rather gifted in bed, and you know I do so enjoy –"

"Yes, I know exactly what you enjoy. Well, you'd better *stop* enjoying it, at least until you get married." He sighed.

"So, what are we going to do about this foolishly devoted... friend of yours?"

"Well, he's coming over tonight for more... enjoyment." She grinned at him. "Don't worry, he has a key to the side door, and always makes sure he's unobserved. Not even my maid knows about him – I'm not stupid."

"Fine. Then he'll get something he's not expecting tonight."

"Please..." Murine held up her hand. "Can it wait until *after*? If I've got to give up sex for the foreseeable future, I'd like to go out on a high."

Nephir rolled his eyes. "Fine – one last romp." He glared at her as a sudden thought struck him. "You're not..." He indicated her stomach.

"Pregnant? Oh, cousin, how much of a fool do you think I am?"

"Let's not get into that. As long as you're certain."

"I am very certain. You needn't worry that the king will have an heir within nine months."

"Good." Nephir looked at her again and shook his head. "The things I do for you," he muttered.

"Deeply appreciated," she murmured back, and then grinned. "I'd be happy to show you *how* appreciated any time." She glanced at her bed.

"I'm not one of your besotted lovers," he growled. "Speaking of which, I do hope that none of this boy's predecessors are likely to show up?"

Murine shrugged. "Not unless you can raise the dead. I do like to be tidy."

"Yes," he agreed. "It is one of your better traits." He started to leave when he felt her hand on his arm. "Now what?"

"You haven't said which of us gets to kill him yet." Murine licked her lips. "You want to throw dice to decide?"

Chapter 5

Melayne felt horribly lost. Events were spinning out of her control – perhaps out of *anyone's* control – and she simply didn't have a clue how to go about solving any of her problems. Above all, she missed her children terribly. How was little Cassary coping with her mother gone? Ysane was a dear friend and Melayne was certain the blonde girl was doing a splendid job looking after Cassary. But – a girl needed her mother, and Melayne was stuck here, in this old castle, and fortifying for a fight, when all she really wanted to do was to get her children and Sander and simply go somewhere to hide. But hiding wasn't an option.

It was hard to believe that just a few short years ago she was simply a farmer's daughter, one whose greatest responsibility was looking after chickens and geese and her younger brother. And now? Now, it seemed, she'd become some sort of war chief, though she had never intended for it to happen. Events had somehow forced themselves upon her and here she was, stumbling about in the dark, juggling. She had a terrible fear that she was going to mess everything up and ruin it all, and get people killed…

"Brooding isn't going to help, my love."

Melayne looked up, her spirits rising slightly. Sander was there, in the doorway, eyeing her with a mixture of love and concern. "Everything's falling apart," she replied. "How can I *not* brood?"

"It's not all on your shoulders," Sander said, crossing to where she sat and taking her hands.

"No?" Melayne gave a bitter laugh. "Well, everybody seems to be looking to me for solutions, and I don't have any. Whose shoulders is it on, then?"

"It's your own fault," he said, gently. "People look to you for answers because you somehow always manage to make them appear. No matter what you've been up against, you've always made your way past them."

"So you're saying I shouldn't be so good at doing things if I want a quiet life?" She snorted. "Sander, I miss our children. All I want is to retire somewhere and live a peaceful life. Instead – " She threw out her hands. "Well, look at it. I'm helping to prepare for war, and half the people out there expect me to lead them."

"You're quite wrong about that," Sander replied. "*All* the people out there expect you to lead them. And so do I."

Melayne felt like screaming. "But why *me?*" she demanded. "I'm nobody – just a simple farmer's daughter. You – well, you were raised to be lord of Dragonhome. You trained for battle; I trained to muck out pigs. You were born to lead; I was born to have children."

Sander went down on one knee in front of her and stared hard into her eyes. "Melayne, stop this nonsense. Oh, I know it seems very daunting right now, and that your emotions are all churning inside you so that you can't see straight. But let's get one thing clear – being raised to do something doesn't mean that you have the ability to do it. Yes, I was born into the nobility, and yes, I was trained to lead and to fight. And yes, you learned how to muck out pigs. But we are none of us limited by what we were born to do, and we are none of us necessarily ready for what we're expected to do. Sometimes our abilities don't reach to those heights – and sometimes they exceed everything we expected.

"You're the latter. It doesn't matter what you were trained to do, or intended to be. You're not limited by those things. Do you have *any idea* why people follow you?"

"No," she replied. "And I wish they wouldn't rely on me so much! I never wanted it, and I never asked for it."

"They follow you," he said, ignoring her protests, "because you have vision. You look at things and you don't see how they *are* – but how they could be. Should be. And you set your eyes on that goal. You aren't distracted by power, or greed, or self-interest. And you let nothing get in the way. I don't always know quite how you manage it, but somehow you always manage to reach those goals. And you know what happens? You inspire other people to be better than they are. You make them see the possibilities. You show them that having ideals to work toward isn't foolish or impossible. Melayne, people follow you because you're going in a direction that they want to go themselves, if only they had the strength or courage to do it." He kissed her hands. "Look at me – before you came along, I was in hiding from the world. I was in hiding even from myself. I was afraid to love, I was afraid to even move. And then you came along and wrenched all of my illusions away and showed me what I was capable of. What I *should* be doing instead of hiding. And look where it's gotten me."

Melayne gave a strangled laugh. "Hiding out in Dragonhome again."

"No. I'm *not* hiding. I'm all done with hiding. Now I'm standing here in Dragonhome beside my beautiful wife, the mother of my children, the leader of an army that will one day change the face of this world of ours. I'm out in the open, and glad of it. You've made me what I should have been all along. And I love you and I am so, so proud of you."

Melayne looked at him and saw that – as always – he was telling her the absolute truth. Somehow, even though her problems hadn't retreated a single inch, she felt a lot, lot better. "You'd better bolt that door," she said softly, "because in one minute I am going to ravish you…"

"There you go, taking the lead again," he said, grinning. "You can't help yourself…"

Somewhat later – when her heart had slowed back to its normal pace and when she'd managed to find all of her clothing again – Melayne dressed and looked down at where Sander was sleeping. He had to be exhausted after all the energy he'd expended in bed... She'd let him rest, even though she couldn't. He had helped her out of her broodiness – her skin still tingled all over and she always felt better after they had enjoyed one another – but the problems still remained. She couldn't simply pretend they weren't there, and they had to be faced and solved. Sander had helped convince her that maybe it was possible to find solutions to at least some of them.

She left her room and headed back to the main hall. As she approached it, she met Devra and Poth, which was fortunate. They were two of the people she wanted to talk with. Devra looked cross, but then Devra always looked cross. Probably Poth had said something crazy to her that had annoyed the other girl. Poth did have a rather disconcerting effect on people.

The elfin Seer grinned and reached out to gently stroke Melayne's arm. "That must have been fun," she said, brightly. "Though I wish it were me with Sander."

Melayne blushed; Poth, somehow, knew what she'd been doing. For some reason beyond Melayne's understanding, Devra blushed as well. Maybe it was because she didn't have a man of her own; Melayne would have to have a chat with Corri and see if they couldn't somehow find a partner for Devra one of these days.

"I'm glad I ran into you," Melayne said. "Both of you. I wanted to talk with you."

Poth clapped her hands in delight. "Oh, good – tell us all about it!"

"*Not* about that," Melayne said firmly. Honestly, Poth was too much couldn't she see how she was making Devra squirm? "We have to make plans for the future, and I need Devra's advice and your insight." She opened the door to the hall, and she saw that Corran and Sarrow were already there. "Looks like we're having a larger meeting than I expected."

Corran bounced to his feet. "Melayne! Sarrow's had a great idea!"

Melayne and her two companions joined the boys. "Good, because I'm in dire need of good ideas. What is it, Sarrow?"

"Well," her brother said, "it may not be a *good* idea, but it is an idea. Melayne, you know I'm truly sorry for what I did to you –"

She gripped his hands. "I know, and it's all done with," she said, gently. He had betrayed her through his childish fears, but he was completely recovered from those now.

"But I still want to make amends," he insisted. "There isn't much I can do here –" He waved his hand to indicate Dragonhome. "But I may be able to do something else to help. Send me to the Far Isles as your representative, and I'll sort out this mess with the King and Queen and your children. It will take one burden off your back, at least."

Melayne had never thought of that, and her eyes widened. "With your Talent for Persuasion, I'm sure you probably could," she agreed slowly. "It might work."

"No," Devra said, flatly. "It couldn't."

Melayne glanced at her friend, puzzled. "Whyever not?"

Devra rolled her eyes. "Look, I'm sure that traitor-boy here is now the apple of your eye again, and all is forgiven. But have you forgotten Ysane and Bantry? They're in the Far Isles, and all they know about Sarrow here is that he sent the slayers there to kill you. If he shows up and claims he's working for you now, they're apt to get just the teeniest bit suspicious of him, aren't they?"

As usual, Devra had spotted the problem. Melayne sighed and bit at her lower lip. "I hadn't thought about that," she admitted. Neither, obviously, had Sarrow, because he sat back down, looking worried.

"Couldn't somebody go with him that they know and trust?" Corran asked brightly.

Devra scowled at him. "Sarrow has the Talent of Persuasion," she reminded him. "They'd just think that he'd forced the other person to do as he was told."

Corran's face fell. "I hadn't thought of that." Then he brightened again. "How about if Melayne writes them a letter?"

"Again, he could have Persuaded her to do it. I know you didn't think of that, but trust me, *they* will," Devra assured him. "It looks like that idea's out."

"Not necessarily." Poth had a gleam in her eye. "How would you manage to get to the Far Isles?" she asked Sarrow. "I mean, you can't just sneak out of the castle, cross Farrowholme and catch a ship there, can you? There's a small matter of the King having troops all over the place, and I doubt you'd be able to Persuade all of them to allow you to pass. One arrow, and phhttt." She made a face, tongue lolling. "Dead, no help to anyone."

"I did realize that," Sarrow growled. "I was thinking of borrowing a dragon and flying there. It's a lot quicker, anyway."

Poth clapped her hands. "There you go, problem solved."

Devra leaned forward. "Excuse me, miss bats-in-the-belfry, I don't see how that is any kind of solution. There's still the problem of his credibility."

"Well, aside from the fact he could just *tell* them, and they'd have to believe him because of Talent of Persuasion," Poth said, sticking out her tongue, "why can't I predict the future with any certainty anymore?"

"Because the dragons interfere with your Talent," Devra said.

"There you go."

Devra rolled her eyes. "I swear, Poth, I am going to punch you any minute – and you won't need your Talent to see that one coming."

Understanding hit Melayne, and she laughed aloud. "No, Devra – she's right! A dragon is the answer."

"Don't exclude the possibility of my punching you as well."

"If the dragons interfere with Poth's Sight, then a dragon would interfere with Sarrow's Persuasion. Sarrow could never use his ability on a dragon, so if he goes back riding one, it's clear that it's because we let him. And if the dragon vouches for him, then Ysane and Bantry will accept him."

Devra opened her mouth to reply, and then shut it again. After a moment, she admitted: "You may have something there."

Corran clapped his hands. "So that's solved, then."

"Not quite," Devra said. She gestured at Sarrow. "The dragons aren't too happy with him, you know. After all, he was the one who set the slayers after them, isn't he? They may not be willing to cooperate with him. They may think it's a great idea to take him up a few hundred feet and drop him on his head."

"I'll talk to them," Melayne said. "They wouldn't lie to me."

"How do you know?" Devra countered. "If everyone else's Talent goes wonky around dragons, surely yours does, too?"

Melayne shook her head. "It's nothing to do with my Talent," she said. "Dragons think differently to people – they don't even consider lying. It's beneath them. If they promise to take Sarrow safely to the Far Isles, they will keep their word."

Corran jumped to his feet. "Come on, Sarrow," he said, excitedly. "Let's go and talk to Ganeth. I'm sure she'll help out." He rushed to the door.

Sarrow stood up with more grace. "Children..." he muttered, and then followed the other boy.

Left alone with her friends, Melayne turned to Poth. "Thank you for your help," she said. "That was a clever idea."

"Oh, she's too clever by half sometimes," Devra muttered.

"Don't be ungracious, Devra," Melayne chided her. "I think Poth did well."

"Do I deserve a reward?" Poth asked, brightly. "I could wake Sander up in a most pleasant way…"

"And then again…" Melayne sighed.

Chapter 6

"Are you going to visit them?"

"Hmmm?" Baraktha looked up from the campfire he was cooking a rabbit over, and saw Shara looking down at him, an odd expression on her face. Almost... hopeful.

"Your family," she explained. "You said you have a sister who lives near this Dragonhome place."

"Do you have any family, Shara?" he asked her, realizing it was a question that had never occurred to him before to ask her.

"Maybe. I don't know. I have no way of knowing, and they live over in the east, and we're not going anywhere near them. But we're going where your family lives."

Despite everything that they had been through together, somehow Shara had never lost her optimism. Baraktha couldn't understand this, though it was one of the things he loved about her. "You're all the family I have," he told her. "I don't need any more."

"But..." She floundered for words. "Your *sister*. Don't you want to know what happened to her?"

"No." He could see the disappointment in her face with his reply, and he struggled to find the right words to explain his reasons. "Talents tend to run in families," he explained. "I'm a talent, so she's probably a Talent too. In which case, as soon as it became obvious, she'd have been shipped off to war. She's probably dead by now. And if I Look for her, then I'll know. If I don't Look, then maybe, somehow, by some miracle she's still alive. But if I Look, then I'll *know*."

"Oh." She sat down beside him as he turned the rabbit so it wouldn't char too badly. "Did you ever Look?"

"Of course I did, when I was first conscripted." He didn't like talking about this, but he couldn't refuse to answer her. He had told her the truth, that she was the only family he had now, and he couldn't refuse her anything that was in his power to give her. "I was so horribly scared and lonely back then, a lifetime ago. As soon as it was obvious what my Talent was, my parents didn't wait – they called in the Seeker immediately and turned me in." Their betrayal still caused pain, but it was an old wound and he could almost ignore it.

"They must have been very loyal to the King," Shara suggested.

"No; they were terrified of me. I was able to Look, and I could find out all of their secrets." He shrugged. "I was too young to understand why they were scared of me, just that they were." He smiled, sadly. "You know what they funny thing is? I never Looked at them. I still don't know what it was that they were so afraid I'd see." He laughed. "You know what I did Look and see? There was this girl who lived in my village, very pretty, a couple of years older than me. Growing in all the right places, you know what I mean? Well, I Looked at her when she was bathing one day..." He blinked. "I hope that doesn't disappoint you?"

"Given your Talent, I'm surprised you didn't do it to more than one girl." She scowled. "Or do you still do that?"

"You're the only girl for me, love – you know that. Besides, you know I can only Look at a person when I've got something of theirs to touch."

She smiled to show him she wasn't really upset. "And your parents found out?"

He shrugged. "She had a mole on her left buttock. I told a friend and in days everybody in town knew about it. She was furious, and my parents were scared, and that was it. I was shipped off the next day. I didn't have much warning – the only thing I brought with me from home was a lock of my sister's hair, wrapped in a cloth. When I was scared or really lonely, I used to take it out and Look at her growing up." He sighed. "At first, I used to do it quite a bit, but as the years passed, I just slowly stopped. The last time I Looked, she was just about old enough for a Talent to start showing. Then I got terrified I'd see her being shipped off to die. I haven't Looked since."

"Poor dear." She leaned in and kissed his cheek. "Do you still have that hair?"

He gestured at his pack. "It's in the bottom of that. I don't Look, but I won't ever lose it."

Shara sighed. "I wonder about my family all of the time," she confessed. "I was an only child – my parents married late in life. But I had a lot of cousins, and we were quite close." She smiled at him. "I used to cry myself to sleep every night when I was conscripted. My Talent couldn't help me get any information about them, unlike yours."

"If…" he said, slowly. Then: "Do you have anything of theirs?"

She shook her head. "No. I didn't get a chance to bring anything with me. My parents tried to hide me from the King's Men, but the Seeker found me and dragged me off." There was a tear in her eye. "I don't even know if my parents were arrested and punished for trying to save me."

"They sound like really good people," he said gently. "I wish mine had been more like that. I'm sorry I can't help you to know."

She sighed again. "Maybe, after this battle is over, we could go east?" she suggested. "Just to see…"

"Love, you're crazy," Baraktha said, though he tried to say it as gently as possible. "We may be heading off to Dragonhome to fight, but there's no way that the King won't start up the wars again as soon as that's over and then ship us all out again."

"Oh, I'm sure that's what he *intends*," Shara agreed. "But once we're away from the wars – how is he ever going to be able to force us to go back? We're an army of Talents, love, and he doesn't have enough men to control us. If he did, he wouldn't need us to attack this renegade lord of his. He'd use his own men instead."

"True enough," he agreed. "And you know I'm in favor of that." He gestured at the encampment, where the rest of the army was cooking, working or resting. "But we don't have a leader, and everyone will want to go their own way. If we're in twos and threes, then we'll be pretty easy to pick off."

"Then what this army needs is a leader – a *real* leader, not that non-Talented idiot we've got in charge of us right now. Somebody that the other Talents will follow."

He knew where this was headed, but he had to ask. "You got somebody in mind?"

"You, of course." She gripped his hands. "You keep our squad going, and you could do the same with the rest of the Talents if you had a chance. People trust and like you, and they'd follow you if you led them. What do you say to that?"

"I say you'd better let go of my hands so I can turn that spit. Trust me, you don't want to eat burnt rabbit."

Shara glared at him. "I'm serious!"

"So am I." He pulled his hands free and smiled gently at her before turning the rabbit. "Look, I agree with your aims and I definitely agree that we need a Talent to lead us. But I don't think it's me, love. All I really want to do is to get far away from fighting, settle down with you and raise kids of our own. And I will *not* be like my parents, I promise you that."

"And that's what I want, too," Shara agreed. "And there's just one way that can happen – if we don't return to war. And the only way we won't return is if we take control of our own lives. We have to make certain that the king never gets control over us again, and that means we have to fight for ourselves and not for him. And for that we need a leader. And the only person I'll follow blindly is *you*."

He felt so lucky that he had found this woman; she truly did complete his life. But she just didn't see the realities of life. Despite all, her optimism hadn't been crushed.

He hated to be the one to do it.

"Do you like bosh nuts?" he asked her.

"What?" She was confused by the change of subject. "Yes, of course – I loved them as a child. I haven't had any in years. What does that have to do with anything?"

"There's a town not far from here. As soon as we've eaten this overcooked rabbit, I'll take you there. There must be someone there who sells bosh nuts. I'll buy you some."

"We're supposed to march on after our food," she pointed out.

"We'll slip away and catch up with the march later," he promised her. "There's something I have to show you."

She shrugged, and accepted her half of the rabbit. It was very hot, but she bit into it, and the juices ran down her chin. "You're right, this is overcooked," she agreed.

"Next time you cook, then," he said, grinning around a mouthful of meat.

As Baraktha had expected, there was a marketplace in the center of the small town. They got a lot of funny looks as they walked through the streets to reach it, and a couple of people even spat as they passed. Shara must have seen this, but she chose to ignore it.

People knew that they were Talents, of course. News traveled faster than an army could march, so these townsfolk knew that the Talent army was passing their town. So when two strangers armed with swords and bows came among them, it was obvious who they had to be.

Baraktha ignored the looks and whispers also. There was no point in taking offense at everyone. Instead, he moved through the market until he found a nut seller.

"You got bosh nuts?" he asked the man, gently.

The man spat on the ground, inches from Baraktha's feet. "Not for the likes of you," he said. "We don't serve Talents here."

Baraktha shrugged. "Probably because you don't get many," he said, affably. He jingled a couple of coins in his hand. "We can pay."

"I won't take your money, and I won't do business with you," the stall holder said. "Neither will anyone else in this market." He spat again, this time closer to Shara's feet. "We don't want your kind around here."

Baraktha turned to Shara. "See?" he said, simply. "We can't simply slip back into society again – regular folks don't like us and don't want us."

"You got that right," the merchant agreed. "Now get away from my stall, and take your stupid, ugly bitch with you."

Baraktha had been expecting hostility, which was how he had managed to keep his temper until control so far. But he couldn't let anyone insult his woman like that. "Friend," he said, gently, dangerously, "it's not very wise to insult a Talent, especially when you don't know what he can do. But you're lucky you're dealing with me, because my Talent is a gentle one. I simply Look." He reached out and gripped the man's arm, tightly. "Ah, your wife handled these clothes, didn't she? Why don't I take a Look at what she's doing?"

The images started to form, overlaying reality. "Oh, she's very pretty, isn't she? At least, if it is her I'm seeing. Blonde woman, about my girl's height. She was wearing a red dress earlier, right?"

The stall holder glared at him angrily, but he couldn't jerk his arm from Baraktha's grip. "Yes, that's her," he agreed. He was starting to look worried.

"Small scar on her thigh," Baraktha continued. "About here." He used his other hand to show where he meant on his leg.

"She dropped a knife a few days ago, and cut herself," the vendor said. He'd stopped trying to pull free now. "How can you know that?"

Baraktha smiled, tightly. "Because her dress is on the floor of your bedroom, and she's..." His smile grew. "Do you know someone a bit taller than me? Dark hair, *very* hairy chest. Friendly grin, missing a tooth –" He tapped his lower right incisor.

"My neighbor. We're good friends."

"You'd have to be, considering what he and your wife are doing," Baraktha said. "He seems to enjoy playing with her breasts..."

"The *bastard!*" the vendor hissed. This time he did pull free, and he turned and ran. "I'll kill them!"

Baraktha turned his attention back to the now unoccupied stall. "Ah, he *does* have some bosh nuts – I thought so." He picked up a small bowl of them. "Want one?"

Shara glared at him. "You did that deliberately!" she accused him. "You Looked for something to hurt him."

He shrugged. "I knew I wouldn't have to look far. He's a very unpleasant man, and people always pay his sort back, one way or another." He crunched one of the nuts. "Delicious – go on, have one."

Shara was still annoyed. "He'll kill them, now that he knows what they're doing."

He shrugged again. "Maybe they'll kill him instead," he suggested. "The neighbor has a knife in his belt. Of course, the belt is on the floor, along with the rest of their clothing. And they *do* seem rather preoccupied..."

"Don't you *care?*" Shara demanded.

"No," he said, honestly. "I *don't* care. Shara, look around you – these people all hate and fear us because we're Talents. Try and understand that this will happen wherever we go. We can't just retire from the army and become ordinary citizens because we're *not* ordinary, and the ordinary won't let us be. We're *Talents*, and at the moment that means that we're not wanted by the majority of the population." He held her hands gently. "Look, love – I'd like to be able to retire and grow old with you and raise lots of kids. But it simply isn't going to happen. It can't."

There were tears in her eyes. He'd hurt her, and he was sorry for it. But there was no help for it. She had needed to understand how life really was, not how she imagined it to be.

"Then what can we do?" she whispered.

"Two things," he said, gently. "First, try to forge a new way of living somehow. Once this battle is over, we'll have to find some way to avoid going back to the endless wars, and find a life we *can* live. Unfortunately, I simply don't know what that can possibly be."

She used the sleeve of her tunic to wipe away her tears. "We'll figure it out, somehow," she vowed. "And what's the second thing?"

"Oh." He picked up the nuts again. "Eat these all up – they *really* are as good as I remembered them."

Chapter 7

"I cannot take being a prisoner any longer!" Tura reared up, her wings spreading, clutching at the sky.

"Sister, stop being so dramatic," Loken hissed. "People will start mistaking you for a human. You're not a prisoner, you're an invalid. Your wing is not yet healed."

"I am fully healed!" Tura insisted. "Did I not fly around the Far Isles yesterday?"

Loken glared at her sister dragon. "And am I not aware of the pain you suffered last night? You are being foolish. You must rest. The flight to rejoin Melayne is hundreds of miles, much of it over the ocean. You will do neither her nor yourself any good if you exhaust yourself over the sea, fall and drown. Leave foolishness to humans and think like a dragon!"

Tura knew her sister was speaking the truth, but it was a truth she did not wish to see, nor to acknowledge. They were both perched on the cliffs beside the crashing waves on the edge of Far Holme. The castle and villages where most of the local humans lived were quite some distance, and here there was simply peace and nature. Except for two quarrelling dragons, each focused on differing goals.

"Melayne needs me," Tura said, for at least the hundredth time since they had been separated. "You know what she is like – she is certainly in trouble, and I feel as though I am betraying her by not joining her."

"Sister," Loken snapped, "I am well aware of how intemperate Melayne can be. And she is *always* in trouble, because she cannot mind her own affairs and leave others to do the same." Before Tura could protest, Loken held up a claw. "Yet I know that without her passion, the five of us would have perished years ago. We all owe her so much, not just you."

"But she is *my* human and not yours," Tura pointed out.

"Also true," Loken agreed. "I have my own human." Ysane, of course.

"And your human is *here*," Tura hissed. "You cannot know what I am experiencing, I who am so far from my human."

"I can empathize," Loken said. "And your human charged me and our brother to keep you safe. That I aim to do, with or without your consent. We will allow you to fly to Melayne only when we are certain that you can survive the journey."

"Then I *am* a prisoner!"

Loken was clearly running out of patience. "Have it your own way, then," she snapped. "If you will not stay as an invalid, then you will stay as a prisoner. But in either case – you will stay."

Tura faced off against her sister. "If I am a prisoner, then," she said, 'you will have to restrain me."

There was a clatter of wings in the air above them, and then their sibling Shath settled to the rocks beside them. "Are you two fighting again?" he asked, bored. "You two are so emotional about everything. What is it this time? Oh, the usual." He shrugged his great shoulders in an almost human fashion. "Stop it, both of you, or I shall claw you both so badly you'll take a year to heal."

Tura wasn't at all certain he could – or would – make good on that threat, but with the two of them here, she knew that she could not possibly get away now. She *might* be able to dodge or fight off Loken, but there was no way she could beat the two of her siblings. She would be forced to remain here at least another day.

And, if she was honest, her wing still hurt from yesterday's exertions...

"Very well," she sighed, and settled back.

"Good." Shath seemed to be alert. "Now the two of you have finished acting like humans for a while, smell the air, my sisters."

Puzzled, Tura gave a great sniff, and started to analyze what she could smell. There was the salt from the ocean first and foremost. Mingled with that, there was the smell of fish... a school of them, off about a quarter mile at sea. Her stomach started to rumble at the thought of them. Atop that, there was the scent of burning logs from the human inhabitations, and mingled strongly with that the stench of the humans themselves. There were delicate fragrances on the air from the flowers of the islands, and the stronger scent of the birds.

And then, faintly but clearly, a *new* scent. But not a new scent...

"A *dragon*," she said, softly. "Could it be Brek or Ganeth back again?" She missed her two siblings.

"Is your nose as damaged as your wing?" Loken snapped. "That is not their scent. Yet it *is* a dragon..."

"A *new* dragon," Shath exclaimed, happily. "We are *not* the last survivors of our kind, clearly – there is at least one more. And a *female*." He hissed happily to himself, and Tura knew that he was thinking the obvious – a potential mate. Well, she could hardly blame him – for there to be any further dragons, they would all need to seek mates from outside their sibling clutch.

"A female with the smell of a male about her," Loken said, somewhat meanly. "You're a little too late there, brother."

"Pfah!" Shath cried. "Well, where there is one female, there may well be more."

"Perhaps she has a sister," Tura said, gently.

"Or a brother..." Loken said, hopefully.

"She will be here shortly," Tura said. "We can interrogate her then."

"Why is she coming here?" Loken asked suddenly. "How could she know that there are other dragons here?"

"Perhaps she didn't know," Shath answered. "Perhaps she was simply passing, and caught scent of us, as we caught scent of her."

"No," Tura said. "We are too far from any land here for any dragon to pass accidentally by. Somehow, then, she *knew* we were here..." She took another deep breath and analyzed the scents. It was faint, but she discovered one that she knew well. "The male she has been with – it is our brother, Brek."

"True!" agreed Shath. "I scent him now, too. Then... *he* must have told her how to find us. But why is she here alone, and not with our brother?"

"Perhaps if you can restrain your curiosity for a short while," Tura suggested, "we will discover the answer when she arrives."

Shath gave an aspiration of annoyance, but settled beside them. He was impatient, and she could tell that he wished to fly and meet this new dragon in the air. But it made more sense to wait here, so that this new dragon would know whose lands she was flying into.

"There is a human with her," Loken said, suddenly. "And the scent is somehow familiar..."

Tura inhaled, and agreed with her sister – there was a human, and it smelled like one she had met before, though she couldn't quite place it.

"Another mystery," Shath murmured. "This is proving to be an intriguing day, is it not?"

Now their eyes could make out the dragon, a growing speck in the sky. Tura felt excitement growing within her as she watched the new dragon approaching. In moments, the new female was overhead, killing her speed, and falling down to join them on the rocks. Her human slipped off her back and stroked her neck. The two were clearly bonded.

There was something vaguely familiar about the young human male, though Tura still couldn't place him. But she had seen him and smelled him before...

The new dragon bowed her head in respect. "I am Kata," she announced. "Sister to the great dragon Hagon. I am mated to Brek, your brother."

"You are welcome, mate of our brother," Tura said, before either of her siblings could respond. "I must ask you – do you have news of Melayne?"

Kata laughed. "Ah! You must be Tura, then! Yes, my new sister, I have messages for all of you, and I shall deliver them in turn. But first, there is something that must be clarified." She inclined her head to the man-child with her. "This is Sarrow, brother to Melayne."

Sarrow! Now that he had been named, all three of them remembered him – brother indeed to Melayne – and traitor! Tura hissed angrily and rose to strike. In that, she was matched instantly by Loken and Shath. Kata moved swiftly to interpose her body between the three dragons and the oddly unmoved human.

"Stay!" Kata cried, urgently. "He is not the same child he once was. He has changed, and become staunch ally to his sister."

"He is traitor to his sister – and to us," Shath exclaimed. "He betrayed us to the humans, and sent slayers to hunt us down and kill us."

Tura flexed her injured wing. "It is solely because of his actions that I am unable to be with Melayne," she growled. "Let me have him, and he will pay for his crimes."

"No!" Kata would not back down. "I dispute none of what you say – but he has changed, and he is *my* human now. I will allow none of you to harm him."

"Do you truly believe that you can stop all three of us?" Shath asked.

"Perhaps not," Kata conceded. "But there is no reason for us to discover the answer to that. Sarrow is here on an important mission for Melayne, one that none of you would wish to interfere with." She looked at them each in turn. "Allow us to pass and to speak with the humans here. You will find that what I say is true."

Shath looked to his sisters. "Can we believe this?"

"I do not trust her," Loken spat. "And I most certainly would not trust *him*."

"And yet," Tura said gently, "dragon cannot lie to dragon. Can you not feel that what she tells us is true?"

"It is not *true*," Shath argued. "It is merely what she *believes* to be true. Do you not recall that Sarrow has the Talent of Persuasion? He can compel all to do his bidding."

"All *humans*," Tura corrected him. "Talents cannot affect dragons."

"As far as we know," Loken said. "But we did not previously know that other dragons existed. It may be that there *are* Talents who can affect dragons, and that we simply had no earlier example of this."

There was a measure of truth in what Loken had suggested, Tura knew. Simply because they had no experienced something before was no proof that it was impossible. Still… "If Sarrow can bend Kata's mind to his will, then surely he could do the same with ours?" This seemed logical to her. "And yet he has not done."

"She and he are linked," Loken answered. "He cannot communicate with us, so he cannot affect our minds. If we allow him to go to the other humans, he will be able to control them. We three must stop him, here and now." She glared at Kata. "If we have to slay our brother's mate to prevent this evil, then so be it."

"Dragon does not kill dragon," Tura said. "Only humans kill their own kind."

"But she is not in her right mind," Shath argued. "Sarrow must be killed, and if we have to slay Kata first, then we must."

"You are wrong," Kata said coldly. "I am in full possession of my own mind, and not affected in any way by this human Talent. And he is here on behalf of Melayne."

"So, we are to simply believe your word and allow him access to other humans who he quite certainly *can* control?" Shath shook his head. "No, Melayne would not wish us to do that."

"She wishes you to allow Sarrow passage and to join with me in supporting him," Kata stated. "If you attempt to stop us, you will be disobeying Melayne."

"And if Sarrow is controlling Melayne's thoughts?" Loken asked. "What then? We cannot trust so deeply without proof."

"And you will not accept the proof you are offered," Kata answered. "We are at an impasse, it would seem."

"One quite easily resolved," Shath replied, "by your death..."

Chapter 8

Sarrow had been paying careful attention to the dragons. He couldn't understand the three new dragons, but he could understand Kata. From what she was saying and the body language and tone of the other three, he could see that things were getting rather nasty. It seemed almost certain that these siblings were intending to attack Kata. Strong as she was, Kata wouldn't really stand a chance against three dragons in a fight.

In the past, Sarrow had been terrified of the dragons. They seemed so wild and unpredictable, so uncontrollable. A lot of his fears had been erased by Melayne, and the terrifying pressure he had felt all of his life to simply survive had been lifted. He'd been able to approach Kata with only minimal hesitation, and had been quite amazed when she had decided that he was her human. He'd looked into those dark, mysterious eyes, and somehow he *knew* that they were connected. It had been an astonishing transformation, and he found that he could suddenly somehow understand it when she spoke.

And he had discovered a friendship that he had never imagined could be his. It was as if he'd had a part of himself missing all of his life and it had suddenly turned up. There was a connection between the two of them that went beyond words or even thought: it simply *was*. It had to be how he imagined love must be, something so simple and so right, and so all-fulfilling. He and Kata were bonded.

He simply couldn't allow her to be hurt. Almost without thinking, he stepped in front of her to protect her. His rational mind was screaming at him: *They're dragons! They'll kill you in seconds!* But his heart simply ignored such protests.

For some reason, the trio of dragons paused. He'd probably confused them.

"Kata," he said, slowly and clearly. "I know that they can understand me, but I can't understand them. You'll have to translate for me."

"What are you doing?" she asked him, urgently. "Step behind me so that I can protect you."

"I'm very proud of you, Kata," he said. "And very grateful that you would even consider fighting three of your kind to protect me. But I can't allow you to sacrifice your life; this is a battle you couldn't possibly win." He stared at the closest of the three dragons. Its purplish skin was tinged with green, and there was a healing wound in its wing. "You must be Tura," he said. "Melayne has talked a lot about you, and how she misses you. I know you think you're protecting Melayne this way, but, believe me, you are not. I am here on a mission for her."

The dragon growled and hissed. Behind his shoulder Kata said: "She says that you cannot use your Talent to talk her out of killing us. I believe she is correct."

"I'm not using my Talent at all!" Sarrow exclaimed. "And it wouldn't work on dragons if I did. I am simply being honest with you all. Yes, I betrayed my sister, and yes, I tried to have you all killed. Melayne has forgiven me, but I don't expect you to do the same. But simply listen to me for a few minutes. If you don't believe I'm telling the truth – well, *then* you can still kill me, can't you?"

There was a bunch of growling and snapping between the three dragons before Kata said: "They agree that you can speak, but warn you that it is unlikely to influence their decision."

"I'll take that chance." Sarrow looked from one dragon to the next to the next. He knew his life was hanging by a thread – and Kata's, too – but, somehow, he wasn't afraid. That sick, gnawing feeling he'd felt for so long was completely gone now. "I did what I did," he explained, "because of fear. I wanted so badly to *live*, and I had this power to force people to do whatever I wanted, so I used it, often without even thinking. I was just a child, and it was all that I knew to do. It led me to manipulate and betray my sister. And when I met you, I was terrified of you - and jealous. I thought Melayne loved you all more than she loved me, and that she was being a fool to even keep you alive. All I could see were large fangs, a ferocious face and claws that could rip my flesh apart in seconds. I didn't know you, and I didn't want to know you. I just wanted to live.

"Melayne came to me, and I was ready to murder her to try and keep myself safe. I was so crazy with fear, I was ready to do almost anything. But Melayne finally managed to get through to me. She made me see what I was doing, and why, and how the fear was controlling me, making me do bad and insane things. She helped me to face that fear - and I decided that *I* was in control of my life, not it.

"And when I did, I finally felt at peace. I understood how wrong it was to force people against their wills to do only what I wanted. And I understood how the fear had warped my way of thinking, my way of seeing what was happening about me. And I was bitterly, bitterly ashamed of myself."

He looked at the three of them, He couldn't tell if he was getting through to them, but he had to hope he was. "You three must remember what I was like back then - how scared and angry and horrible. Look at me now - do I seem like that person any longer? Am I driven by fear?" He half-turned and stroked Kata's scaly neck. "Am I terrified of dragons, or has one of your own accepted me, despite all that I have done? I admit to you that I was wrong - more than wrong, *evil*. But I have changed, and I want to make amends for what I did in the past.

"Now I am helping my sister because I believe in what she is doing. She is afraid now - afraid for her children - and she wishes me to look after them."

The closest dragon growled; was it his imagination, or did it sound less angry than before?

"She says that Melayne's children are safe, and that there is no reason for her to fear," Kata reported.

"Physically safe, yes," Sarrow agreed. "I know you would never allow danger to come to them. But the rulers of this land have a plan to take the children from Melayne and keep them as their own."

The dragon roared a reply, and Sarrow knew that was an angry one. Kata murmured: "She says that *nobody* will steal Melayne's children – she would kill them first."

"No!" Sarrow exclaimed. "It doesn't have to come to that! These people are not evil – they simply have their own worries and concerns. And here is something I can do – I can talk to them and convince them to give up this foolish plan of theirs." He gave a small grin. "And my Talent *will* work on them, where it won't on dragons." He spread his arms. "That is why I am here – to set Melayne's mind at rest that she will not lose her children. Now you must believe me or not. If you do not, then kill me – but don't harm Kata." He stroked her neck again. "She is only trying to protect me, and I love her for it. But I will not allow her to die to save me."

"Sarrow –"

"No," he said, firmly. "Kata, no matter what happens, do *not* fight your kin. If they do kill me, go back to Melayne and tell her that I failed." He turned his back on her and faced the other dragons. "Now – make your decision." He folded his arms and stood still, trying very hard not to feel scared.

The three dragons conferred. Voices were raised, claws extended, heads swayed back and forth. He had no way to know what they were saying, but every moment he wasn't killed was a good one. Despite what he'd said, Kata stayed close by him, her head just over his. He could feel her breath on his hair and knew she was looming over him to protect him. Gradually, though, she seemed to lose her tension.

The argument was quite heated, clearly, but the voices slowly settled down from their level of anger, and Kata finally said: "They have accepted what you say. Somewhat reluctantly, it is true, especially on the part of the male dragon. He seems to be rather stubborn – but males as a whole are like that. The females are more receptive, and Tura believes what you say completely. As she is Melayne's dragon, the other two have agreed to abide by her decision. Ah – they do warn you that at the first sign of betrayal they will reverse this decision and reluctantly devour you." He could hear a touch of humor in her voice. "The reluctance isn't because of killing you, but because human meat tastes very bad."

"I understand," he said, feeling a great deal of relief. "And I thank them for their kindness and intelligence. I know how hard it must have been for them to reach this decision, and I am very, very glad they did."

Kata nuzzled him. "What impressed them the most," she murmured, "was that you were trying to protect me from them. I think that is why they decided eventually in your favor."

He stroked her face. "I couldn't let them hurt you," he said. He had never imagined he could ever be friends with a dragon, but now he knew he didn't ever want to lose her. It would hurt more than dying himself. He smiled at the other dragons. "Now," he said, "let us go to the castle so that I can do my job, shall we?" He leaped onto Kata's back, and she spread her great wings.

The four dragons rose into the air together. Once again, Sarrow felt the surge of joy that swept through him from being astride Kata, and simply flying.

It was a short journey to the castle of the rulers. In minutes, Kata spiraled down, the other dragons with her, and she touched gently down in the courtyard. The other dragons flanked her, shaking out their wings before settling down. Sarrow climbed down from Kata and looked around.

"Hey, you!" somebody cried out, and then there was a small band of armed soldiers heading toward him. He held up his hands to show that he was unarmed. The men formed a circle about him, the swords drawn and watching him until their leader arrived.

Sarrow recognized him. "Bantry!"

Bantry recognized *him.* "Sarrow!" he exclaimed, keeping his own weapon leveled firmly at Sarrow's heart. "What are you plotting now?"

"Here we go again…" Sarrow muttered.

Chapter 9

If another man were standing here, he might have found the sight inspiring – perhaps even scenic. From high on the ridge, the plain was spread out beyond. It was possible to make out three villages, nestled by streams, surrounded by pleasant woods. The mountains that served as backdrop were quite spectacular, their jagged tips layered in snow year-round. And, in the center of it all, the castle.

From this angle, the repairs to the castle were quite visible. After a century of slowly falling apart, it had been rebuilt and reinforced in the past couple of years. The walls looked sturdy, the place was inhabited again by more than a lonely lord and his handful of retainers. The grounds were bustling, and there had to be several hundred people living there now.

People – and dragons…

Another man might have enjoyed the view – but to Corrig, it was all irritating. It made his job harder, and ate at his patience – never his strongest virtue, even when he was happy. And he was not happy now.

"This is no way to fight a war," he growled.

His aide, Aimon shifted slightly. "They are not a common enemy, sir," he pointed out.

"No," Corrig agreed. "They're freaks, Talents allowed to run wild. *This* is why they all have to be killed." He gestured down at the castle of Dragonhome. "If they're not exterminated, they'll end up believing that they're as good as normal people. And yet we sit here, doing *nothing*."

"On the orders of the King and General Krant," Aimon said, tactfully. "It is not your decision. They have ordered you to wait."

"Wait!" Corrig glared at the castle. "Waiting is no way to win a war!"

"We have them surrounded, sir," the aide pointed out. "They can't escape."

"They're not *looking* to escape, you idiot!" Corrig shook his head. "They're fortifying the place, and the longer we wait, the more time they have to strengthen themselves."

"But we'll have a tactical advantage once the Talent army arrives."

"The *Talents*?" Corrig shook his head. "Do you think I'm going to let a bunch of freaks steal the victory that should be mine by right?"

"But what else can we do?" Aimon asked, plaintively. "If they were a normal enemy, we'd have them at our mercy right now. With our men surrounding them, they wouldn't be able to get any supplies into the place. We could just sit and starve them out. *If* they were a normal enemy. But they have dragons, and the dragons can bring in anything they need. Why, just this morning I saw one of them drop two whole cows into the courtyard."

"Don't you think I know that?" growled Corrig. "As long as they have those damned dragons, they have an advantage over us. They can afford to sit there and try and wait us out. And we're forced to do nothing…"

"We can't fight dragons," Aimon said, sighing.

"What about those men who trained as Slayers?" Corrig asked. "Can't we find even *one* of them?"

Aimon shook his head. "All the known Slayers were called here just a short while back. They all went off somewhere, and not one of them has returned." He shrugged. "There are plenty of stories of what happened to them, of course. Some say they're on a quest after the mother of all dragons, and that if they succeed, all dragons will die out. Some say the message luring them here was a trap to exterminate them. Some say they died in battle. The truth? Well, I don't think we'll ever know. But it means that we can't look for help from them."

"Then we're forced to fall back on what we know," Corrig said. "And what I know is that it's a foolish mistake to sit here and do nothing, allowing those rebels to grow stronger every day. We need to fight them, and we need to do it *now*."

"But our orders –"

"Are issued by... people who are not here and do not see what we see, or know what we know. General Krant is merely a politician, not a seasoned warrior. He's good at licking the boots of kings, but he's hardly fought a day in his life. You and I, Aimon, have seen more action in a day than he has in a lifetime. As for the King – well, Aleksar was merely a noble until a few weeks ago. What kind of a king he'll be – who can say?" He shrugged. "Anyway, none of that is any of our business – our business is *fighting*, and we know it. And we both know that simply sitting here isn't going to win us anything – and it might just lose us the battle."

Aimon looked worried. "But what can we do?" he asked.

"What we'd do in the normal course of events," Corrig replied. "Attack. I've ordered the engineers to ready the siege machines. As soon as I get the signal to tell me that they're ready, I aim to move in and breach those walls. Once we have them down, then – dragons or no dragons – our men will be able to get inside the place, and we'll have the advantage." He smiled grimly. "And *then* the killing will really begin..."

Corran let his ability to become Unseen slip away as he hurried back toward Dragonhome. He'd been able to observe and hear the two soldiers talking without either of them being aware he was standing right beside them. And he'd learned quite a bit by simply being there.

He was a little worried, though – not over the soldiers' plan, but over what his father and step-mother would say once he reported in. They were likely to be rather angry with him for risking himself like that... But if he hadn't, then they might not know about the impending attack, and people might have gotten hurt. Knowing what the enemy was up to was worth a risk, and his Talent made him rather a good spy.

He felt rather proud of himself, right up to the point when the arrow slammed into him...

Ganeth felt the sharp agony, as if some great spear had pierced her. She screamed, and straightened as the pain abruptly died away. She was shaking, and knew with absolute certainty that Corran had been injured.

She didn't waste a second. Her powerful wings beat and carried her immediately aloft. There were voices behind her, but she barely heard them and they didn't register. Whatever they were saying didn't matter – *Corran was hurt!*

Instinct, the bond she had with her human, the scent of his fresh blood – whatever it was, she *knew* where he was, and she flew directly toward him. There was a sheen of terror for him, and an anger at whoever had harmed him, that should have clouded her thinking. Instead, however, it left her sharply focused. She could see humans below her as she dived from the sky to where Corran's body lay bleeding on the forest floor.

The humans there were soldiers, and they panicked, firing arrows at her – as if such puny weapons could break a dragon's scales! With a roar of fury, she tore into the frail bodies, slashing with her claws, whipping her tail at them. In a matter of seconds, all that was left of the patrol that had ambushed her human were fragments of bone and flesh scattered across the clearing. Not even pausing, she gripped Corran's limp form gently in the claws that had rendered his attackers, and then she hurled herself into the air again and back toward the castle.

"There's trouble."

Melayne looked at Devra as the girl stumbled into her

room. She had obviously run up to find Melayne, and was breathing heavily. "What is it?" she asked.

"Don't know," Devra said. "One of your dragons screamed and shot out of here. The others seem very upset. You'd better come and talk to them. I don't know what's going on."

The dragons? Melayne nodded, and hurried down the stairs. Devra followed as fast as she could. Melayne had no idea what might be happening, but anything that could make a dragon scream was obviously something to be concerned about. Devra couldn't tell one dragon from another – except Hagon, of course – so it was no use asking her which one seemed in pain. Once Melayne was in the courtyard, though, it was obvious that it was Ganeth that was missing.

"What's the matter?" she asked the others. "Where's Ganeth?"

"Chasing her human," Hagon rumbled. "Something has happened to him."

"Corran?" Melayne felt a stab of fear. "Something's happened to Corran? What?"

"I do not know," Hagon replied. "Ganeth didn't say – she just left." He sniffed the air. "She is returning, and I smell blood – lots of it, all human."

Melayne looked up, and saw a distant speck in the sky growing larger. There were other people with her now, but her mind couldn't register them. She was willing Ganeth to hurry back. As the dragon drew closer, she could see that there was a limp body in her claws. Melayne felt faint and sick – Corran?

Then the dragon was back, and she could see that it was, indeed, Corran. He was limp and pale, and the stench of blood was strong. For a second, Melayne was afraid that he was dead. She could see the arrow still lodged in his back, and his blood-soaked clothing. Ganeth was frantic, and it took several seconds until she heard Melayne instructing her to let

Corran go. She finally released him, and Melayne gripped her step-son gently. She could see that he was still breathing, though deathly pale. And there was so much blood…

"It's not all his," Ganeth said, as if she read Melayne's thoughts. "He was attacked by soldiers, and I killed them. But he's hurt!"

Melayne looked around, and saw Sander pushing through the small crowd that had gathered. She could read the fear and anguish on his face. Poth was there, too, with another Talent.

"My son!" Sander cried.

"He's still alive," Melayne assured him. "But he's badly hurt."

"Out of my way, you morons," she heard Poth screaming. "Healer coming through. Move it, you tortoise!" The seer pushed people aside, and Melayne could see that she'd brought Hovin the Healer with her.

"Bless you," she said, gratefully.

"I Saw a need for him," Poth confessed. "How is the boy?"

"Bad," Melayne said. "But it could have been worse." She turned to Hovin, who was peering at Corran's wound. "What do you think?"

"I think we'd better get him inside immediately," Hovin said, firmly. "I need to examine him and to work on him."

"I'll carry him," Melayne said.

"You'll do no such thing," Hovin snapped. "I'm the Healer here, and I don't need scared parents bothering me." He pointed at a nearby soldier. "You look good and strong – you bring him. And be careful." He glared at Melayne and Sander as the soldier did as he was ordered. "You two stay away. I'll send for you when I have news." He glanced around. "Poth, Devra – you're elected nurses. Come on!"

Melayne watched the small party heading inside, and felt drained and helpless. "Oh, Sander," she whispered. "Will he be all right? I..." She couldn't say any more. She was terrified for the boy she'd grown to love.

"He's strong," Sander answered her. "He's a fighter. And Hovin is the best we have. If anyone can help him..." His voice trailed off. Melayne knew why, because she was thinking the exact same thing – what if no-one could help him? She wasn't sure which organs the arrow might have penetrated, or how badly hurt Corran might be.

Corri was there, somehow, and she held Melayne's hands. "Oh, Melayne," she said, her voice filled with sympathy.

"What was he doing out there?" Melayne yelled, anger replacing the numbing fear. "How could he have been so stupid? How..." And then her thoughts dissolved into tears. "Oh, Corri – I don't want to lose him for nothing!"

Corri clutched her hard and let her cry, stroking her hair and murmuring. If she used words, Melayne couldn't make them out. She just wanted to hold and be held.

She had no idea how long this went on. Her mind was too torn to be able to understand anything. Fear, anger, rage and shock warred in her mind, and her emotions shifted and changed, dragging her along with them. Eventually, though, some measure of sense replaced the maelstrom in her mind, and she was able to wipe her eyes and nose and to focus on Corri's face again. "I'm sorry."

"For what?" Corri demanded. "I know how much that boy means to you. I'd have been more worried if you hadn't..." She gestured at Melayne's face. "You're a real mess, you know."

"I don't care." Melayne looked around, but the two of them were now alone. "What's happening? Where is everyone?"

"Sander went off with some of the soldiers." Corri cocked her head. "I think everyone else went off to dodge the tears. They can be catching." Now that she'd mentioned it,

Melayne could see that her friend's eyes were watery, too, and there were dried streaks on her cheeks.

"I'm sorry," she said again. "I'll be better." She straightened up. "Is there any news about Corran yet?"

"No – but you know what Hovin is like – he chased Sander away again, and insists on working with just his two nurses." She managed a pale smile. "Devra's not too happy, I hear, but Poth is surprisingly attentive. I honestly don't know what to make of her, Melayne – sometimes I'd like to rip her ears off, and then she does something kind and gentle like this."

Melayne shrugged. She wasn't going to try and analyze Poth's motives – difficult at the best of times. "Who can say with her? And who cares? Just as long as Corran gets better." She glanced around, and saw Ganeth curled tightly in a corner of the courtyard. "I need to speak to the dragons." She marched across and slid her hand down the ridges on Ganeth's face. "I know how this must hurt you," she said, gently.

The dragon's great eyes opened. "He is my human," Ganeth said, in a whisper. "I cannot bear this."

"I know." Melayne looked at her. "Ganeth, do you know what he was doing out there on his own?"

"He did not tell me," the dragon replied. "I was unaware that he had left the castle. I knew nothing until the pain…"

Corri laid a hand on Melayne's shoulder. "You know Corran," she said. "He was probably trying to help somehow."

"Yes," Melayne agreed. "I am sure that's exactly what he had in mind. And since he's Unseen, he clearly thought that he wouldn't be running too great a risk. He forgets how young and inexperienced he is."

Hagon raised his immense head and glared over at Melayne. "The humans have injured my beloved's human," he rumbled. "They must be punished."

"Many of them are innocent," Melayne replied. "They did nothing to hurt him, and I don't think we should hurt them for it."

Corri stared at her. "Melayne, they *all* want to kill you and everyone here. Set the dragons on them – it's no better than they deserve."

"No," Melayne said firmly. "Those soldiers are mostly young men, some not much older than Corran. They are forced to do as they are told, or they will be punished for it. They have no will for war, and I don't want their deaths on my conscience."

"Then remain out of it," Hagon replied. "I have no compunctions about taking their lives."

"Hagon, we must punish the guilty, not the innocent – otherwise we're no better than they are. And to punish the guilty, we must discover who they are." She looked around the courtyard and spied Greyn. Like a dog, the wolf was prostrate in a patch of sunshine, dozing. Soldiers and servants alike were giving him a wide berth. No matter how dog-like he might seem, he was still a wolf. "Greyn! Up, you lazy creature!"

Greyn barely raised his head to look at her. "It's so nice in the sun," he complained. "Do I *have* to?"

"I have a task only a true wolf can accomplish," Melayne told him. "It calls for cunning, stealth and cleverness."

Greyn sighed. "Yes, that certainly sounds like only I qualify," he agreed. He shambled to his feet and shook his entire body. "What do you want me to do?"

Melayne gestured toward the ridge where Corran had been found. "Our enemies are up there," she said. "I need you to slip into their lines and to find out where their main camp is. I want to know where their commander is." Then she looked at Hagon. "Once my sly friend here has done that, then I think you can have your revenge..."

The dragon licked his lips. "Very well. I shall wait. But those humans must pay for damaging the boy of my beloved."

"Oh, I promise you, they will pay," Melayne agreed. There was a cold, hard ball of hate inside her. "They will pay indeed."

Chapter 10

Aimon slipped into Corrig's tent and saluted. Corrig glanced up from the map of the area he was studying. "What is it?" he growled.

"One of the patrols has been... killed," Aimon said, hesitantly. "By a dragon, it seems. The bodies are scattered over quite an area."

"So they're feeling brave, are they?" Corrig scowled. "I *knew* that just surrounding them and waiting was the wrong move – it emboldens them. They think we're weak against them." He stroked his chin. "Perhaps we can use that belief to our advantage. If they think we're too timid to attack, they won't be expecting anything. Are the siege towers ready?"

"They're being manned as we speak," Aimon replied. "They will be ready to move whenever you give the order."

"Good." Corrig gestured down at the map. "I've been studying the lay of the land. They're built up the fallen walls again, but the ones along here on the east haven't been strengthened as much as the others. That's where we should concentrate our attack. If we can breach the wall there, then with our numbers we can simply overrun the castle."

Aimon looked nervous. "But what about the dragons?"

"They only have a handful of them!" Corrig yelled. "They can't be everywhere, and we can prevent them from getting too close to our men. I've had the engineers build long spears, metal-tipped, for a number of the soldiers. These can be used to prevent the dragons getting in close to fight. And the siege towers will also protect our men. These rebels think they're safe behind their castle walls and with dragons to do their fighting for them, but we will soon show them the true spirit of fighting men, Aimon!"

"Indeed, sir," his aide agreed. "What are your instructions, then?"

"Send runners to the troops stationed on the northern hills and the western forest perimeter. Tell them to draw out two-thirds of their forces and for them to move to reinforce the men on the eastern assault. But the ones that remain have to look and act as if all of the troops are still there, so the rebels won't suspect the movement. We'll be able to pour more men into the assault than these Talents imagine."

"Understood, sir."

"Meanwhile, I'll start forward with my troops and the siege machines – we'll begin the direct assault as soon as we arrive. These cowardly rebels won't know what they're in for..." Corrig smiled grimly. The moment he'd been waiting for had now arrived. "Oh – and make certain that all of the troops know what happened to our patrol."

"Ah... aren't you afraid that might demoralize the men?" Aimon asked, worriedly. "I've been keeping it quiet for that reason."

"You underestimate our men, Aimon," Corrig said. "This news will anger them, and fire them up so that they fight harder, to avenge their fallen comrades!"

"If you say so, sir," the aide agreed. He saluted again and withdrew.

Corrig looked at the map and smile. In a very short while, he'd have a fallen castle and good news to send back to the King. Things were going very well indeed...

Greyn ran through the forest, his pack pacing him with ease. This was the life! To run free, to hunt and to play! Much as he loved Melayne, there was simply no way that even she could understand the heart of a wolf, the need for this rush. Well, she was only human, after all, so she was to be pitied rather than blamed. She did what she could, and she could not be a wolf.

Even though there were a dozen of them, racing along, they made barely a sound. Their paws hardly touched the earth, and they stirred no leaves and broke no twigs to give warning of their passing; they were wolves, not startled and scared creatures like deer or rabbits. This was their domain, and there were none to challenge them here.

There was the stench of humans all around, a mixture of sweat and dirt, of charred food and alcoholic drinks. Greyn led the pack in the direction of the strongest scent, knowing this would be where their main encampment would lie. He didn't need to give vocal commands; the pack followed his lead instantly and unhesitatingly.

And then the trees narrowed, so Greyn slowed to a lope, the pack matching his stride. He slipped forward to peer from the cover of the bushes, so that he could observe the men.

They were clearly getting ready for a fight. He grinned at the thought. The men were donning protective armor and checking their weapons. They didn't have good, true claws like wolves, so they had to make and carry artificial ones of metal. They didn't have the cunning and speed of wolves, so they had to rely on numbers. The pack could probably take out thirty or forty of these soldiers without a problem, and the desire to do so was strong in Greyn. But Melayne had ordered him only to survey, not to attack, so he reluctantly fought back his instincts. Melayne could be quite a spoil-sport at times...

Some of the men were working on large artificial structures. They were made from wood, from trees hacked down and cut and joined. These constructions were vast, as tall as a tree, but hollow. This didn't make any sense to Greyn – but, then, very little of what humans did made any sense to him, and he dismissed it from his mind.

What was quite clear was that these men were getting ready for a fight, and they had only one enemy... Greyn backed into the woods a way, and his pack gathered around him. He singled out Tarka, his favorite female and the swiftest runner in the pack. "Go back to Melayne," he instructed. "Tell her that the men prepare to fight."

"What of you?" Tarka asked.

Greyn grinned. "We wait here; there may be a chance and a need to fight."

"I should stay and fight with you," Tarka argued.

"Melayne needs to know where we are and what is happening; you will go and tell her because you are the bravest and swiftest."

Tarka scowled. "I am to miss a fight because of that?"

Greyn laughed. "Oh, Tarka, you are the swiftest – you can take this message and still be back in time to fight beside me."

She cocked her head, considering the point. "You are right," she finally agreed. "I go." And go indeed she did, vanishing into the trees.

Greyn settled down. There was nothing else to do for the moment; he might as well get a little rest...

Kaya the falcon wheeled high in the sky, his sharp eyes surveying the ground below. There were men down there, many men, all bustling to and fro as men did in their inexplicable way. Kaya didn't know why Melayne had sent those silly wolves off to act as scouts – his eyes were sharper, his senses keener than any wolf's. And he could fly high, above the heads of the soldiers below. None would suspect his task, for humans always felt so superior to birds.

He was glad when Melayne had asked him to do this simple task. He had been raised since he was a chick to attack and kill slower, weaker birds for the pleasure of his human masters. But Melayne had freed him from that, and showed him that there was so much more that he could do. He owed her everything, and he was ferociously loyal to her. Whatever she required of him, he would gladly perform.

And so he watched the foolish humans below scurry about like mice, doing their strange and incomprehensible things. One thing was quite clear, though – a number of them were slipping away from where they had been on the hills and were moving off to join with others of their kind to the east. Kaya had no idea what all of this meant, but he knew that Melayne would; she was very clever. But she needed Kaya to carry her the news, and the falcon felt proud that he was able to contribute. He whirled about and sped back to the castle to report in...

Melayne sat, lost in thought, considering what her two scouts had reported in. Tarka paced impatiently in front of her as she waited word releasing her to return to the pack, but Melayne wanted to be certain she was doing the right thing before committing any of her allies and friends to action. Kaya simply sat, grooming himself, unconcerned with outcomes. Birds did tend to be lost in the moment.

What to do? There was no question that they had to defend Dragonhome. She had not expected an attack this soon, and plans she and Sander had made were sketchy at best. Even Poth had thought that the attack wouldn't commence until the Talent army arrived. The problem was that even the Seer couldn't foresee everything changeable humans might do. Evidently, the local commander had grown restless simply following orders and waiting.

The problem was that she *really* didn't want to hurt the small army that was on the move. As she'd said over and over, most of the soldiers were young and indoctrinated. They believed what their commanders told them, and had been trained to blindly obey orders. Should they be punished and killed for that?

She wished she could consult with Sander over this, but her husband was with his injured son, and Melayne didn't want to interrupt him. Almost all of the time, Sander's opinion was the one sure rock she had to fall back on. But with Corran injured and perhaps dying even Sander might succumb to thoughts of revenge. Anyway, he had more than enough to think about for now. So it was up to her.

She made up her mind and turned to Tarka. "Wise wolf," she said, gently. "Swift wolf, brave and true – go to Greyn and tell him my decision. If it is safe for the pack – and only *if*! – then you are to seek out and attack the leaders of this army. Do not attack any others of that pack unless your own lives are threatened. Do you understand me?"

"No," Tarka replied honestly. "We should kill everyone we can. But –" she said, swiftly "– I shall convey your exact words, and we shall confine ourselves to precisely what you wish."

Melayne hugged the wolf affectionately. "Thank you, my loyal friend. Run swiftly."

Tarka barked a laugh. "Is there any other way?" And she was gone.

Kaya looked up from his grooming. Melayne smiled. "You have done your task, keenest of eye. Rest now."

"As you say." There was a certain measure of relief in this response.

Melayne crossed the courtyard to where the dragons impatiently awaited her. Margone, she noted, was with Hagon. She hoped that their bonding was proceeding well. It was an odd mixture – dragon and ex-slayer – but stranger things had worked out. Hagon's head reared up and he looked down at her.

"Have you decided, human?" he asked in his cold mental voice.

"I have," she informed him. She glanced at Ganeth. "The two of you should suffice for what I have in mind."

Ganeth hissed, angry and worried. "I hope that it is painful and terrifying for the humans responsible."

"I think you will find it so," Melayne agreed. "Listen to what I suggest..."

Corrig watched his army's progress with smug satisfaction. The extra troops he had brought in from the outlying areas were augmenting his main forces. His watchmen indicated that there was no change in the routine in the castle ahead of them, so it looked as though the freaks were unprepared for this assault. Typical! Anyone could appoint themselves a general, but it took talent and intelligence to actually fight a war – attributes these rebels were clearly lacking. This wouldn't be an assault – it would be a massacre. He smiled in pleasure at the thought. Wait for the Talents to arrive, indeed!

He could see the six huge siege towers moving forward, propelled by men and horses. Surrounding each of them were a contingent of special troops with the extra-long, extra-sharp spears that should fend off even a dragon. Once the towers were in place, nothing would stop the walls of Dragonhome from falling.

There was a cry from the walls as the defenders finally saw what was about to befall them. He smiled again, picturing the panic that had to be spreading amongst the defenders. This was what he had been born for – the crushing of foes and the anticipation of their screams.

Then he heard the screams – prematurely, and a lot closer at hand. Also a loud crash. Surprised, he looked around, but saw nothing – save some of his men milling about a pile of broken wood and bodies... What had happened?

Then he saw that there were only five of the siege towers. The broken wood and mangled bodies were all that remained of the sixth.

"What happened?" he demanded. Aimon, standing beside him, looked confused.

"I don't know, sir. The siege machine simply... broke apart."

As he watched, a second tower suddenly exploded into fragments of wood and body parts. There was a second loud crash and screams of injured and dying men. Again, there was no obvious cause.

It *had* to be the rebels. But – how?

The destruction of two of their major weapons caused the army to slow its forward pace slightly, especially since nobody seemed to know what had happened to them. Angrily, Corrig yelled: "Advance!" and waved his men onward. Whatever happened, the attack would go forward. But he had to know what had destroyed his two towers, seemingly out of the blue...

There was a shadow moving across the ground toward the siege engines, and he glanced upward.

"Dragons!" he exclaimed. Two of them, wheeling in the air, far, far above their heads. As he watched, one of them released something it held in its claws, and he saw the object falling...

It was a rock, huge and heavy, and it dropped hundreds of feet in seconds, gaining momentum as it did so. It slammed from the sky almost invisibly into a third tower, which exploded into fragments of shattered wood and broken bodies.

That dragon flew off, obviously to fetch another rock, and the other one zeroed in on the fourth tower. He watched in shock as the dragon opened its claws, another rock fell, and the fourth tower exploded...

There was *nothing* he could do to stop this! That high in the air, he had no weapons that could even reach the dragons, let alone harm them! They were vanquishing his great siege engines with impunity, and there was nothing he could do about it! And without the towers, it was impossible to assault the castle walls.

His entire attack was being stopped by two dragons with boulders! He had barely seconds to realize that he'd been defeated in a matter of mere minutes. The thought tortured him, but he knew that he had to give the order to retreat, to return to camp to lick his wounds until he could think of another strategy. General Krant would not be happy to hear of this failure...

Then he didn't have to worry about any of that any longer. He heard the sound of movement, and vaguely saw a rush of shadows. Aimon, beside him, gave a strangled, cut-off cry, and went down spraying blood from a ripped-out throat.

He barely saw the wolf that attacked him, and the dreadful pain of his own throat exploding under savage fangs lasted only seconds...

Chapter 11

Ysane clutched the two babies closer as she glared at Sarrow. She was in the great hall of Far Holme, one of the few people allowed to be seated while Darmen and Perria were on their thrones. The court here was small, but they still observed the formalities.

Ysane's husband, Bantry, escorted – or guarded? – Sarrow as he walked into the room and then made a deep bow before the throne.

"This here's Sarrow, your majesties," Bantry said by way of explanation. "He's the brother of Melayne, come from Dragonhome. Says he has a message for you from her."

'Indeed?" Darmen asked, coolly. "I had heard that he was estranged from his sister – our very good friend."

Bantry shrugged; he'd never quite managed to get used to how to address royalty. "He claims things have changed." He gestured over his shoulder with his thumb. "He's got a dragon out there that backs up his claims."

"Indeed?" Darmen peered at Sarrow. "Dragons tend to be... rather particular who they associate with. Very well, we'll hear him."

Bantry gave Sarrow a nudge with the butt of his spear, and the youngster stepped forward, though not before giving Bantry a glare.

Ysane was proud of her husband. She wasn't at all convinced yet that the brat had reformed. It was hard for her to forget and forgive what he had done. And she couldn't help thinking that whatever he was here to say might simply be another of his schemes.

Sarrow inclined his head again, though not as far this time. "Lord Darmen," he said, gently, "I bring you greetings from my sister, as well as news. She now holds Dragonhome with her husband, and is well – though she misses her children, of course." He glanced about the room. "I should very much like to meet my niece and nephew when this audience is over."

Ysane clutched her son, Falma, and Melayne's son, the Silent One, tighter. She wasn't at all sure she liked the idea of letting Sarrow anywhere near the children. Cassary, thankfully, was in her room with the nursemaid, and out of Sarrow's reach.

"That should be possible," Darmen agreed, "provided we are certain of your motives for being here. We have heard many disturbing things about you in the past."

"All true, I'm afraid," Sarrow admitted. "But I ask you to bear in mind that I was a terrified child – I had seen my parents killed, and was on the run with my sister my only protection. I did what I thought was necessary to survive. I wasn't really aware then of my Talent and what I could do with it – or how powerful it was. I only knew that I was able to manipulate people to my will – and my will was to live. Melayne made me see what I had become, and I loathed myself for it, and determined to change. I assure you that she and I are now back on excellent terms and with true affection for one another. This is why she entrusted me with this mission."

"And what, precisely, is your mission?" Perria asked, sharply.

Sarrow glanced around the room. Everyone was silent, of course, listening to what was being said. "Ah... I would suggest that be for your ears only – though Melayne insisted that Ysane and Bantry also be present, as they are her friends. But I can tell everyone this much: Melayne and Sander are safe and well, and in full control of Dragonhome. We have discovered new dragons – the one who brought me here is one – and the dragons look set to breed and thrive. However, Melayne has fallen afoul of the local king, Aleksar, and we expect an attack on Dragonhome at any time."

Darmen's brows furrowed. "Then Melayne needs our help?"

Sarrow shook his head. "By the time you or your men would be able to arrive, any fighting would be over." He chuckled wryly. "You know Melayne – she's ever the optimist, and is convinced that she will win, even without further help. Luckily, I had begun to recruit a small army, and they now fight for her. And with the dragons, and Devra and the other Talents, she might well be right."

Ysane knew she should keep quiet, but she couldn't restrain herself any longer. "You were ever the trickster," she snapped. "How do we know that this isn't simply a ruse of yours so you can use your Talent of Persuasion on us?"

Sarrow turned to look at her. "Ysane, I know why you distrust me, and I honestly can't blame you for it. But if you remember, Melayne pointed out that my Talent works best when people are unaware of it. You and everyone else here know about it, and if I were to attempt to influence you, you would know about it immediately and be able to fight me. The very fact that you can raise suspicions about me proves that I'm not attempting to use my Talent."

Bantry cleared his throat and gave her an apologetic look. "Shath assures me he's telling the truth, love. And he certainly can't use his Talent on a dragon."

Ysane's suspicions waivered slightly, but she was determined not to be taken in by Sarrow again. "Maybe," she agreed, guardedly. It was her responsibility to look after Melayne's children, and it would take a deal more evidence than that to convince her that he wasn't up to some trick.

Sarrow turned back to Darmen. "Now, my lord," he said, gently, "I ask that we might have a private conference – the rest of Melayne's message is for the two of you, Ysane and Bantry alone. I assure you, it is of a... delicate nature."

Darmen considered for a moment, and then nodded. "Very well," he agreed. "The court is excused." He looked around the room.

The various nobles and soldiers took the ungentle hint and left. There was a murmur of talk as they did so, no doubt everyone speculating on what the rest of the message was. Bantry went with them, and shut the door as the final few courtiers filed out. He then returned to stand firmly by Ysane, his spear held firmly upright. She knew that if Sarrow gave the slightest hint of betrayal that Bantry would act. Clearly, Sarrow knew this as well.

"Thank you, my lord," Sarrow said. He bit his lower lip before speaking again. "This part is a bit... personal," he apologized. "Please forgive me if I'm rather blunt – I've never been schooled in courtly etiquette, I'm afraid."

"Get on with it, then," Darmen growled.

"One of the Talents in Melayne's team is a Seer," Sarrow said. "She has informed Melayne of your plans for her children."

Ysane was puzzled, but this clearly meant something to the Lord and Lady of Far Holme. Both of them flushed and gave each other guilty glances. Ysane scowled; whatever could Sarrow mean?

The youth held up his hand. "Don't worry – you know Melayne, she's not mad at your planned betrayal of her trust. In fact, she completely understands what you're planning and why."

"What are you talking about?" Ysane demanded. "What plans? What's going on?" She glared at Darmen and Perria – neither of whom could meet her gaze. Then there *was* something being plotted!

"The Lord and Lady of Far Holme have no heirs," Sarrow said, softly. "They are both of them extremely fond of Melayne and had considered adopting her, making her their heir. But they realized that Melayne and Sander hold Dragonhome, and that will always have the first claim on their hearts. Realizing this, they are planning on keeping Melayne's children, adopting them instead, and making the boy the next Lord of the Far Isles."

Ysane looked at the nobles and saw written in their faces that everything Sarrow had claimed was true. Everything. "How *could* you?" she cried. "How could you betray Melayne like that?"

"It's not exactly *betrayal*," Perria answered in a strangled voice that gave the lie to what she was saying. "We *do* love Melayne – and the children! They would become our heirs! They would inherit everything we have!"

"But lose their parents!" Ysane cried.

"Ysane," Sarrow said, in a firm voice. "Please. Melayne knows what they're planning – they have done *nothing* wrong yet! – and she understands and forgives them. Lady Perria is quite truthful – the children would undoubtedly be loved and well cared-for. But it is, of course, unthinkable."

Ysane held tight to the Silent One. "Indeed it is!"

Darmen hung his head in shame. "Now that it is known and being spoken of... You are both right. It *is* a shameful act of betrayal we were planning against of true friend Melayne. And it is one we cannot go through with." He held his wife's hand and squeezed it tightly. "I do not know what we can do about our problem, but it will not be the enforced adoption of Melayne's children, I promise."

"Good." Sarrow gave a broad grin. "Because Melayne and I have an excellent alternative suggestion for you."

Darmen looked up, his anguish changing to hope. "After what we were planning, she still thinks of us?'

The youngster laughed. "Oh, come on – you must know what Melayne is like by now! She's always taking other people's problems on her own shoulders. Honestly, that sister of mine is a bit crazy at times, you know. But in a good way," he added hastily, seeing Ysane about to erupt.

"That's true enough," Perria agreed. "But, please – the solution to our problem?"

Sarrow threw his arms wide. "Adopt *me*."

Both Darmen and Perria looked stunned at this suggestion. Ysane felt like exploding. "Are you crazy?" she yelled.

The youngster shrugged. "Possibly. I know I *was*. But, honestly – isn't this the best solution to everyone's problems?" He started ticking off the points on his fingers. "Melayne and Sander have Dragonhome back, and they certainly don't need me there to complicate matters for them. My men are now sworn to support Melayne, and *they* don't need two commanders around. Secondly, they want their children back – though not while Dragonhome is in danger, obviously. Third, Darmen and Perria need an heir and fourth – well, this one is a bit selfish, I'll admit – I need a home. And parents. I'm not as crazily worried about being protected as I was, but I'm still a child, and I *would* like somewhere to belong. Melayne thinks very highly of Darmen and Perria and thinks they might make me excellent step-parents. Let's face it – in this situation, everybody wins, don't they?"

"If we can trust you," Ysane snapped.

"Ah, yes, there's always that," he agreed. "But if you can't believe me, can't you believe your own dragons?"

"I *do* trust Loken," Ysane agreed slowly, worried that this was still somehow another trap.

"Then go and talk to her; hear what she thinks." Sarrow gave her a winning smile. "Please?"

Bantry laid his hand on her shoulder gently. "He does make a good case," he said. "Perhaps we'd better go talk to the dragons and listen to what they think."

It wasn't easy for Ysane to smother her suspicions about Melayne's brother – he *had* betrayed her, and then sent the slayers here – one of whom had been meant to be his sister's assassin... How could she possibly forget or forgive any of that? But if he *was* telling the truth, and he and Melayne had reconciled – how could she not do what Melayne wanted?

If only she knew what to believe!

"I'm just a simple farm girl," she said. "Nobody expected me to do anything more than milk cows, feed chickens and get married and have lots of babies who'd grow up to do the same. I was never raised to make big, important decisions like this. The future of dynasties..." She shook her head. "To be truthful, I'm totally out of my depth here. But Melayne left me with responsibilities to look after her children, and if *she* trusts my judgment – well, then, maybe I should, too."

Sarrow laughed, and it sounded completely genuine. "Ysane – Melayne wasn't raised to make those sort of decisions either. We, too, were children of simple farmers – at least, as far as we know. Our parents never spoke of their past. And now she's off waging a war to free all the Talents from these endless wars. She's taking on Kings and Generals – and she's winning. We aren't just what we were born – we're what we make ourselves into. My sister has become a great leader, even though that's something she never sought and probably still doesn't want to be. But she is what is needed now, and I for one am going to do everything I can to help her. Right now, that means being here and ensuring that you will be able one day to restore her children to her. I don't care what you *were* – right now you're Melayne's trusted friend. She didn't give her children into your care because there was nobody else who could do the job – she did it because she trusts you above all to look after them. And if Melayne has that much trust in you – can't you learn to trust yourself as well?"

Bantry nodded. "I may not agree with everything the lad says," he said. "But I agree with every word of that, my love. It doesn't matter what you were born, you're much more than that now. I know you're smarter than I am, and that you'll work this out. And I'll stand beside you in whatever decision you make."

Perria leaned forward, smiling. "Ysane, both of them are right. You weren't born noble, but so what? Far too many high-borns turn out badly, like this King Aleksar. I wish we had more like you instead."

Ysane found herself blushing. No matter what they said, she *was* out of her depth. But... "You're right, Sarrow – if Melayne believes in me, I should believe in myself. If you'll excuse me, I'm going to talk with the dragons. If they back Sarrow up – well, then, so will I, for whatever it's worth."

"Thank you," Darmen said. "In the meantime, my wife and I will talk about this ourselves." He gave Sarrow a glance. "Alone, if you don't mind; we have quite a grave decision to make."

"I understand," Sarrow said. "Maybe somebody could direct me to the kitchens? I'm still a growing boy, and I'm starving."

"Oh, of course," Perria agreed. "Bantry, if you please?"

"Of course." He turned to Sarrow. "Come on then, lad – I could do with a bite or two myself, to be truthful."

They all started toward their various destinations. Ysane took the two babies back to her chambers, leaving them with the nurse and Cassary – who loved playing the older sister to both children. Then she went to the courtyard.

Her Loken was there, with Shath and the ever-impatient Tura. There was also a new dragon, who had to be Sarrow's Kata. The four seemed to be getting along well enough, though Ysane could only communicate directly with Loken. She stroked her dragon's nose, and Loken rested her chin on Ysane's shoulder for a moment in greeting.

"There are more dragons!" she said, excitedly. "Ganeth has a mate, and will lay her eggs soon!"

"That is good news," Ysane agreed, happy for her friend.

"And there may be a male for me, soon," Loken continued. "I'd like to have hatchlings of my own, as you do."

"One day," promised Ysanne. "It will be wonderful when all dragons and humans can live together as friends, as we do."

"It will happen," Loken said. "I have faith in Melayne."

"So do I," she agreed. "But if I only knew what to believe about her brother." She sighed. "I was so sure he was evil, but now..."

Loken nuzzled her. "Kata says that he has changed, and that he is telling the truth. Human beings sometimes seem like they *wish* to be deceived, but dragons can always tell. Humans can lie to one another, but they cannot lie to dragons. If Kata says that Sarrow is now honest, then he is honest. You may believe it, without doubt."

"Oh, I *want* to believe it," she said, hugging the dragon. "But I have such a great responsibility. If I decide wrongly, then I will be betraying my friend, and possibly bringing great harm to her children and to the Far Islands. It's such a great burden to bear. I really wish I didn't have to do it."

"But you must," Loken said gently. "And you will. I, at least, have faith in you."

Ysane wept, and clung to her friend.

A short while later, Bantry and Sarrow were eating leftover pie in the kitchen. Bantry wasn't sure what to make of any of this, but he knew enough to know that he couldn't help out here. He was a simple soldier, good at following orders. But he needed other people to make the decisions that led to those orders. Above all, he trusted his wife, who was so much cleverer than he was. She'd make the right decision, he knew – even if he didn't know what that decision would be.

He glanced up and saw her standing in the kitchen doorway. She was carrying the Silent One and holding Cassary by the hand. Sarrow followed Bantry's gaze and stopped eating.

"Sarrow," Ysane said firmly. "You're acting as Melayne's agent as well as her brother in this. I thought it was only right, then, that you met your niece and nephew for the first time. Family is family."

Chapter 12

Nephir had to admit that the coronation had been most impressive. It had taken place in the throne room, with the High Priest placing the crown firmly on Aleksar's head. The cheering from the gathered nobles was only partly inspired by fear. There were some, it seemed, who were actually glad that Aleksar was on the throne. Some of those might even have believed that Aleksar was the best man for the position; others were glad that it would be someone else's neck on the block in the event of a revolt.

He himself was among the latter. He supposed that he might have been able to seize power – but why bother? It was a lot simpler to manipulate whoever did take the throne and achieve his ends that way. Let Aleksar take all the glory; Nephir would take most of the money, and money was what mattered, not some glittery show of monarchy.

Aleksar was fairly glowing, having achieved the pinnacle of his desire – he was king, crowned and sealed by the blessings of religion and the acclaim of the nobility. Nephir doubted that the reality would match the image Aleksar had, but he wouldn't be the one to burst the new king's bubble. Instead, it was time to ensure that his own grip on the throne was secured. And that meant ensuring that Murine would be the new queen.

And the place to cement that was at the celebratory feast. The Great Hall had been set up in high style, ready for the feasting. All of the nobles of Farrowholme were gathered – none would have dared to stay away, whatever else might be on their minds. In the first place, it was a great feast, and most of the nobles loved to gorge themselves – especially when somebody else was paying for it. In the second place, they had to demonstrate their loyalty to the new king.

And in the third place, like Nephir, they had to cement their position in the new ruling order.

This would be a time of scrambling for power and influence, with few of the nobles restrained by tact or sentiment. It was everyone for themselves, and to the winners – everything. Nephir had to ensure that he ended up on top of the heap, and everything hinged on Murine.

Nephir couldn't help but admire her. She had been born blessed with beauty, and she knew full well how to take advantage of it. Her hair was streaming, with a simple tiara drawing attention to her face – lovely and flawless as ever. The dress she wore was long and flowing, in various shades of green, and drew attention to her cleavage. Many of the men present could barely drag their eyes away from her. If Nephir hadn't known her true nature, he might have been suckered in as well. Still, it didn't matter how many others found her bewitching – the only important one was Aleksar.

At the feast, Aleksar was head of the high table, naturally. Both Nephir and Murine were at the table, on the new king's right hand. There were only a handful of other people so honored, but they included Caramin and his daughter, Shera.

Caramin was an older man, his russet hair and beard streaked with gray. He'd been a close friend of the late king, and was clearly maneuvering to retain his position. Aleksar favored him from time to time, and Nephir had to hide his irritation. The lord owned large tracts of land and fielded a good number of soldiers, so it was important that he back Aleksar, and the king knew this. Nephir certainly couldn't look as if he disapproved, but he also couldn't allow the man to weasel in too close to the king.

And… Shera.

Now *there* was a real problem. She was quite resplendent. She had inherited her father's shock of red hair, and it framed her face like a halo of the sun.

And Nephir had to admit that her face was very attractive. She had bright, merry eyes and a ready smile – it was impossible to know how genuine the latter was – and a pleasant, low-toned voice. She laughed in all the right places, and cast her eyes demurely down if a ribald comment or two were made. She was the picture of feminine innocence and attractiveness.

The cunning little bitch...

Naturally, Murine was her match, smile for smile, laugh for laugh, modesty for modesty. But which was making the greater impact on the king? Nephir couldn't say. And that annoyed him, though he had to keep it from his demeanor.

The feasting went on. The head cook had outdone herself this time. There were so many dishes that even the rotund Lord Tarrbin couldn't sample them all! Roasted birds, tender baked meats, voluminous pies, fish of all sizes and flavors... There were shellfish and vegetables, stews and soups. There were tidbits and pastries, and great, steaming loaves of fresh bread. There were fruits and tarts, and even rare ices. All washed down by gallons of sweet wines, spiced meads and hearty ales. There was enough to feed an army, and there would be ample left over for the servants to enjoy a few rare treats of their own overnight.

And there were musicians and jugglers, clowns and even a few dramatic readings. One silly poet had written an ode to the new king, and insisted on reading all sixty-seven stanzas. Thankfully, the wine made it endurable, but Aleksar seemed pleased enough with the nonsense to accept a copy, and to give the poor fool a handful of gold coins for his troubles. Nephir was tempted to have one of his men cut the idiot's tongue out as he left, but decided against ruining the mood of the party.

And, finally, there was dancing – though how anyone who'd eaten and drunk as much as they all had was expected to be nimble on their toes was beyond Nephir. And, to be honest, he despised dancing at the best of times. If there was a way, he'd have begged off. But Aleksar decided that a few turns around the floor would be a good idea, so everyone had to join in.

And now came the moment of decision... Who would the king chose as his partner in the first dance? Nephir saw that Caramin was leaning forward as intently as he was as the king wiped his hands reasonably clean on a cloth before taking to his feet.

Aleksar looked to his left and then his right. "An almost impossible choice," he said softly. "Two lovely, charming ladies." He shook his head. "My Lady Murine –" and she leaned forward, eagerly "- I am afraid you will have to be second – at least in this." He held out his hand to Shera. "My Lady Shera, if you would..." Shera, naturally, sprang to her feet and accepted the offered hand.

To her credit, Murine's smile didn't slip into fury, though Nephir could see it was a close call. He gripped her hand, quickly. "My lady, if you would be so kind," he murmured, and almost dragged her to join the dance.

"That bitch," Murine whispered into his ear as they danced, the smile still illuminating her face.

"A temporary setback, no more," he assured her. But he was thinking furiously; had the king already chosen? If so, then Caramin would wield the greater influence in council, and rake in the greater rewards. Nephir could not let that pass without fighting.

"I can always kill her," Murine suggested. "I'd love to carve out her scheming heart and eat it."

"I'm sure you would," Nephir said gently. "And you'd be the first suspect if something... unfortunate happened to her. No, for our sakes, she has to stay alive – at least for the time being. Perhaps later you can indulge yourself. No, we need as effective a way of removing her from his thoughts as possible, but one that won't lead back to us in any way."

"I suppose I could get someone else to kill her." She sounded quite disappointed with the prospect. "At a time when we are with the king, so we cannot possibly be guilty."

"The same problem, my dear," he said. "It would simply be assumed that we hired an assassin. No, forget shedding her blood – we need a different approach..."

"We could disfigure her," Murine said, a little more eagerly. "Carve up that pretty face so that no man will ever be able to look upon it with anything but repugnance."

"You're not paying attention. It has to be some way without harming her *physically*."

The king seemed to be enjoying the dance, Nephir noted. At least, he seemed to be enjoying holding onto Shera. And who could blame him? There must be a lot of men in this room very envious of him...

And there was a possibility! "My dear," he whispered to his cousin, "you have admirers everywhere, don't you?"

"Of course,' she agreed. "What is there about me not to admire?"

Her bloodthirsty nature, for one – but he knew better than to mention that.

"And the Lady Shera is almost as attractive as you are," he said, thoughtfully. "She must have admirers of her own."

"One or two, probably," Murine conceded, ungraciously.

"See if you can find out who they might be," he said to her. "Perhaps she has even had lovers – looking the way she does, I can't imagine that nobody has tried to get a closer look at her."

"If they exist, I'll uncover them," Murine promised.

"And if they don't?" he prodded her.

"Then I'll create them," Murine vowed.

"That's my girl," he said, approvingly. She was catching on quickly. There was no need to destroy the other woman physically – as long as her reputation could be ruined.

The dance finished, and everyone bowed to their partners. Aleksar came over to Nephir, a smile on his face. "If you have no objections, my lord, I should like to dance with the fair Lady Murine next?"

Nephir bowed. "I would be honored, sire – as would my charming niece." Murine dropped a very fetching courtesy, and even – somehow! – managed to blush. Nephir watched them move off as the second dance began. He then became aware of a shadow at his elbow and turned to see Caramin standing there.

"They make a handsome couple, don't you think?" Nephir asked.

"Almost as handsome as the king and my daughter," Caramin replied. "Almost."

Nephir laughed. "It is, perhaps, a trifle early to start comparing fore-runners in this race, don't you think?"

"It's never too early to start looking to the future," his companion replied. "I see that we are both… forward-looking men."

Nephir inclined his head as if this was meant as a compliment. "I do believe we are."

"But, as in any race, there can be only one winner – and a lot of losers."

"I fear that is so," Nephir admitted. "Isn't it a shame that there is no prize for the runner-up?"

"I'm sure you will soon discover that," Caramin said.

Nephir smiled, enjoying the verbal fencing. "Only second-hand, I'm afraid – watching you lose."

Caramin glared at him. "I am not a gracious loser," he promised. "Are you?"

Nephir turned and half-bowed. "I'm afraid I have no idea – I have never lost." And then he moved away. It was rather fun to leave Caramin fuming. But the man had declared his open enmity, so Nephir knew that he would be in for a fight. Caramin wouldn't go down easily or quietly.

And that would make Nephir's victory even sweeter…

Chapter 13

"Come on, come on, come on, come on!" Poth barely paused between the words. She had a firm grip on Devra's hand, and was dragging her along.

"What's the urgency?" Devra grumbled. "What's going on in that cracked mind of yours?"

"Opportunity!" Poth laughed. "Strike while the iron is hot! Seize the day!"

"I'll seize your neck if you don't tell me what this is all about," Devra warned her.

"I told you – opportunity!" Poth gave her lop-sided grin. "Melayne is depressed."

"And that makes you happy?" Devra asked. "You really are cold-hearted, aren't you?"

Poth sighed. "She's depressed, you cheer her – you get closer to her heart. And we get closer to splitting her and Sander. Simple!"

"If you ask me, *you're* simple," Devra growled. It didn't seem right to be deliberately taking advantage of Melayne's moods... But, then again, if Melayne truly was depressed, she'd need cheering up. Without any agenda. It would only be the right thing to do. Wouldn't it?

Why was this all so confusing? Devra almost wished she didn't have feelings for Melayne. It would have been so much simpler if she didn't care, the way that most people actually believed she lived. Instead, she was in love with a girl who was happily married and completely oblivious to her true feelings.

Wouldn't it be better for Melayne to leave things as they were? Devra was used to being alone, and she could endure it. Probably. But... didn't she have any right to strive for her own happiness? To be able to love?

"Come on!"

Poth didn't have any of these doubts. She wore her heart on her sleeve. *Eveybody* knew what she wanted, even if they didn't take the crazy girl seriously. Poth had no hidden depths, no secrets – she blurted out whatever came into her mind without any censorship. Devra couldn't do that – she preferred to be private, even if it meant she came over to other people as cold and aloof. She *wished* she could just let her feelings pour out, that she could simply tell Melayne how much she loved her, how she wanted to kiss her and touch her and –

No! It simply wasn't possible. If she admitted what she felt, if she told Melayne... Well, she knew that Melayne would never be offended or upset by the confession. She might even be touched by it. But she could never return her feelings. Melayne was simply far too much in love with Sander to even *think* about anyone else.

Devra was almost certain that there was no chance of winning Melayne's love – at least, her *romantic* love; she had absolutely no doubt that Melayne loved her as a friend. But that was not enough for Devra. She wanted more – much more. And, despite all of her doubts as to the wisdom of trying – how could she stop?

They had reached Melayne's chambers now. Poth barely paused, giving a quick knock and then dragging Devra inside before Melayne had even had a chance to respond.

Melayne looked slightly startled by the intrusion, but she smiled wanly when she saw Devra. "I'm afraid I'm not good company right now," she admitted. "Or is there a problem?"

"Yes," Poth said, cheerfully. "The problem is *you*. You're taking things far too seriously, and you need to relax."

Melayne shook her head sadly. "I *have* to take things seriously," she said. "This is all my doing, after all. It's because of me that Dragonhome is under siege, that this mad King wants to kill us all and that there's a Talent army on its way to destroy us."

Devra couldn't bear to see Melayne wallowing in self-pity and self-blame like this. "Don't be silly," she growled. "It's not your doing, it's *his*. He's the one who is oppressing people, he's the one attacking people and he's the villain of the piece – not you."

Melayne smiled and shook her head. "You're a good friend, Devra. And I am so glad to have you with me. But it *is* my doing. I sent the dragons and wolves against the poor soldiers who surround us, and I had them kill their leaders. *Me*. Not that King."

Devra laughed harshly. "Listen to yourself, Melayne! *They* are attacking us, and *you* blame yourself for stopping them! These *poor soldiers* have minds of their own, and they could opt out of this any time they feel like it. Instead they obey the orders of an evil leader and attack innocents. You don't merely have a right to defend yourself, you have a responsibility to defend those who love you. You have done *nothing* wrong, and everything right."

Melayne jumped to her feet and abruptly hugged Devra. "Oh, it's so good to have you for a friend," she said. "I guess I needed to hear somebody tell me I haven't turned into a monster."

"Monster? You?" Devra laughed. "Honestly, Melayne, you do have the craziest ideas sometimes. Maybe Poth is rubbing off on you."

Poth giggled. "I'm a very bad influence." She winked at Devra over Melayne's shoulder, and then inclined her head and nodded at Melayne. It was abundantly clear what she was suggesting, but Devra couldn't bring herself to make even the mildest pass at her friend. If anything, just *thinking* about it made her muscles seize up.

Of course, Melayne was completely oblivious to the emotions that she'd stirred up in Devra. She laid her hand on Devra's bare arm – it was all Devra could do to stop herself shivering with pleasure – and smiled. "You do cheer me up."

"How is Sander?" Poth asked, perkily.

"Worried," Melayne admitted. "Corran appears to be recovering, but he's very weak. Sander won't leave his side."

"I could go and... cheer him up," Poth offered. "He likes looking at my backside, you know."

"I like looking at your backside, too," Devra informed her.

Poth grinned. "Really? I didn't know I had that effect on you."

"When I see your backside," Devra explained, nastily, "it means you're leaving."

Melayne gave a little scowl. "Come on, now, Devra – don't be so cruel. Poth can't help herself."

"Poth wants to help herself to your place in Sander's bed," Devra pointed out.

Melayne shrugged. "Well, there isn't any chance of that, is there? And she's not trying to do it behind my back – she's quite honest about what she wants."

"Yes," Poth said, sticking her tongue out at Devra. "Everybody knows my feelings. Does everyone know about *yours*?"

Devra felt the fury building up inside her, and knew her face was flushed. How *dare* she try and force her to say something? "Poth," she growled, "one of these days I'm going to –"

"Devra!" Melayne glared at her sternly. "Poth has been through a lot. Try and remember that." She winced slightly.

Immediately, Devra's concerns shifted. "Melayne – what's the matter?"

"Oh, it's nothing." Seeing Devra's glare, Melayne admitted: "It's just aches. Tension, you know."

Poth grinned. "Devra's very good with massages," she offered. "Let her rub your shoulders – trust me, you'll feel a lot better. If anyone can promise that, I can."

"I don't want to bother –"

"Don't be silly," Devra said, firmly. "Sit." Meekly, Melayne obeyed. Devra started to knead her friend's shoulders. She could feel the tension in the muscles – well, considering everything that was happening, it was little wonder that Melayne was so stressed and tense. At least, this was something she could do to help.

And, to be honest, touching Melayne like this was making *her* feel good. Then she felt guilty for that. This massage didn't mean the same thing to Melayne that it meant to her...

"Oh, that *does* feel good," Melayne murmured. "Thank you, Devra." Her muscles were loosening up, as Devra's fingers worked their way across them. The trouble was, she was starting to get tense herself, from an entirely different cause...

Then she caught sight of Poth, who was off to one side, out of Melayne's line of sight. Not that it mattered much, as Melayne had her eyes closed, enjoying the massage. Poth had her head cocked to one side and was making kissy-faces at Devra, and urging her on. And that killed Devra's mood more effectively than anything could. She stopped the massage before her own tensions made her grip Melayne too tightly.

Melayne opened her eyes, as Poth blanked her face. "Thank you, Devra – that was wonderful. But I think I'd better get on – there's so much still to do. If you'll excuse me." She abruptly gave Devra a hug and then hurried out of the door.

"Well, you wasted a good opportunity there," Poth remarked. "You could have had her clothes off in a few more minutes."

"Shut up!" Devra yelled. "Just shut up!" She was burning, and furious, and ashamed at herself for her own thoughts.

"Oooh, that is *so* mature," Poth mocked.

Boiling with anger – and other emotions she didn't want to even start to examine – Devra grabbed Poth's shoulders. "I swear, one more stupid word from you and I'll beat the crap out of you. You can see the future – you *know* I'll do it."

"Yes, you would, too," Poth agreed. "You'd take out your own guilt on me, wouldn't you? Devra, face facts – you *want* Melayne. I'm only trying to help you get the girl you love. What's so wrong with that?"

"What's wrong?" Devra really wanted to haul her fist back and punch that elfin face. "You don't have the first clue about love, do you? You're only interested in what you *want*. But love – true love – means that you put what your loved one wants ahead of your own desires. And what Melayne wants is Sander and not me. And if you loved Sander – truly loved him – you'd feel the same way about him."

Poth scowled. "You think I don't deserve any happiness? I'll show you." And she began to unlace her clothing.

Devra felt a moment of panic. "What are you doing?"

"What do you *think* I'm doing?" Poth asked, discarding her tunic. "I'm taking off my clothes, you idiot."

"Somebody might come along and see you!"

"Do you think I care?" Poth asked, sending her leggings flying. She was dressed only in a shift now. "Anyway, as you so rightly pointed out, I can see the future. There won't be anyone along for a good twenty minutes." She allowed the shift to drop and stood there, naked, her fists on her hips. "Well – what do you think?"

Devra stared at Poth. The other girl was a little underweight, but there was no denying she was beautiful. "Think about what?" Devra asked her. "What's the point of this?"

"Do you think I'm lovely?"

"Well, yes," Devra said, stammering a little. "You look very nice. But – so what? What are you trying to prove?"

"This." Poth turned slowly around, and Devra gasped.

Her entire back was a mass of scar tissue, from her shoulders to her pert little behind. It was mostly healed, but some of it was fairly recent and reddish.

"What... what happened?" Devra asked, appalled.

"Melayne's brother happened," Poth replied. "The Burning God. Whenever things didn't go as he wished, whenever he was angry..." She gestured to her back. "Sometimes it was simply that he wanted to hurt someone." She ran a hand through her short blonde hair. "He burned all of my hair off once," she said. "I learned to keep it short after that."

"That's horrible."

"Yes," Poth agreed. "It was. It is. I wanted him to love me, but he was a God, and far, far above loving a mere mortal. But not above hurting me. That's what he enjoyed – hearing me scream, burning his hands into my skin..." There were tears in her eyes. "So – don't you think it's time I got to have some love? To have someone touch my back and my body because they want to *love* me, and not hurt me? Or don't you think I deserve some love?"

"Of course," Devra agreed. "And I really, really hope that you find it. Do those scars hurt now?"

"No – the nerves are mostly dead. But it hurt *then*. You know how they sometimes say you forget pain? Well, you don't. Not ever."

Devra reached out and hugged Poth. For once, the Seer seemed to be absolutely startled, as if she hadn't Seen that coming. Then she released the elfin blonde. "You do deserve happiness," she said. "But you *don't* deserve to steal it from other people. So let me tell you this: if you do *anything* that will make Melayne unhappy, then I will pay you back. I can Find anything." She trailed a finger along one of Poth's scars. "I can Find the exact spot on your body that will cause you more pain than any of these scars ever did. And you won't ever be able to hide from me, because I can Find you wherever you go. If you thought that mad brother of Melayne's was nasty, you don't have a clue just how nasty I can get. I'm not going to help you in your stupid quest to gain Sander's love because Melayne's happiness means more to me than my own does. And if you try to continue with your plans without me – then there will be a *lot* of pain in your future. Trust me, if I can't have my fun with Melayne's body, I will have a very different kind of fun with yours." She could see from Poth's reaction that her threats had hit home. The one thing Poth wanted more than Sander was to avoid pain. And there was only one way she could manage that...

Devra spun on her heels, but hesitated as she started to leave the room. "And put your damn clothes back on," she said as a parting shot.

Chapter 14

Baraktha sighed as he saw the captain heading in their direction. "This has to be more trouble," he grumbled. He knew how things worked – whenever someone with a little authority headed in your direction, he was going to start throwing his weight around.

Warra chuckled. "Maybe he's just lonely, and wants to say hello?" The others around their campfire laughed at the thought. All but Shara, who was cooking their supper of thin soup. She'd been lost in her thoughts for quite some time. Baraktha hoped it meant she was coming around to his point of view, losing her naïve beliefs and seeing the world as it really was.

Rotten.

The captain stood just outside their circle, scowling. Baraktha knew he was waiting for an acknowledgment of his rank, but he'd have a long wait. Neither he nor his friends set any store in military discipline. Eventually, realizing he'd get neither salutes nor even anyone standing up, the soldier scowled again and inched forward.

"The rations have almost run out," he stated.

Baraktha snorted. "Think we don't know that?" he asked. He gestured at the pot. "That's soup's so thin it's barely more than water. And you expect us to march on food like that?"

"Yes," one of the other Talents put in. "If you expect us to march, let alone fight, we're going to need better than piss to eat."

"We need supplies," the captain said, stating the obvious. "And that means we need a farm – better yet, several of them. Maybe a town. I've scouts out, but none of them know this area." He looked at Baraktha. "But you can Look for them, can't you?"

For once, the captain made some kind of sense. Baraktha shifted on the log he was using for a seat. "Aye," he agreed. "I can that." He allowed his surroundings to slip slightly out of focus as he concentrated his Talent. It was difficult to explain how he managed it, but it was as if he were no longer inside his body, but floating freely, rising in the air. He could Look around and from that vantage point he could see the local terrain spread about him like a map. It helped when he had something to touch – like that merchant earlier, but he could manage without.

The road they were taking through the woods carried on for miles ahead, the only break in the trees for quite a while. Then, perhaps ten miles ahead, there were clearings that became fields, and fields that became farms, surrounding a small village. Maybe thirty or forty buildings in the main area, so not a large place.

He gestured. "That way, maybe a dozen miles," he said. "Just off the road we're taking. You could send the scouts out in the morning and they could arrange for what we need." The captain nodded, spun on his heels and walked away. "You're welcome!" Baraktha called to his retreating back, and his friends all sniggered.

"Think they'll have any luck?" Warra asked, poking the fire with a stick.

"What do you think?" Baraktha snorted. "They'll all say they need whatever supplies they have to live through the winter, and they've nothing to spare."

Shara looked up from the pot. "That's probably true," she said. "I grew up in a small village like that. There's probably little to spare." She glanced around the clearing at the dozens of campfires. "Certainly not enough to keep a couple of hundred soldiers going for very long."

"I'm sure you're right," Baraktha agreed. "Let's be optimistic and say they even *want* to help us out, there's not likely to be enough for more than a few days for all this lot."

"We need a larger town, then," Shara said.

"We can't wait for a larger town," Warra growled. "I'm wasting away as it is. We need food now."

"Agreed," Baraktha said. "And they're not likely to *give* it."

Shara frowned. "What are you saying?"

"You *know* what I'm saying." If he didn't love her, he'd have been annoyed by her constant naivety. "What they won't give, we have to take. It's as simple as that."

She stared at him. "If we *take* their food, then they'll be starving."

"Sooner them than us," one of the Talents called out.

"There are *children* in that village," Shara pointed out.

"There are *always* children," Baraktha said. "Peasants breed like rats. And they're not our concern. We're passing through this stinking area on the King's business. It's their duty to help us, plain and simple. If they don't – ha! *When* they don't! – then they'll leave us no choice. And speaking of no choice, isn't that soup ready yet? It's weak and tasteless, no doubt, but my stomach needs something in it."

Later, as they settled down to sleep, Shara turned to stare at him. Baraktha sighed again. "What is it, woman?"

"Are you seriously asking us to rob that village?"

"We're on King's business," he said, patiently. "We're allowed to requisition supplies. It's their duty to give them to us."

"But you don't think they will."

He snorted. "I'm quite certain they won't."

"So you're planning on taking the supplies anyway, and leaving these people to starve, come winter?"

"*These* people are my concern," he said, waving his hand at his men. "I have to keep them fit and fed and ready to fight. To do that, I need food. Look, I'm sorry if it means hardship for this village, woman, but if it's them or us – well, I choose us every time."

"And let these people suffer?"

Baraktha shrugged. "They're not my problem; let the King worry about them – they're his subjects."

"The King is a long way off, and he most likely doesn't even know these people exist."

Baraktha chuckled. "Oh, trust me, when it's tax time, *then* he knows these people exist."

"So *if* they can make it through the winter somehow, without sufficient food, *then* they'll have the joy of being told they're being taxed for it?"

He sat up. "What do you expect, Shara?" he demanded. "I know this isn't a perfect world. If I were running it, things would be different – but I'm not, and they aren't. I've told you before, I'm a realist. I'd love it if everything were all sweetness and happiness, but it isn't. This is a real world we're living in – and that means that there's suffering and death – yes, and farmers starving to death sometimes. And yes, I know that sometimes I add to their problems, while I'm trying to solve my own. But that's just the way of this world, and you have to harden your heart and just accept it."

"There has to be a better way," Shara insisted.

"If you find it, let me know. In the meantime, deal with the world as it is. The reality is that it's just us, together – there's nobody else looking out for us, nobody else willing to do us good. We can only trust each other."

She turned away from him, physically trying to reject the bitter truth. "It may not be the way you say it will be," she muttered.

"Oh, it will be," he assured her. "Trust me on that one."

As it turned out, he was wrong.

It was worse than he'd said it would be.

It was impossible to keep the approach of a couple of hundred soldiers quiet. As a result, when they reached the village, they were met by a barrier of carts, behind which the farmers and their families had gathered. They were armed – if *armed* was the right word – with pitchforks and scythes, axes and some with just large sticks.

It was, frankly, pathetic. And annoying.

The captain, dim as ever, rode forward to the barrier and stared at the men behind it. "What's going on?" he asked.

Their spokesman considered, and then spat deliberately on the ground. "What do you think?" he asked. "Yon band of ruffians marching toward our village."

"We're not ruffians," the captain protested. "We're the King's soldiers. *Your* King."

"Is that a fact?" the man asked, clearly not impressed. "Well, in that case, you'd best be on your way, hadn't you? I'm sure he must have some pressing need for you, if you're marching like this."

"We intend to be on our way," the captain answered. "Just as soon as we get some supplies. Our food is running short."

"Planned badly, did you?"

That annoyed the captain, at least; he liked to think he was a smart man. "We had our marching orders unexpectedly. We're in a hurry and need to requisition food."

"You do?" The farmer spat again. "And just what's the difference between *requisitioning* and *stealing*?"

"Requisitioning means that the King will pay you back."

"Really?" The farmer turned to his friends. "When was the last time that the King ever paid us a single coin, friends?" That brought a harsh laugh from a dozen throats. He faced the captain again. "No, I don't think so," he said. "If he'd like to pay us first, then maybe we'd be able to find some scraps for your rabble. Kings have notoriously bad memories when it comes to paying debts."

The captain was getting annoyed. "That's treason."

The farmer shrugged. "If the King wants our supplies, then he'll have to come here and tell us himself, won't he? And then pay us for them." He leaned forward. "Friend, look around you – we're simple farmers. We're not rich, and we raise only enough to feed ourselves and our families. And a bit extra, so come tax-time we can pay what's demanded of us. Even if we wanted to, we don't have food enough to give away. Go somewhere else to do your thieving, and leave us in peace."

Baraktha was getting impatient. That fool captain looked set to spend the rest of the day arguing, when it was quite clear that talking would get them nowhere. What was needed was action.

"Warra," he growled, "I think we need to show them what they're up against. Why don't you do something about that barrier of theirs?"

"Why not?" Warra agreed, grinning. He stepped forward and gathered his Talent. Then he threw a stream of fire at the wooden carts.

The captain's horse reared and panicked as the flame surged past. It was all the rider could do to stay in his seat. The rickety carts ignited, sending a blazing jet of fire skyward. The men manning the barricade fell backward, yelling and panicking. One man's sleeve caught fire, and he rolled in the dirt, howling, to extinguish it.

"What are you doing?" the captain yelled out, struggling to control his mount.

"Cutting out the crap," Baraktha snapped. He gestured for his squad to move forward.

"I'm trying to negotiate for what we need," the captain protested.

"Your way takes too long," Baraktha informed him. He glared at the villagers' spokesman. "Right, you – hand over what we need, or there will be more of that."

"You're *Talents*," the man said, spitting again. "Filthy, inhuman scum." He raised his pitchfork. "You get *nothing*!"

"Wrong," Baraktha said. "Now – we get *everything*." He gestured his men forward.

Shara grabbed his arm. "What are you doing?" she asked him.

"Requisitioning supplies," he said. "Didn't you hear the captain?"

"There's no need for this," she protested.

"Wake up, Shara! You heard what he said – and you saw the look on his face when he realized we're Talents. We need this food, or we starve. They won't give it – so we take it. It's that simple." Much as he loved her, her weakness sometimes annoyed him.

"I won't be a party to this," she snapped.

"Then stay out of my way." Baraktha urged his men on.

The villagers tried to fight, but they were farmers. The whole lot of them *might* have been able to hold off a dozen ordinary soldiers, but they didn't stand a chance against Talents. Scythes were nasty weapons if you could get in close – but the farmers weren't allowed to close in. Warra, laughing, simply threw fireballs at them from a distance. Bollo, the Lifter, simply tossed large rocks, crushing bones. It wasn't a fight, it was a massacre. The villagers didn't stand a chance.

Some tried to hide, but Baraktha simply used his own Talent to find them, and his men killed them. Not one of the Talents suffered even a cut, but the adult villagers were all dead within a very short time.

The captain found him as he was directing the killing of the cattle and sheep. There would be plenty of food for them once the butchering was done. Other men went through the houses, hauling out the food within, and everything that had been prepared and stored for the winter.

"This is murder," the captain said, appalled. "We're soldiers, not bandits."

Baraktha was getting really tired of the man. "They wouldn't give us what we needed," he said. "That's treason. The penalty for treason is death. They're dead. Stop whining."

"When the King hears about this, he'll have us all executed!"

"No, he won't," Baraktha explained. "First of all, as I said, they were traitors, and got what all traitors get. Second, the King *needs* us to take out the other Talents at Dragonhome, doesn't he? So he can't afford to execute us. Now, if you're not going to help, get out of the damned way." He turned his back on the captain and went back to supervising the collection of supplies. As he'd expected, the soldier didn't bother him further.

Things were going quite smoothly, except in one respect. The adults had all been killed, but there were still children, most of them silent in shock, but with plenty of them whining, sniveling and crying. Baraktha had them all gathered together in the central part of the small village. There were about forty in all, of both sexes, ranging from babies to teenagers – most of the latter girls; the boys had died attempting to fight.

Warra and Shara were staring at the survivors as Baraktha eyed them. "What do we do with this lot?" the Fire Caster asked.

"You kill them," Baraktha answered.

"You can't!" Shara exclaimed in horror. "They're just children!"

Once again, he found himself in the position of explaining common sense to her. "We're taking all the food," he pointed out. "There are no adults left alive. If we simply leave them, they will all slowly starve to death. Killing them is a kindness. I take no pleasure in it, but it must be done."

"All of them?" Warra asked. He glanced at Shara. "We're not all as lucky as you, and there's a few ripe-looking girls among them. The lads would appreciate them."

Baraktha shrugged. "If you want to share your rations with them, fine. Pick out the ones you want, and kill the rest." Warra grinned and hurried off.

"But... they'll *rape* those girls," Shara protested.

Baraktha nodded. "I'm sure that's what they have in mind, yes. But maybe the girls will get smart and realize that they might as well enjoy the inevitable."

"That's horrible."

"That's the way of things," he informed her. "At least they'll live – isn't that what you wanted?"

"Not at this price."

He turned to her. "Then kill them. All those poor girls who are destined to be raped. You have the power – all you have to do is kill them. You'll save their virtue – if they even have any. They're peasants, you know, and they've probably been doing it for years." He waved at the small group of girls who were being singled out. "You've got my blessing – go on over there, and kill any or all of them. I'll make sure nobody stops you."

As he had known, she simply couldn't do it. She was powerful, but weak, held back by her emotions. She simply couldn't grasp reality. Instead, she stood beside him, pale and tortured, as the Talents slit the throats of the babies and the unselected children.

Soon enough, the village was quiet.

Chapter 15

"What?" Morgone asked, appalled.

"You heard me," Hagon growled, glaring down at him. "It's time for you to learn to fly."

Morgone swallowed. "I can't fly."

Hagon somehow managed to roll his huge eyes. "No, of course you can't – but I can. All you have to do is to get on my back, and I'll do the rest." Then he grinned. "Oh, and *stay* on, of course."

Margone had never before considered that he might be a coward, but for the first time he wondered about it. The idea of just leaping up into the sky, supported only by a dragon he wasn't entirely sure liked him, seemed... somewhat foolhardy.

It wasn't helping his state of mind that Corri was giggling.

"It's all right for you," he muttered. "*You* can fly."

She managed to stop making fun of him long enough to say: "I'll come along with you. If you fall off, I'll catch you."

"That's all very well," he protested, "but I'm a lot heavier than you. I doubt you'd be able to support me in the air."

She eyed him critically. "You *have* put on a bit of weight," she agreed. "Oh well, I'd probably be able to slow you down at least, so the fall wouldn't kill you. You'd probably only break both of your legs."

"And *that's* supposed to encourage me?"

Hagon sighed. "You won't fall off," he promised. "Well, not as long as you do what I tell you. I can't answer for your inherent stupidity."

"I repeat my last statement."

"Oh, stop being a baby," Corri said. "Climb onto Hagon, and let's get going. Once you're in the air, you'll forget all your worries." She grinned. "Just think, you'll be able to experience a bit of what I enjoy. Honestly, there's nothing like flying through the air. It's so liberating."

"I'm just worried it will liberate me from my life."

Hagon growled. "I picked you as my human because I thought you were one feeble creature that I could actually respect. I'm starting to wonder if I made the right decision."

"Fine," Margone said, throwing his arms wide. "I'll fly with you. How do I get into position?"

The dragon talked him through clambering up onto his back, and sitting just in front of the huge wings. Margone felt horribly exposed. "Shouldn't I at least have a bridle or something?"

The dragon shuddered. "If you think I'd humiliate myself enough to wear a bridle," he said, "I'll drop you on purpose. Now, stop complaining and hold on."

"To what?"

"Enough!" Hagon roared, and then spread his huge wings. Their scales glittered in the sunlight, looking like they were on fire. Then the dragon took two steps, gave a great down-beat and leaped into the air.

It was all Margone could do not to scream. Air rushed past him, and he gulped for breath. He hardly dared look down, but could see that they had cleared the walls of the castle and were climbing as Hagon's wings beat with steady intensity. When they were a hundred feet or so in the air, Hagon leveled off.

"I'd normally go a lot higher than this," he said. "Best way to avoid down-drafts. But, seeing how scared you are, I thought lower might be better for the time being."

"Lower?" Margone looked down, and then wished he hadn't. The ground seemed to be a long, long way off. The castle was behind them now, and they were above the first trees of the forest.

There were birds flying *below* them...

A second later, Corri popped up next to him, a big grin on her face. "Isn't this amazing?" She didn't have to flap her arms or anything, and she almost looked as if she were simply standing on the ground, though the wind was plucking at her clothing.

"It's certainly *something*," he agreed, nervously.

"Look out ahead of you," she said. "You can see for miles. There's so much more to see from up here than when you're stuck on the ground."

He looked where she was gesturing, and he could see the forest stretching away from them into the distance. There was a sparkle of water – maybe a far-off lake- and a few clearings where there were towns and farms. He had to agree, the view from up here was certainly very different than from the ground. The air seemed to be cooler – though whether it was actually cooler or simply the result of the wind, he didn't know. It was also fresher; Dragonhome was a lovely place, but there were a lot of odors... Some good, like the scent of fresh bread cooking in the kitchens, some bad, like when you got too close to the latrines. Up here, the air was clearer and crisper.

There were clouds overhead – lacy, bubbly things that seemed to be a lot different than they seemed seen lower.

He realized that he was actually starting to enjoy the experience. Hagon's wing-strokes were strong and assured, beating regularly, keeping them up in the air. Corri spun and danced in the sky beside them, clearly loving every second of this. He wondered how she could ever abide being on the ground when she had the freedom of the skies. He was fairly certain he was in love with her, but, for the first time, he was starting to understand her life. She existed on the ground, but she lived in the air.

His horrible sense of vertigo and his fear of falling were starting to recede. It wasn't that he was exactly *comfortable* – but he was a lot less disturbed than he had been.

"You can go higher if you like," he told the dragon.

With a happy cry, Hagon leaped joyfully higher and higher. Margone was still scared, but he discovered that he was actually more thrilled than afraid. This was amazing... He looked down, and saw the lake he'd vaguely glimpsed before, and the river that wound its way through the forest.

He also saw the enemy camps, scattered all around Dragonhome. There their foes watched and waited. But they couldn't keep the three of them enclosed. Margone, Hagon and Corri had the freedom of the air, and there was nothing those troops could do about it.

He let out a happy cry of his own.

Corri flashed in, grabbed his face and gave him a quick kiss, and then danced away. "Now you're starting to understand me," she said.

"Yes," he agreed. "I am." He hugged Hagon's neck. "Thank you."

"Don't cut off my circulation," the dragon warned him. "Not a good idea." But Margone knew it was just Hagon's way of trying to sound as if he wasn't pleased. And Margone didn't care.

He was *flying*!

Sander didn't know how long he had been sitting here. He vaguely remembered Melayne trying to comfort him and bringing him food that he ignored. He remembered every time that Hovin had stopped in the sick room to examine Corran's wound. Each time, he had the same answer for the bleak look in Sander's eyes: a shrug. If even the healer didn't know whether Corran would recover, who would?

Well, Sander would, of course. All he had to do was to take off his glove and touch his son's clammy skin and *he* would know, absolutely, whether his son would live or die. All he had to do...

And all he couldn't bring himself to do. In this instance, knowledge terrified him.

Oh, it would be wonderful if he knew that Corran would live – but what if he discovered that his son would die? How could he possibly endure that? No matter how tempting it was to *know*, he was too much of a coward to do it.

Memories washed over his mind, ebbing and flowing in no particular order. Corran's birth, his mother Cassary, holding him so proudly. Then Cassary's death, leaving Sander with only their son as a link to his first wife. The terrors of raising Corran, knowing that he was a Talent, and that he would be sought by the King's Seeker, and taken off to war. Hiding his son for so long alone, until, finally – miraculously! – Melayne had shown up one day and agreed to help share Sander's burden.

After that, Melayne was impossible to unweave from his son's story. She had fallen in love with the boy as much as Cassary had ever loved her only child, and she was fierce in his defense. Sander's emotions were thoroughly mixed, thanks to Melayne. He'd been afraid to love a woman again after foreseeing and suffering through Cassary's death, but it had been impossible for him *not* to love Melayne. The three of them had become a family, and now there were two more children.

But Corran was still special to him, of course. Both for his own sake, and for the sake of Cassary, Sander's first love. It had broken Sander's heart and spirit to lose her – and he simply couldn't bear the thought of losing their child as well.

Poth stopped in from time to time as well. She, like Sander, could see the future – though he saw what *must* happen, and she saw only what *could* happen – but she could see almost nothing in Corran's lifeline. She said that it was because of the dragons, who interfered with her powers. In Corran's case, because of his close ties to Ganeth, her abilities failed miserably in foretelling anything. She tried in her own foolish way to cheer him up, but there was only one thing that would cheer him – and so far that had not happened. And it might never happen...

He looked down at his son – still in a coma and unresponsive to touch and healing Talent alike – and carefully wiped the sweat from his brow, and then held his son's hand again – his own hands being firmly gloved, of course.

Sometime, somehow, he slept, but when he jerked awake, he could see no change in anything. Corran was still limp and pale and still, his eyes closed, his breathing shallow. But he *was* still breathing.

Hovan came by a short while later, and glared down at him. "When did you last eat?"

Sander shrugged. "It's not important."

"It is to me – I don't need any further patients. If you don't get some food inside you, I'll ban you from this room." As Sander was about to protest, Hovin held up his hand. "I swear to all the gods, I will. And I'll have plenty of people to back up that edict, I promise you. Melayne, for one – you're scaring her, you know, and she doesn't need any extra distractions at this moment."

Melayne? "How is she doing?" Sander asked.

"Don't change the subject. She's almost as bad as you, but in her case I have Corri and Devra to watch over her and force her to eat and sleep. Do I need to appoint a nurse for you as well to make certain you look after yourself? There's always that Poth – but she bothers me. I wish my Talent included healing minds as well as bodies, because she's one demented nitwit. But enough about my problems – are you going to behave?"

Sander didn't want to, but even he could see the healer's point. It would do Corran no good for him to starve himself, and it must be worrying Melayne dreadfully. Hovin was right – she had so much on her mind trying to plan the defense of Dragonhome, and she didn't need any further problems. He sighed. "Have Poth bring me some food," he said, "and I promise to eat it. But I'm not leaving this room until my son recovers."

"I suppose that's the best I can get from you," Hovin grumbled. He pointed a finger at Sander. "But if Poth tells me you didn't finish your food, I'm getting some soldiers and locking you in a cell if I have to. And I expect you to eat every meal after that as well." He glared at Sander. "And it wouldn't hurt you to wash your face and comb your hair, either."

Sander nodded, barely understanding what he was agreeing to. "Is there any change in my son?"

"If there was, don't you think I'd have told you?" Hovin snapped. "No. He could wake in a minute, a month or never. Or he could simply fade away." He touched Sander gently on the arm. "Look, I know how worried and scared you are for your son, but he's been very badly wounded. I've managed to heal the entry point, but he lost a lot of blood by the time we found him. His body is very, very weak. I can knit up the damage to it, but that may not be enough. Or it may be. All we can do is to wait and pray." He bit at his lip. "I'll be honest with you, because I know you'd want nothing less – sometimes the injuries he sustained cause so much blood loss that the mind is affected. It's as if it closes down somehow. His body is making more blood all of the time, but that doesn't mean his mind will heal. There could have been too much damage caused, and his mind might never recover. There is a real possibility that Corran will be as you see him for the rest of his life – his mind unable to recover. However, that's only a possibility, and I don't know how strong it is. To be blunt, I'm in the dark here. I've done all I can, and it's now up to your son – if he's still with us, and his mind isn't already a blank slate." He looked sympathetically down. "I wish I could give you better news, but I can't." He laid a gentle hand on Sander's shoulder and then turned and left the room.

It was probably a good thing that Sander felt so numb, otherwise he'd probably have been plunged into greater despair by this report.

He knew, logically, that his son might die. But he had to hope that he wouldn't. How could he live otherwise?

If only he had the courage to take off his glove and discover the truth…

But he knew he would never do that.

Chapter 16

Lord Nephir strode into his sitting room, to discover that his cousin was already there, sipping a drink, waiting for him. He raised an eyebrow. "Drinking, Murine? Isn't it a trifle early in the day, even for you?"

"I have to do something," she snapped. "And if you got up before noon, you wouldn't consider this early in the day."

"You seem a little tetchy," he said, waving away the servant who had come to see if he wanted food. "Is your search not going well?"

Murine waited until the servant had closed the door behind him before replying. "Shera is either as pure as spring water, or else she's very good at covering her tracks." She took another sip. "I believe it's the latter, because nobody with her looks could be *that* pure."

"So you've found nothing, then?" He was annoyed and disappointed. He had been certain that Murine would have produced results.

"Not nothing, exactly," Murine answered. "But I need money."

Nephir raised an eyebrow. "Isn't your inheritance enough to keep you in clothes and lovers anymore?"

"Not for that, dear cousin. I don't live beyond my means. I need the money to bribe one of her retainers."

"You've found someone willing to talk, then?" That was more like the Murine he knew.

"So he's indicated. But he's an old family retainer, and it will take more than I can afford to convince him to switch his allegiances. People like him sell their morality at premium prices."

"Can't you offer him... other inducements?" He pointedly stared at her breasts.

"Aside from the fact that I do have certain standards," she snapped, "I doubt he remembers what to do with a woman's body."

"I'm sure you could... jog his memory, so to speak."

"His memory, certainly – but not other parts of his body, dear cousin. Men are so fragile, they wear out a lot quicker than women do. And he wore out more than a decade ago, I'm certain."

Nephir sighed. "Well, the prize is worth the expenditure, I suppose. Very well, I'll underwrite this bribery scheme of yours. Did this decrepit retainer give you any idea what he will be able to sell you?"

"He knows where the bodies are buried."

"Literal bodies, or merely allegorical ones?"

"Corpse in the ground kind, he claims."

Nephir smiled with pleasure. "Ah, the best kind of proof. Very well, inform him that I'll pay half of the... fee in advance. He'll get the rest *if* his information proves accurate. Ah – you might point out to him that what he will get if his information is *not* accurate will be a lot less to his liking."

"I believe he understands that portion of the negotiations," Murine said, smiling. "I have a meeting with him at suppertime. When will you have the money I need?" She named a very large sum.

Nephir whistled. "That will take... By tomorrow at this time," he decided. "Tell him he'd better come here, and be prepared not to return to Shera's house. Once we begin, his life will be in grave danger if she suspects anything."

"Certainly, dear cousin." She stood up. "I'll be on my way, then, and leave you to your lunch – or breakfast, or whatever it is." She moved to the door.

His hand reached to ring for the servant to see her out, and then stopped as a thought occurred to him. "Do *you* have one?"

"One what?"

"An old family retainer who knows where the bodies are buried?"

She frowned slightly. "Well, of course – old Druce. You remember him, don't you?"

Nephir did indeed – a lanky, ancient streak of misery. "Is he the only one?"

"Of course – I wouldn't have trusted anyone else. Druce has been with the family for three generations. I had to have help with the graves, and carrying the bodies."

He couldn't imagine that old man being of much help in either circumstance, but that wasn't really the point. "If he's served the family that long, then I think it's about time he retired – don't you?"

She frowned again. "You don't mean to kill him, do you?"

"Of course I do, you idiot. You just said he's the one person who could possibly betray you."

"But... *Druce*?" She shook her pretty head. "He'd never do that."

"And I'm sure that Shera would say *exactly* the same thing about the ancient retainer you're bribing." He glared at Murine. "We're playing for very high stakes here, my dear, and you can't afford to get sentimental on me now. Sooner or later Shera will think of doing to you what we're planning to do to her. It would be better if Druce weren't to face temptation, don't you think?"

For once in her self-centered life, Murine looked as if she were experiencing a crisis of conscience. She quite obviously had affection for the old servant that she'd known all of her life. Good memories, too, by the look of things. But, as he'd said, this was no time for sentiment, and eventually she clearly realized this. "I suppose you're right," she said. "We don't really have a choice." Her face fell. "But... *Druce*..."

"He's merely a servant," Nephir reminded her, "and you will be queen – provided your secrets remain safely buried. I had better accompany you – even if he is an old man, you'll need help to bury this body." He rang the bell this time, and sent his servant to make sure Murine's carriage was still waiting and ready.

Then another thought came to him. "Aleksar will be expecting his queen to be a virgin. Do you think you can fake that well enough to convince him?"

She snorted. "Trust me, once he's been between my legs, I'll be able to convince him of *anything*. And a small vial of blood, discretely hidden and spilled at the appropriate time will complete the illusion."

"I'm glad you've thought that through."

"I've been forced to play the virgin before, dear cousin. Trust me, I can be very convincing."

The servant returned to lead them to the waiting carriage. During the short journey to Murine's home, Nephir kept up a non-stop rambling conversation about the latest court gossip. You could always guarantee that the coachman would be listening with half an ear to whatever his passengers said, and Nephir didn't want to chance Murine even hinting the wrong thing.

Murine's house was not as ostentatious as Nephir's, and her household was a lot smaller. She had only a handful of servants, two maids and her cook. Once inside her receiving room, she gave her maid her cloak and sent her to find Druce. Once Nephir had declined a drink, she dismissed her servant, and they were alone again.

Nephir could see that Murine was still having qualms about what must be done. Typical female – she could see it *had* to be done, but she was allowing her feelings to interfere. Thankfully, she'd never been like this with any of her lovers when it was time to dispose of those. In fact, she seemed to have enjoyed killing them as much as bedding them. It was annoying, then, that she should have such affection for a servant, and such a struggle coming to realize that he had to die.

Women! What could you do about them? If he didn't need her as a part of this plan, he'd never have even begun this.

There was a tap on the door, and the maid returned. "Please, miss, I can't find Druce nowhere."

Murine scowled. "Has he gone on an errand for cook again?"

"Please, miss, cook says not."

"Drat the man! Where can he be?"

"The garden?" suggested Nephir, starting to get worried.

"Oh, no, sir, he ain't out there," the maid said. "He's not nowhere to be found."

That wasn't good... Nephir glanced at Murine, then snapped at the maid: "Lead me to his room, girl."

"But – it's in the servants' quarters, sir."

"Of course it is," he agreed. "I didn't think he'd have the master bedroom. Get a move on."

Flustered, the maid led the way to the top floor, Murine trailing behind. Nephir had never been in any servants' halls before; this one was quite dismal, the walls a flat beige color, with no ornamentation or paintings. He hadn't realized quite how dull their lives were before. The maid led him to a closed door, and stood beside it, wringing her hands.

Nephir opened the door and strode into the room. It was quite stark – just a bed, a smallish chest, a chair and a table. On the table was a bowl and pitcher for washing. There was nothing else. How could even a servant live with so little?

The bed was neatly made. "Has it been slept in?" he asked Murine.

"How should I know?" she snapped. "I've no idea what he does." She glared at the maid. "Well?"

"I dunno, miss," the girl replied. "We makes our beds when we gets up, so they're always tidy like that."

"When was the last time you saw Druce?" Nephir demanded.

The girl thought for a moment. "Last afternoon," she finally said. "He were carrying wood for the cook. But I doesn't usually see him much at all, sir."

"Very well," he said. "Go and ask the cook and the other servants when he was last seen, then hurry back."

"Yes, sir." She gave an awkward curtsey and fled.

"You think something has happened to him?" Murine asked, anxiously.

He opened the small chest, but it contained only clothes. He didn't know if that was at all unusual, or whether there should be anything else present. He looked around the room a little before answering the question.

"This Druce – did he have a beard?"

"No, he's very fussy about his appearance – he's always close-shaven. Though he had the shakes a bit, so he sometimes cut himself."

"He had the shakes?" Nephir said, eagerly. "What was his health like?"

"You think he might be sick somewhere?" Murine asked anxiously.

"That would be the best solution, yes," he agreed.

"He seemed healthy enough, except the slight unsteadiness in his hands."

"Damn."

"What is wrong?"

"Look around you," he snapped. "Don't you see? There's no sign of a shaving kit. A fastidious man would have one, probably beside the bowl on the table. Yet – no kit."

Murine was finally starting to get the point. He saw understanding dawn. "You think he's left the house?"

"I think it the likeliest answer, yes."

At that point the maid returned, panting. As soon as she could, she said: "Nobody's seen him since last night."

"Damn," he said again. He glared at the girl. "Go and make sure the carriage is still ready and waiting," he ordered her. The girl, still gasping for breath, nodded and shot off again.

"What do you think has happened?" Murine asked him, following him as he strode from the room.

"I think Shera has had the very same idea that you had," he replied, angrily. "Only first. That's what I think."

"Oh, gods!"

"Quite." He was rattling down the stairs. "Get your cloak – we have to go immediately."

"Go? Go where?"

"To wherever it is that you buried that last body, you idiot. We have to make certain it's not been found yet. If it hasn't, we'll move it. This way Shera will think Druce is lying to her."

"What if he hasn't gone to her? What if he is lying sick somewhere?"

"Then extra caution on our part can't hurt," he told her. "You'd better pray he's sick or dying somewhere, otherwise you could be in very serious trouble." As they were approaching the front door, he snapped to the servant there: "Fetch me a shovel – quickly!" The man looked puzzled, then hurried off.

By the time he'd helped Murine into the carriage, the man had returned with the shovel, which was stowed beside the coachman. Nephir took his seat beside his cousin and glared at her. "Tell the coachman where we're going," he growled.

"Oh. Yes." For the first time, Nephir could see that she was flustered. She was so used to being in control of everything in her life that finding her plans gone astray had thrown her. She ordered the man to drive to the small park just outside of town.

He was starting to wonder if he'd chosen the wrong person for this task. He'd always been impressed with her skill and planning in the past, and the revelation that she could become so unraveled so easily was disturbing. They were silent as the coach rattled through the streets, forcing people to get out of their way or be trampled. There was no time to spare.

He prayed that he was wrong somehow, that the old servant had just gone out for a drink and dropped dead in the street. But he couldn't take a chance on that, not with Murine's latest victim still relatively fresh. And not while they were playing for such high stakes. He couldn't afford for his cousin's reputation to be blackened in any way, not even by innuendo. He'd worked too long and too hard to fail at the last moment.

It seemed to take forever, but eventually the town gates were left behind, and they entered the small park. "Wait here," he ordered the coachman, and dragged the shovel out. He turned to Murine. "Lead the rest of the way on foot." Subdued, lost in her own thoughts, she did so.

At least they seemed to be the only people here. Murine took a side path into the woods, and then stopped near a tall tree. She gestured to a hollow in the ground nearby. "It's in there," she said, distractedly.

Then there was still a chance to salvage all of this. There were no signs that the body had been disturbed at all. He had to admit that Murine had selected a good place to dispose of it. Unless you knew there was a grave in that spot, you would never have been able to see it. He hurried to the spot and dug the spade into the ground.

He caught sight of movement out of the corner of his eye, and spun about.

Aleksar had stepped out from the small copse where he had been concealed. Beside him was Shera, a smug look on her bitch-face and they were accompanied by at least a dozen armed men, emerging from their own hiding places...

"Why, Lord Nephir," the king purred. "Fancy meeting you here! And looking so busy, too!" He turned to a couple of his men. "Come along, there – lend Lord Nephir a hand. We wouldn't want him to tire himself, would we?" Those men and several others moved forward. One took the shovel from his unresisting hands and started to dig.

Nephir was too stunned and disappointed to be able to react properly. He simply stood there, staring at the king. Aleksar was clearly enjoying himself.

He turned to Shera, who had that insufferable cat-got-the-cream look on her face. "What *do* you think he was digging for? Don't you just *love* treasure hunts?"

"I'm sure we'll all be surprised," Shera purred. "Well, *almost* all of us…"

Aleksar turned to face Nephir. "My dear Lord Nephir," he drawled. "I think we all have a little talking to do, don't you?" He glanced at Murine. "Especially that lovely cousin of yours…"

It was all over…

Chapter 17

Ysane found Sarrow seated on a rock, staring out to sea. He was clearly lost in thought, watching the waves crash, the birds wheel, and the sparkle of the sun on the waters. She hesitated to disturb him, but then he looked around and saw her. To her surprise, he smiled. "I'm not disturbing you, am I?" she asked him, anxiously. "I mean, it's nothing important."

He laughed, and gestured to the rock beside him. "Please, I'd love you to join me. I was just..." He broke off and frowned slightly. "Did Melayne ever tell you that we were from a farm near the sea, originally?"

"Yes, she did mention that." She followed his gaze out over the ocean. "Do you miss it?"

"You know, I never realized how much until I came here. Once we fled those raiders, I really didn't think about home very much. It was too painful..." He sighed. "I'd felt so safe there, but when our parents were killed and we had to run... I didn't feel safe again for a long time." He looked at her. "I'm not trying to excuse what I did. I was young, and scared, and selfish, and when I found I could kind of nudge Melayne into doing whatever I wanted... Well, I couldn't stop myself. It was wrong, and I know it was wrong, but at the time – well, it didn't *feel* wrong. It felt like the right thing to do. The *smart* thing to do. But I only mention that to explain what I'm doing here." He gestured out across the waters. "It feels so *right* to be here again, beside the sea. Like I've retreated into my childhood again."

"Sarrow, you're only eleven – I think you're *still* in your childhood."

He laughed. "I don't know – so much has happened to me – to all of us. I think we shot right out of childhood somewhere along the way. I mean – Melayne has two children! And I'm an uncle. You can't be a child and an uncle at the same time, can you?"

Ysane laughed. "I think it's possible, yes. Don't be in such a hurry to grow up. Sit here as long as you can and enjoy the sea."

"I think it's too late for that," he replied soberly. "And I'm not complaining. But when I look at Cassary – and especially the Silent One – well, *they're* children, and I feel almost an adult, and very protective of them. And that's odd, because until recently, I hadn't even thought about being an uncle. But I like them both, and I like being their uncle. As soon as I'm able, I'm going to spoil them dreadfully, you know."

"We all do." Ysane stared at him. "Sarrow, can I be honest with you?"

"I wish you would," he said. "I'm not very used to people being honest with me, to tell you the truth. When you can influence people, you don't care much about what they think or feel – you can always change it. So people haven't really been honest with me much."

She nodded. "Well, you know I wasn't very fond of you."

He grinned. "Yes, I did catch that. And I can't blame you for it."

"You were a brat, and you were hurting Melayne, even if she couldn't see it, and Melayne is my best friend. There was a time I'd gladly have beaten the crap out of you."

"I'm hoping that *was* is significant..."

"It is." She sighed. "When you first came here, I was pretty sure it was another of your tricks, and I kept a close watch on you. But you seemed to be telling the truth, and that dragon vouched for you, and it's hard to disbelieve dragons. And I've seen you with Cassary and the Silent One, and it's clear to me that you *do* care about them."

"I do," he agreed, firmly. "In a way I've never cared about anyone else before. I'm trying to learn how not to be selfish."

"Well, I think it's working. Empathy with others is important for personal growth. Learning to see what is best for other people and not just ourselves – well, that's vital, you know?"

"I'm starting to understand that, yes."

Ysane nodded. "Well, I'm not a good speaker, like your sister, or some of her other friends. I'm only a backwoods farm girl who's often way out of her depth. And I know I'm not very smart, and I'm always amazed when I'm treated like I'm somebody. Me and my Bantry – well, we're simple people, and we've found ourselves in a funny sort of position for people like us – hobnobbing with royalty and such – but, well..." She stared firmly at him. "For what it's worth, I believe you. I believe you've changed, and that you're trying to be a better person, and I can't tell you how glad I am about that. And I want you to know that you've got a friend here, even if I'm not much use for anything."

To her surprise, Sarrow burst into tears and then grabbed her and hugged her tightly. She felt rather uncomfortable, but she put her arms about him and hugged him back until he finally stopped. He wiped his eyes and his snot on the back of his sleeve and then let her go.

"You're the first person ever to say that to me that I haven't *made* say it," he told her. "Sorry if I embarrassed you."

"That's alright," she assured him. "I'm used to being embarrassed."

"Anyway," he continued, "you're wrong, you know."

Her eyes narrowed, and she felt a pang of fear. "What?"

"About not being much use for anything, and about not being somebody. Believe me, that couldn't be further from the truth. Melayne trusted you with her children, the most precious things she has. She wouldn't do that if you were *nobody*. She knows you're the person that she can rely on the most in her life, after Sander. And I can see the inner you, the person that Melayne sees. You may not be the smartest person in the world, and you may have been brought up on a farm – but so was I, and so was Melayne, don't forget. And look at her now – a Lady, with a castle, and kids and a husband who adores her." He grinned. "Pretty much like you, in fact, though you don't actually *own* this castle. If Darmen and Perria had any sense, they'd make *you* their heir, and not me."

"Get away with you." She punched him gently on the shoulder. "What use would I be as a Lady? I haven't the manners, nor the sense for it. I'm happy as I am, thank you very much."

"Well, I wouldn't want you to change," he admitted. "So, okay, you can stay just the way you are. And I am *so* glad that you've decided to be my friend. It truly does mean a lot to me."

"Get away with you," Ysane said, laughing. "You know, even without using your Talent, you can still get your way, can't you?"

He looked at her, surprised. "You know, that's actually true. It's because my way is now a sensible path instead of a selfish one. Isn't that wonderful?

"As long as you behave yourself, yes." To Ysane's surprise, she found that she was actually enjoying his company. "Anyway, it's about time for the midday meal, and I've never known you to pass up food yet…"

He hopped to his feet, grinning. "Then we'd better get back, hadn't we?" He cocked his head to one side. "I'd challenge you to race me back, but you're such an old lady it wouldn't be fair."

"Cheeky little beggar," she growled, making a mock swipe at him. He laughed and ran on ahead. He might have changed somewhat, but he was still an eleven year old boy. On the other hand, there was a slice of truth in what he said – she didn't run much these days. Maybe becoming a mother drained some of the fun out of you and poured it into your children?

They were certainly the most important things in her
life – her own boy, and Melayne's two. Even just being away
from them for a short while made her uneasy, as if she was
shirking her duties.

She reached the courtyard of the castle, and stopped,
puzzled. In the middle were three dragons – her beautiful
Loken, Melayne's Tura and Sarrow's new one, Kata. Sarrow
was arguing urgently with the latter, and the other two
appeared to be very agitated.

"What's wrong?" she asked Loken, anxiously.

"Tura is being foolish," she snapped back. "She is
insisting on flying to join Melayne. Her wound is barely
healed – such a flight might cripple or kill her. And that
new... bitch is supporting her."

"What?" Ysane knew that Tura had been wanting to
rejoin Melayne for the longest time, but Loken and Shath had
so far managed to convince her not to go. Now this new
dragon seemed to have tipped the scales, so to speak. Ysane
turned to Sarrow. "Why is Kata causing trouble?"

"She's not causing trouble," Sarrow snapped, his good
humor evaporated. "She simply agrees with Tura that she's
well enough to return to Melayne."

"What does she know?" Loken roared angrily. "Tura is
my sister – I know her better than some foreign dragon ever
can!"

Sarrow translated Kata's side of the argument for
Ysane: "You're too close to her and too worried about her to
see that the best healing she can get is to rejoin her human!"

"It's a long flight over the sea," Loken growled. "She
may get tired and fall and drown."

"And she probably won't," Kata snapped. "If that is all
that worries you, I will fly with her and look after her. She
doesn't have to make this trip alone."

"*We* will fly with her," Sarrow added to his dragon.
"I'll stay with you, of course."

"Do you really think this is a good idea?" Ysane asked Sarrow. "I mean, can't you see Loken's point of view?"

"Of course I can," he agreed. "She's worried about her sister – I understand that perfectly, trust me. But – well, Ysane, think about it. If *you* and Loken were hundreds of miles apart, would either of you be very happy?"

"No, of course not." She stroked Loken's dark nose. "I wouldn't ever want to be parted from her."

"And that's precisely how Tura feels about Melayne," Sarrow said gently. "Trust me, she'll heal a lot faster if she's with Melayne than she ever will here, pining for her human. Surely you can see that?"

"Yes." Ysane could. She knew how she would feel in these circumstances, and turned to Loken. "Can you see that, too?" she asked her, gently.

"Of course I can!" the dragon replied. "But – she is not well enough to travel."

"I think we'll have to let her be the judge of that," Ysane said. "We can't keep her here against her will. And if Kata goes with her, she won't be alone. If she gets into trouble, Kata will help."

Ysane could sense the struggling emotions in her dragon, fear fighting against love. Eventually, though, Loken bowed her head. "You'll have to help me tell Shath," she finally said. "I know he's not going to be happy about this."

"I will," Ysane promised. She turned to Sarrow. "Well, it looks like you'll be going back, then."

"Yes." He stroked Kata's neck. "I've gotten awfully fond of this old girl, and I can't let her go off alone."

"Well, there will be plenty to talk about over lunch, I can see," Ysane commented. "We'd better tell Darmen and Perria first thing."

They left the dragons and hurried inside to the small dining hall, where they ate most of the time. The banquet hall was reserved for special occasions, thankfully – it was too big and imposing for Ysane's tastes. The nurse had brought the children, and Ysane went to help feed them all. Darmen and Perria were already there, with Cassary perched between them. Perria was helping the child to play with her food. Sarrow crossed to join them and explained what had been decided.

"Kata and I will accompany Tura, to make certain she gets safely back to Dragonhome," he finished.

"And then what will you do?" Darmen asked.

Sarrow shrugged. "That rather depends upon you, my Lord," he replied. "Am I welcome back here?"

Darmen glanced at his wife and inclined his head. Perria smiled. "Well, we were going to speak to you later," she said. "But I suppose now is as good a time as any. Sarrow, we've decided that we would like to adopt you as our heir. So, yes, *please* do come back again."

Sarrow stood there for a moment, quite still. Then a tear rolled down his cheek. "Thank you," he said, catching his breath. "You have no idea how much this means to me."

"And to us," Darmen said, slightly gruffly.

Sarrow moved forward and gave Perria a tight hug. "Thank you so much." He brushed away the tears. "Does this mean I start calling you mother and father?"

Perria's eyes were full of tears also. "I certainly hope it does."

Cassary looked up from her plate and frowned, realizing she was being ignored. "Is something happening?" she asked Ysane.

"Yes, my love," Ysane replied, her own voice catching. "Something quite wonderful."

"Oh," Cassary said. "That's all right, then."

Chapter 18

Melayne had called another council of war. She didn't like doing it, but she really had no choice in the matter. Whether she liked it or not, Dragonhome was under siege, and the marching army of Talents was still on its way. Instead of the usual chambers, though, this was being held in a smaller room near Corran's sickroom – it was the only way that Melayne could get Sander to agree to attend. He wanted to be close at hand in case anything happened to his son.

She couldn't fault him for this, because she was just as worried and concerned about Corran. She wasn't his mother by birth, but she couldn't love him more if she had been. But she was trying to force down her fears and hopes about him in order to focus on other matters.

Sander was there, though his attention didn't appear to be. So were Devra and Corri, Margone and, inevitably, Poth. The latter was staring at Sander, but obviously not out of concern for Corran.

Devra was in her usual mood. "Is this going to be a council of war?" she growled. "Or a council of putting-off-making-decisions-as-usual?"

"You know how I feel about this, Devra," Melayne said. "I really don't want to be responsible for the taking of innocent lives."

"None of us do," Devra answered. "But these lives *aren't* innocent, are they?" Margone had set up a map on a spare chair, and she gestured at it. It showed the lie of the land around the castle up to about a hundred miles. "There's an army encamped all around us. Their task is to keep us contained and to kill any of us they find outside these walls."

Sander winced at this, since that was precisely what had happened to Corran, but he didn't speak. Devra's expression softened a little at this, but she carried on.

"You can hardly call them *innocent*, can you?"

"No," Melayne agreed. "And we struck back, taking out their commander, the man responsible."

"Who was promptly replaced," Devra said. "We needed to take out the entire army while we had the advantage. But, no, you wouldn't agree. Now they're entrenched, and they've been building protection against the dragons. We lost our advantage there, and may not be able to recover it. Taking them out now would be a lot harder and cost us a lot more men."

"I don't want to take them out!" Melayne protested. "We'd have to hurt them if we did."

"Yes, well, I'm sorry, but the idea of war is to do just that."

"But I didn't declare war on anybody."

Devra sighed. "It takes two to make peace, but only one to declare war. Aleksar started this, and he aims to finish it. Let's face it, he's got to destroy you in order to remain king, doesn't he?"

"If he leaves me alone, I'll leave him alone," Melayne said.

Corri snorted. "Oh, right, like *that's* going to happen! Melayne, the man's a monster, worse than the last king. Even if he leaves us all alone, he's going to do something that will annoy you – probably to his own people. And then you'll have to fight him. Devra's right, we should have struck before this, and now I'm rather afraid we're trapped."

"You *want* us to kill people?" Melayne asked.

"Of course not!" Corri's face went red. "I'd love nothing more than to live quietly and peacefully. But Aleksar isn't going to let that happen, is he? He's the one pushing for war – I'm simply saying that it's about time we stopped trying to pretend nothing is happening and for us to fight back."

"We may be running out of options," Margone added, gently. "I've been out flying on Hagon, and we've scouted out quite far." He gestured to the west on the map. "That army of Talents Aleksar has sent for is getting closer. They're about a week out now, and about to enter the holdings of Dragonhome, and that's going to be a very real problem."

"I certainly don't want to fight other Talents," Melayne protested. "They're just like us – well, most of us, Margone." He, of course, wasn't a Talent.

"But they're *not* like us," Devra snapped. "They're willing to fight for and support Aleksar, even to the point of attacking us and killing us if they can."

"They simply don't understand what they're doing," Melayne said. "When they arrive, I'll just talk to them and explain things."

"Oh, for..." Devra looked like she wanted to punch Melayne. "Look, I know Communication is your Talent, and that you can get through to people, but I wish you could get through to *yourself*! Talking to these killers isn't going to work – they already know who we are, that we're also Talents – and they simply don't care." She glared at Poth. "You – tell her what he chances of talking her way out of this situation are."

Poth blinked. "Too many dragons," she apologized. "The future's all higgledy-piggledy. Maybe this, maybe that. But – talking?" She shook her heads. "They don't want to listen. Even I can see that. Best chance is that they'll kill us all, then go on and kill Aleksar as well. They're not doing this for him, but for themselves."

"And I'm afraid that's not the worst of it," Margone said apologetically. "I've been tracking their path, and this army is very aggressive. It's also very hungry. They're been stealing food from villages as they marched. In two places so far, the villagers tried to stop them, and they simply killed everyone, took what they wanted, and burned the towns to the ground." He tapped the chart. "By tomorrow, they'll be on Dragonhome land – the farms and villages that supply food and so on to keep this place going. If they follow their usual way, they'll either steal all the food they can or else simply kill everyone and take everything. We can't let this happen. Aside from the fact that *we* need the supplies ourselves, those people are dependents of Dragonhome, and Lord Sander is sworn to protect them. If we let this army of thugs start raping, looting and killing, then *all* of the farmers and towns and villages who have sworn allegiance to Dragonhome will see that we won't protect them. In that case, they'll most likely turn against us. We won't be able to hold out for long without their help, I'm afraid."

"Not to mention," Corri mentioned, "that it would be horribly immoral of us *not* to protect them. That's our responsibility, isn't it, Melayne?"

Melayne felt shocked. "I wasn't aware of what they are doing," she said, slowly. "I'd have done something before now if I'd known these Talents were killing innocent people. I wish you had told me this before." She tried to avoid accusing Margone, but she knew it was in her voice.

He flushed. "I only just discovered this by back-tracking them," he answered.

"I'm sorry," she apologized. "I didn't mean to sound as if you'd been withholding information from me. I know you wouldn't do that." She looked at the gathered faces. "But he's right – this changes everything. And Corri's right – we have to protect the people who've sworn allegiance to Sander and Dragonhome. We can't allow this army of killers and rapists onto our lands."

Devra smiled, eagerly. "Then we prepare an attack?" she asked.

"No, of course not. Don't you ever listen to what I say?"

"Far too often," Devra replied, annoyed. "All right, what do you have in mind?"

"I told you already – I'll go and talk to them."

Devra turned to Poth. "How does it feel," she asked her, "to know that for once you're not the craziest person in the room?"

Poth giggled. "I don't know - it's never happened to me before."

Margone scowled. "Melayne, I agree with Devra completely - you can't *talk* to these people. They're on their way to kill us all, and they've proven their intent by their actions to date. Talking isn't going to work."

"Thank you," Devra said, glad that someone agreed with her for once.

"We don't know that talking won't work until we try it," Melayne said simply. "If they listen - well, then we'll have saved a lot of lives, won't we? And if they don't, well, then we can try it your way and have a war."

"The war isn't *my* way," Devra snapped. "*They* are the ones starting it; I simply think we have to finish it."

"In either event," Corri said, "we have to act *now*. By tomorrow they will be on Dragonhome land, and our people will become their prey. I know you're not ready for it, Melayne, and don't want it, but we seriously have to think about a battle." She held up a hand as Melayne opened her mouth. "I know we're not going to be able to talk you out of going to talk to them because we can never talk you out of *anything*. But you have to agree that we must prepare to strike if talking falls through. We can't let that army of Talents get any closer."

Melayne considered this and then nodded. "You're absolutely right, Corri. You, Devra and Margone get our Talents together." She sighed. "I really don't want it to come to a fight, but I agree that we have to be prepared. There's too much at stake here."

Devra nodded. "You do realize that we're seriously outnumbered, don't you? They have an army, and we have - well, maybe sixty in total, and some of those are Healers, like Hovin, and useless in a fight."

"But we have something they don't," Corri said, with a broad grin. "We have dragons."

"And they will be a great help," Margone agreed. "Not the least because it's likely to scare the poop out of even Talents. But if it comes to a fight, I'm not entirely confident we can win it." He looked at Poth. "I don't suppose you can be of any help here?"

The blonde girl shrugged. "The future is a bit iffy," she admitted. "Too many variables, too many dragons. If they listen, it goes one way, if they fight it goes another. I really wish I could tell you better, but..." She looked at Melayne. "When you talk with them, I'm going, too."

"Why?" Devra asked. "So you can knife her in the back?"

Poth laughed. "Didn't even think of that," she confessed. "Better check me for weapons before we go, eh?" Then she turned serious. "We'll be away from dragons, so I'll see clearer. And I can judge how things are going better. I can offer you the best advice."

"And you're not going anywhere without me," Devra said, firmly. "Someone has to protect your dumb ass."

Melayne held up her hands as the others chimed in. "I'm not taking an army with me," she said, firmly. "That's going to look too confrontational. I know you're all worried about me, and I love you for it, but you're not going with me. Except for Poth."

Poth looked surprised but pleased. Devra looked furious. "The only one of us you're taking is the crazy bitch who wants to steal your husband? Do you have a death wish?"

"No, I don't." Melayne smiled, but it was strained. "Poth is right - she'll be able to judge the future better if she's with me, and her help could be invaluable. I know she wants Sander, but I don't think she'd ever hurt me."

"How can you be sure?" Devra growled. "Even *she* admits she can't be sure."

"Because she's one of us now, whatever she says."

"That makes no sense!"

Melayne knew that arguing would get her nowhere with Devra. Instead, she simply reached out and hugged her. "I know you're just worried because you love me," she said, feeling the other girl stiffen up. She released the hug immediately; maybe that had been too much – she knew Devra didn't like physical contact; she was too private for that. "Sorry," she apologized.

Devra appeared confused. She glanced at Poth, who had a big smirk on her face. Melayne didn't know what was going on between the pair of them, but suspected that Devra was mostly put out because she appeared to be favoring Poth. And Poth was certainly not above rubbing that in. Maybe she should reconsider taking Poth? But the girl might well be very useful, and she needed every advantage she could get. This meeting with the Talent army was going to be very uncertain...

There was a rap on the door, and Hovin stuck his face around it. "If you're all done planning our futures," he said, "I thought that you might like to know that Corran just woke up."

For the first time in days, Sander lit up. He jumped to his feet, his face a maze of emotions. "How... how is he?"

"Apparently hungry," the Healer replied. "So I think that means he's getting better."

Melayne's heart sang, and her fears and doubts dropped away. "Can we see him?"

"You and Sander – and only for a short while," Hovin ordered. "He's very weak, but I think it would do him good to see the pair of you. Just don't overstay, and don't exert him!"

Melayne ignored whatever he was saying. She and Sander grabbed each other's hands and virtually ran from the room. Forget the future – Corran was recovering!

Chapter 19

Murine was furious and impotent. She had been – gently – thrown into a cell under the king's castle. She imagined that – as far as jails went – this was quite mild. There was a bed large enough for two people, a table and chair, and a chest for clothes. There was even a carpet on the floor. Still, there were quite obvious indications that this was not meant to be entirely comfortable. The most obvious of these was the door that had been slammed shut and locked behind her. Also, the only window was tiny and placed very close to the ceiling – clearly to dissuade any thoughts of climbing out it. The light in the room came from a large candle holder that stood inside the room beside the table. Though the candle was large, it didn't throw off enough light to illuminate the corners of the room. Finally, the sanitary facilities consisted of a pot. At least it stood in an alcove so that she wouldn't be in view of anyone looking through the bars of the door when she had to use it.

And, somewhere in the distance, someone was screaming. Clearly this place had a working torture chamber.

The fact that she was being treated almost kindly didn't alleviate the fact that she was a prisoner. She! Treated like some common criminal, and she hadn't even been informed of the charges against her. Possibly murder, as if anyone would even miss that idiot lover of hers! She paced up and down the cell, working off some of her anger. As her temper subsided, fear started to creep in.

What did Aleksar have planned for her? Would he really punish her? Or was this some show of force, to cow her cousin into submission? Nephir hadn't been arrested, as she had. Not that there was much that he could do about it, at least overtly. She was sure her cousin wouldn't leave her in this predicament... Well, *mostly* sure. He valued his position and power more than he valued her, if she was honest about matters.

He might stick his neck out for her – but if he did it wouldn't be very far.

She had to talk to Aleksar. Perhaps she could even convince him that this was all a mistake, that it was Nephir's doing, and she had only been helping out her cousin... On the other hand. That bitch Shera had clearly bribed her servant, who would undoubtedly have told everything... If Aleksar believed the stories, then it was unlikely she could ever return to his good graces. But perhaps there was a way to twist this?

Murine was still pondering her options when there was the rattle of keys and her door opened. In stepped the last person she would have expected to see. Rustling her gown, Shera slipped into the cell and nodded to the guard. The door was shut and locked behind her.

"What's this?" Murine asked. "Come to gloat?"

"Can you blame me?" Shera asked. "We both aimed at the same target, and you lost." She grinned, wrinkling her nose in a way men might find pretty. "And part of the fun of winning is getting to crow over the people you've defeated."

"Isn't that rather petty?"

"Is it?" Shera shrugged. "If it is, then I suppose I am petty. But I'm *winning* petty, rather than *losing* petty, like you."

"Well, do allow me to congratulate you then, you bitch."

"Taken in the spirit it was intended," Shera said, still smiling. "I must confess, you played the game well. Against anyone else, you might have won. But I'm an old hand at politics, my dear."

"*Very* old," Murine agreed. "The wrinkles are starting to show."

That annoyed Shera, and wiped that insufferable grin off her face. "You certainly had the right idea, attempting to bribe my servant. Unfortunately for you, he reported your approach to me. Needless to say, I gave him more money *not* to cooperate with you. And dear old Druce was *so* forthcoming – you *really* should pay your retainers better, my dear. *If* you ever get out of here."

"Do you know what Aleksar has planned for me?" Murine asked. She tried to make it sound casual, but Shera was laughing again.

"I imagine whatever he does with losers, sweetheart. Your past indiscretions are catching up with you, I'm afraid. Aleksar *does* so have his heart set on marrying a virgin – he wants to be absolutely sure that the heirs she bears him are his and not some gutter-trash's."

"Really?" Murine raised a haughty eyebrow. "And do you think you can convince him you're still a virgin?"

Shera laughed. "There's no proof that I'm not – at least, none that will ever reach him, my dear. And we both know how simple it will be to fake the wedding night."

"You're no better than I am," Murine snapped.

"Of course I'm better than you are! I *win*." Shera shook her head. "You, on the other hand, lose – badly. You're an amateur in a game only professionals can win."

"The only profession you're proficient in is the oldest in the world," Murine said.

"Tut-tut," Shera chided her. "I do not accept money for my... favors. But it does give me such a delightful idea. Perhaps I can talk Aleksar into allowing you to be useful. You've enjoyed so many lovers, my dear – far more than I have – that you might actually like it if you were sentenced to working in a brothel."

"Perhaps you *both* might enjoy that..."

They both spun around to see that Aleksar was smirking at them through the bars of the cell. Shera went white, and for one delicious moment, Murine thought she was going to faint. But somehow she managed to drag herself together.

"Aleksar," she managed to say. "Dearest... I was just talking with Murine, and making up stories –"

The king raised his hand, cutting off her excuses. "I don't think so, *dearest*. You see, I am not as naïve as either of you imagined. When I announced my intention to get married, I knew that the scheming would begin. Naturally, both Nephir and Caramin, being ambitious men, saw their chance to advance themselves and offered up their sweetest bait. I was sure you'd both prove to be – well, pretty much what you *have* proven to be: liars and whores. But – well, I need the support of your relatives, so I couldn't just walk away from you. Neither could I accept either of you. As you so correctly stated, Shera, I require my bride to be a virgin, so I know any children she produces are *mine*. It's rather a shame, really, because I do so admire a well-played hand – or other attractive anatomical feature. And I was quite sure that you'd both be plotting against each other, so all I had to do was to sit back and wait until one or the other of you struck. And Shera managed it first."

"What you may have heard me saying," Shera said, urgently. "I was *lying* – just having my fun with Murine."

"I'm sorry, my sweet, but I simply don't believe that." Aleksar smiled, a trifle sadly. "You see, I, too, liked the idea of bribing the old family retainer, just as you did. And, like Murine, I found one who seemed to be willing... But I'm a frugal man, and the idea of outbidding you for his loyalty didn't appeal to me. Plus, I think it's a bad precedent to be seen to be bribing people to change sides – it might give my own servants bad ideas." He cocked his head as there came another far-off scream. "Of course, there are other ways to make someone tell everything they know, aren't there? I do hope he finishes talking soon – his screams are starting to really annoy me."

Murine might have enjoyed seeing the shock and fear that enveloped Shera at this moment – if she wasn't in exactly the same position herself. Still, seeing that mocking smile wiped off the other woman's face was almost worth it. Almost.

This was Aleksar's moment, and he was clearly enjoying milking it to the fullest. "It's quite clear that you're both liars, whores and murderesses. Frankly, if you'd done this to anyone else, I might have rather enjoyed this sordid little story. But I can't allow the pair of you to get away with trying to con me, can I? It would look rather bad for me if I did."

He was clearly fishing for a response, and Murine wouldn't give him the satisfaction. Shera, however, couldn't resist. "What do you plan to do with us?"

"Me?" He smiled and spread his arms wide. "I don't plan to do *anything* to you. As you know, I do rather need the support of those relatives of yours. They might get a trifle annoyed if I obeyed my first instincts and killed you both – slowly. So then I had a better idea." He smiled, maliciously, and drew a dagger from his belt. Aiming through the window, he threw it hard enough that its point sank into the surface of the table.

"Now, here's my offer," he said, gently. "In the morning, I'll have this door opened, and *one* of you can go free. But only one of you. The other one will be buried. I'll leave the decision of which of you is which to you." He smiled cheerfully. "I'll be off, now. To one of you – I'll see you in the morning. To the other – farewell, forever." He turned to leave, and then turned back. "Oh, if I were you, I'd try to avoid being the first to fall asleep..." Laughing, he went away.

Murine eyed the knife, and then she eyed Shera.

It was quite clear that they both had exactly the same thought...

Chapter 20

Melayne had been working with frayed nerves for days now. Sander had been so occupied with his worry and grief over Corran, he had been unable to function properly. Melayne knew that one of them had to, so she'd pushed back her own fears and terrors as much as she could to enable her to get through the day. Now that Corran was awake and on the way to recovery, she didn't have to hold those emotions in check anymore. They flooded over her as she watched father and son hugging – gently! Everything she'd forced herself not to feel for days flooded over her. She wanted to laugh and cry, scream and shout for joy, all at the same moment. When it came her turn to give Corran a gentle hug, there were tears streaming down her face.

"I thought you'd be happy," Corran said, puzzled.

"I am, I am," she assured him, brushing his fringe back. "I just show it in a funny way."

"Very funny," he agreed.

"It's just that we've been terribly worried about you for days," Sander explained. "It's a lot of emotions to handle all at once." Melayne smiled – he knew!

"We are so glad that you're getting better again," Melayne added. "You don't know how horrible these days have been."

"Well, they're over now," Corran said, with childish practicality. "When can I get up?"

"Not for some while yet," Sander said firmly. "Hovin would probably kill us if we let you out of bed after all the hard work he's put into saving your life."

"So you'll stay there until he says it's okay for you to get up," Melayne put in. "And you'll do *everything* he tells you – understand?"

Corran grinned. "Even if he tells me to jump off a

bridge?"

"Well, if he tells you that," Melayne said, laughing, "then I'm sure it'll be because you've driven him crazy."

"Speaking of which," Sander added, trying (and failing) to sound severe, "can you tell us what you were doing in the woods when you were shot?"

Corran looked down, a guilty expression on his face. "I wanted to help out," he said, quietly. "I'm Unseen, so I thought there really wasn't much risk, and I figured I might be able to find out something useful by sneaking into the enemy camp. Only on the way back, I got tired from being Unseen for so long, and I guess I dropped it a bit too soon. One of their patrols found me..." He looked up, unhappy. "I just wanted to help out, to make you proud of me."

"Oh, you silly thing," Melayne said, hugging him again. "Corran. We're *always* proud of you! There's no need for you to risk your life trying to impress us!"

"Quite the contrary," Sander agreed. "We'll be happier if you stay here and look after yourself. It would be one less thing for us to worry about."

"I'm sorry you had to worry about me." Corran looked up fiercely. "But everyone else is doing their part to help in this war, and I wanted to do something, too."

"We understand that," Sander said, gently. "And your heart is in the right place. But you are still a boy, and our son, and what we want the most is for you to be safe."

"None of us are safe right now."

"We know that," Melayne agreed. "But we're doing our very best to change that. And, right now, the best way for you to help us is to stay out of trouble and get better. This way we won't be distracted from what we have to do because we're worrying about you. You do understand that, don't you?"

"I guess so," he agreed reluctantly. "I'll promise to be good and stay here until Hovin says I can get up. Okay?"

"Very okay," Sander said.

The door opened, and Hovin bustled in with one of the servant girls. "Right, that's long enough a visit," he decided. "The two of you get out of here and let me look after my patient now. You can come back in a few hours." He held up his hand before they could speak. "I'll let you know when. Now – scat!" As Melayne and Sander obeyed, they heard him addressing Corran: "Right, time for a bath – you're quite ripe, my lad."

"I don't want you to give me a bath!" Corran protested.

"I figured that," Hovin agreed. "That's why it's this pretty young lady who'll be doing it. I'm sure you won't object to her." The door was closed before Melayne could hear Corran' reply.

She and Sander hugged one another tightly. She could feel that his tension was letting up, that, finally, he was able to relax, stop worrying and start thinking again. She kissed him gently. "Welcome back."

He smiled ruefully. "Yes, I've been rather out of it, haven't I?"

"Understandably." Melayne stared into his eyes. "I was worried enough, but I knew it was much, much harder for you. But you had to be left to deal with it as best you could."

He nodded. "I'm afraid I really don't remember what's been happening these past few days," he admitted. "Has anything happened that I ought to know about?"

Melayne laughed. "Quite a bit, yes. Don't worry, we'll fill you in as we go along. Right now..." Her voice trailed off as she felt... strange. As if something were about to happen, something wonderful, something –

"Come on!" she cried, feeling her emotions welling up again, though for a completely different reason. "We need to be in the courtyard – *now!*" She started off at a run.

Sander was caught by surprise. "Melayne, what's wrong?" He started after her.

"Wrong? Nothing's wrong – something's *right!*" She dashed on, slipping past soldiers and servants who looked startled, but got quickly out of her way. She felt the excitement growing in her, though she could hardly say why. She just *knew* that something good, something important was happening.

She was quite breathless when she emerged into the open air. Sander arrived beside her a moment later. "Melayne, will you please tell me what's going on?"

"I'm not entirely sure," she confessed, scanning the skies. "I just *feel* that I need to be here, to – there!" She pointed into the clouds to the east. Two small shapes appeared, quickly resolving into dragons. Melayne watched, hardly daring to breathe. Her heart was pounding as it had when she had just seen Corran, alive and getting better. "Oh, Sander – it's Tura!"

"Tura?" he repeated, puzzled. He followed her gaze.

Melayne *knew* she was right – she could feel the joy emanating from her dragon as she approached the castle. Flying beside her was Kata, carrying Sarrow. The two dragons wheeled in the air, and then slipped down to settle in the courtyard.

Melayne rushed forward and hugged Tura's neck tightly. "Tura, Tura! You're well again!"

"Melayne," Tura said, sighing happily. "I am *so* glad to be with you again."

"I missed you so badly," Melayne admitted. "And I worried about you."

"I was going to say the exact same things about you," the dragon answered.

Melayne released her and took a step back to examine her. "How do you feel? How is your wound?"

Tura snorted. "I feel better for being back with you. As for my wound, it's virtually healed. The flight did me so much good, just being in the air again." She shifted uncomfortably. "Though I have to confess I'm feeling a bit stiff, and wouldn't mind a bit of a rest."

"You can rest all you want," Melayne promised. "But it is so good to have you back again." She turned to Sarrow. "You too, little brother."

He grinned and hugged her. "I wasn't gone all that long."

"How did you like the Far Isles?" she asked him. "More to the point, how did they like you?"

"Better than I expected," he said. "Answering both of your questions. Darmen and Perria are lovely, and they've agreed to adopt me as their heir." He gave her an odd look. "When I was... bad, I did it all just so I could feel safe and wanted," he said. "And, the funny thing is that when I stopped worrying about it – well, *now* I have new parents and a new home. Isn't that odd?"

Melayne laughed. "Sometimes we don't discover what we want until after we stop looking for it. I guess that's what happened to you."

"I suppose." Then he brightened up. "Melayne, I saw your children! Cassary and the Silent One. They're adorable. I'm going to be a terrible uncle, and spoil them rotten, I just know it."

"Did you have a hard time convincing them of your intentions?" Sander asked him.

"At first, yes. But once Ysane decided I was telling the truth, it all changed." He giggled. "They really do listen to her a lot, don't they?"

"She's got a good head and a better heart," Melayne said. "And everyone but her knows it." Then she sighed. "I miss my children, Sarrow, so I'm glad to hear they're all right. As soon as this is all over, I'm going to go straight back for them."

His good humor evaporated. "And when will this all be over?"

"Well, you've arrived in time for the first part," she answered. "Tomorrow I confront the Talent army, and we'll find out just how tough the fight is going to be..."

"You're not doing this alone," he said, firmly. "I'm with you."

"I agree," Sander said, scowling. "You're not confronting an army alone, and that's for certain."

Melayne smiled, though she was nowhere near as sure of herself as she hoped she sounded. "I have to speak to them by myself," she said. "They need to see that we're not afraid of them, and we're not their true enemy." She held up her hand as they both started to protest. "But I won't be alone." She reached out to stroke Tura's neck. "I have my dragon back again, for one. And, for another..." She glanced around the courtyard. "Where is Greyn?"

The wolf heard his name from where he'd been chewing a bone with a couple of his cubs. He sauntered lazily over. "Is it time for fun?" he asked.

"Very nearly," Melayne replied. "I have a task for you and your pack. But you need to make certain that you're not spotted – you're not just up against regular people this time. These are Talents."

Greyn barked, amused. "If we're seen by anyone, I'm going to give up being a wolf and retire as a dog," he said, scornfully. "What do you want of us?"

Melayne began to explain her plan, hoping that it would work as well as she was hoping...

Chapter 21

Shara looked out over the landscape ahead of them and couldn't help but feel how beautiful and peaceful it appeared. They had come through a small pass in the mountains toward the end of their march at last, and they were looking down on the valley that led to the holdings of Dragonhome. The sun was low in the sky, casting a rosy tint over the forest before them. Beyond that were the mountains, below which the stronghold of Dragonhome lay.

The captain shifted nervously beside her. On her other hand Baraktha cleared his throat and spat. "You know," he remarked, "I almost admire this Melayne."

The comment surprised Shara, but it clearly worried the captain. "You're not thinking of going over to her side, are you?" he asked.

"If I was," Baraktha said, gently, "then you'd have had your throat cut by now."

The captain looked worried again, and then laughed, nervously. "I never know when you're joking."

"If you assume *never*, you won't be far wrong," Baraktha replied. Ignoring the man, he called over his shoulder: "Cavan!" From the knot of Talents behind them, the young Seer ambled across to join them. Shara didn't like the youth – he was a Seer, and very, very creepy. He gave her odd looks from time to time, as if he was mentally stripping her. Given his abilities, perhaps he was.

He grinned nastily at Shara and then moved between her and Baraktha. "You need me." It wasn't a question.

"Yes." Baraktha gestured toward the mountains ahead. "The rebels are down there. I'm assuming they know we're here. If I were this Melayne, I wouldn't allow us to get much closer."

"Nor will she," Cavan agreed. "We'll be seeing her tomorrow."

"Can you be more specific?"

Cavan gestured at the short plain that lay in front of the forest. "Right there, fairly early."

"And will she bring her army with her?"

Cavan scowled. "I don't think so."

Baraktha's hand whipped out and he grabbed the boy by the throat, shaking him. "*Think*? You're a damned Seer, lad – you should *know*!"

Cavan squealed for a moment, flailing about, until Baraktha released him. He scowled, rubbing his throat. "It's not that simple," he whined. "She has dragons."

"I *know* she has dragons," Baraktha snarled. "Fat lot of good they'll do her – I've no intention of letting her use them against us."

"That's not what I mean," Cavan whimpered. "There's something about them... They make my Seeing go all wonky. Like it sort of slides off them. The closer this Melayne is to the dragons, the harder it is to see her."

Baraktha laughed. "By the gods," he said, finally, "I'd wondered why she had those stinking beasts about her – and now we know. They throw Seers off, making her actions that much harder to predict. Clever girl, eh, captain? Maybe I'll get me some dragons, too. It could be very useful if you could make sure your enemies don't know what you're doing."

"It might work the other way, too," Shara pointed out.

"Huh? What do you mean?"

"If *we* can't See her actions too well because of the dragons, then maybe *she* can't see ours, either."

"Shara, no wonder I love you – you're one of the few people I know who can use her brains!" Baraktha laughed again. Once such praise would have warmed her soul, but now... Well, Shara didn't know any more. She'd always followed whatever he had said. But...

They had destroyed a second village a few days back. Once again, Baraktha had led the fight, killing virtually helpless peasants whose only "crime" was trying to retain their food against the winter. Once again, babies and children had been slaughtered. Once again, more young girls had been taken to be raped. None of this seemed to bother him at all, but it was preying on Shara's conscience. She had always thought of herself as a relatively moral person. Yes, she'd killed people, but it was in a war, and she was fighting on behalf of her distant king. It was one thing to kill an enemy on a battlefield – but quite a different matter to snuff out the barely-begun life of an infant that couldn't even crawl yet...

"Well," Baraktha said, slowly, "if she can't see us, then perhaps we'd better get ready for her." He gazed out across the short meadow. "If we position men in those trees, she won't be able to see them. At a signal from us, they'll be able to cut her down."

"You think she's coming to attack us?" Shara asked.

"Why else would she confront us?" he asked, puzzled.

Shara turned to Cavan. "What do you See?" she asked him. "Maybe you don't know the details, but you must be able to See *something*."

He gave her a lopsided grin. "She's coming to talk."

"Talk?" Baraktha snorted. "What, she wants to surrender? Or does she expect *us* to give up?"

"I don't know," Cavan admitted. "But she doesn't seem to be the sort of person to give up."

"No," Baraktha agreed. "She'd not have gotten this far if she was a quitter. Well, we'd better be ready for her. We can cut her down as soon as she arrives."

"Aren't you even going to listen to her?" Shara asked.

"To *what*?" he asked. "What do you think she can possibly have to say to us?"

"I don't know," Shara replied. "That's why I think we should listen. That way, we'll find out."

"She's a traitor –" the captain began.

Baraktha cut him off. "She *talked* to the late king," he said to Shara, gently. "And within a week, he was dead. I don't think that's a coincidence – do you? I don't know about you, but I'd like to come out of this alive."

"I've heard tales –" Shara began.

"So have I," Baraktha agreed. "And that's all they are – tales. They tell all sorts of things about her, as gossip is wont to do – and, as gossip does, the tales often contradict one another. Who's to say which are true?"

Shara shrugged. "If we listen to what she has to say, we can make our own minds up."

"She's a traitor," the captain repeated, determined to finish this time. "Anyone who listens to her will be a traitor, too."

"Stuff and nonsense!" Shara snapped, annoyed. "Talk can't do anyone any harm."

"Oh, it can," Baraktha said, softly. "Talk does more damage than battles ever could. Talk makes people *believe* – believe all kinds of things that can't possibly be true. Like those stories that say Melayne is trying to get all Talents to join together – I dare say they're the ones *you've* been listening to, aren't they? They ones that say she wants a world where humans and Talents live together in peace and sweetness?"

Shara blushed, because those were *exactly* the ones she wanted so desperately to believe. "What's wrong with that?"

"It's *crap*," he replied. "We can never live together in peace with simple humans – one or the other of us has to be in charge. That's human nature. At the moment, it's the humans, because they outnumber us."

The captain looked annoyed. "You're getting dangerously close to treason yourself," he warned. "Talking like that."

"As long as it's just *talk*, you've nothing to worry about," Baraktha said. "Which is kind of my point, isn't it? Talk raises hopes and expectations, but gets you nowhere."

Shara didn't want to accept this. "Surely," she said, "there has to be a better life? One that doesn't include all of this fighting and killing?"

"Oh, Shara," Baraktha said gently, "I really hoped better of you. I really thought you had begun to understand. There *is* no better life – just the one we have. There will always be war and killing, and theft and betrayal because there will always be *people*, and that's what people do. Somebody has more than I have – and I want some of what he has. He wants more, maybe even the little I do have. What else can we do but fight over it? That's the way of all life, girl. Look about you – animals do this, too – they fight for mates, for food, for territory. We're human, but there's still the animal in us. And that's why there will never be peace – because it's not in us to be peaceful. We always want something – maybe something we don't have but could get, maybe something that somebody else already has. Either way, we want it, and we use force to take it. Life can't improve because people can't improve."

"That's too cynical for me," Shara confessed. "I simply can't accept it."

Baraktha shook his head. "You mean you simply *won't* accept it. Shara, you're just turning your back on what's real. Let's assume for one wild moment that this Melayne is somehow telling the truth – that, really, all she does want is for everyone to live together peacefully, all love and sparkliness. Does she have any idea how she's going to manage that? Can *you* even think of any way that can happen? All it would take to ruin that dream is one person with a weapon and a will. *One.* And there will always be more than just one who prefer the thought of taking what he or she wants through force than living together in peace. Can't you see that?"

There were tears running down her face. "Yes," she admitted. "Yes, I can see that there will always be people who will want to ruin even the most beautiful of dreams. But does it have to be like that?"

"Yes," Baraktha said, brutally. "Because people don't change. If this Melayne actually does think that, then she's crazy. But I don't think she does. I think that she's actually far smarter than that. I think she's done just what you seem to think – she's found a lovely dream that people can get behind and really desire. And that she's using this dream to worm her way into power. The stories say she was born a farmer's daughter, don't they? And that she's now Lady of Dragonhome? That's quite a rise, isn't it? She's snaked her way up from the dirt and dung of a farm to being a grand lady, with her own servants, and a castle and a noble husband. Oh, I'm not denying she must be very good to have managed all of that – like I said, I could almost admire her! She's taken a bunch of naïve fools and sold them this dream of hers, and used it to manipulate her way into power. And the king's right to be afraid of her, because she's obviously heading that way herself, aiming to kill him and take the throne. People like her won't be satisfied with anything less."

Shara was annoyed with him now. "You don't know *any* of that!" she snapped. "You're just projecting your own hopes and desires onto her, assuming she's just like you. You only think *she* wants the throne because that's what *you* want!"

"Oh, Shara, you shouldn't have said that," Baraktha said, gently. He gave a small gesture with his hand, and Warra grinned and moved. The Fire Caster shot a blast of flame that engulfed the captain. The startled man barely had a second to scream before he collapsed, writhing and burning. There was the sudden stench of burning flesh and Shara felt herself throwing up.

Baraktha's hand rested gently on her shoulder. "Well, that was inevitable, I suppose. I had to kill the captain some time. But when you blurted out my plans, I had no choice in the matter." He waited until she couldn't vomit up any more, and tilted her face back to stare gently down at her.

"His death is your fault, Shara," he said. "Because you talked too much, he had to die. I don't blame you for that, of course, but it does simply prove my point that talk is purely dangerous." He released her chin and turned to look out over the valley below. "Tomorrow, when this Melayne arrives to talk, we will be ready for her..."

Chapter 22

Murine was sitting on the table, waiting, when Aleksar showed up – bright and early, as she had expected. She looked at the door as he entered, and then winced from the black eye Shera had given her. Aleksar gave her an amused glance.

"You look a trifle under the weather this morning," he murmured, with fake solicitude.

"Not as bad as she looks, though," Murine said, gesturing with one foot at the crumpled pile on the floor. The hilt of the knife was just visible between the otherwise nice breasts, and there was a pool of blood on the floor beside her.

"No, that's true enough." The king moved to stand between Murine and the body. He gestured to the guard, who withdrew and then locked the cell door.

"I thought you were going to let the survivor go free?" she murmured.

"Oh, I am," he assured her. "I always keep my promises. I just want a quiet word with you before you walk out of here."

"Fair enough, I suppose," she agreed. "So, what do we discuss? The weather?"

He smiled. "I had rather thought that your future might be more of interest to you right now."

"Trust me, it is. I imagine any wedding plans are off?"

That made him laugh. "Oh, there was no chance of my marrying either of you, my dear – you're both far too... how to express it?... bloodthirsty for my tastes." He glanced down at Shera again. "Though I have to admit, you're rather competent at it."

"I strive to be the best I possibly can be," Murine admitted. "And, to be honest, there are some people that this world would be *much* better off without."

"I've never quite understood female jealousy," Aleksar

admitted. "But I can see that the two of you were both after the same prize, so I can understand how you couldn't get along."

"We had a lot in common," Murine informed him. "It's just that in some races, there can only be a winner and a loser." She pointed with her foot again. "She was the runner-up." She looked at the king. "So, you were going to talk about my future?"

"So I was. But first I have to thank you for taking care of a small problem for me." He gestured at Shera. "I didn't want either of you around – you're far too vicious and efficient for my liking – but as I explained yesterday, I couldn't kill either of you for fear of alienating your relatives. But *you* killing Shera solves all of my problems. I can't be blamed for your actions, and she's now out of my way."

"And me?" Murine asked, curiously.

"Once I let you out of here, I'm certain that Lord Caramin will probably want to have words with you about the death of his daughter. I can quite see that you had to kill her, but I doubt he'll be quite as understanding."

Murine nodded. "That's pretty much the way I thought you were planning this. I imagine that means you have both him and my cousin close at hand – ready for whichever one of us survived?"

"Quite." He smiled again. "I am so glad that you understand. I do so hate women who get all hysterical."

"Oh, neither of us was ever the hysterical type," Murine informed him.

Aleksar smiled again. "And Shera is now the dead type," he said. "And you, my dear, I'm afraid will shortly follow her."

"I don't think so."

Aleksar scowled slightly, his good humor vanishing. "And what do you, alone, imagine you can do about it? Especially since I have a sword and you have no weapons at all."

"Oh, you're wrong there, Aleksar," Murine said, softly, allowing her anger into her voice at last. "I have the best weapon in the world."

He started to speak, but then heard the rustle of a dress behind him. He started to turn, his hand on the hilt of his sword, just as Shera ran the knife she'd held close to her breast across his throat, leaving a red streak that started to pour blood.

Murine sprang into action as he started to crumple, shoving his hand from the sword hilt and drawing the weapon herself. "You really *didn't* understand women, did you?" she mocked him. "You really expected us to try and kill one another simply because that was what you planned."

"It never occurred to you that we would see that, did it?" Shera asked, smiling as he started to choke on his own blood. "Or that we could put aside our animosity for one another in a greater hatred for you?"

"Like all men, you're terribly easy to manipulate," Murine added. "Just show you what you expected to see, and it never occurred to you that we'd seen through your foolish plan."

Aleksar was gurgling and clawing the air, his blood spraying everywhere. He wasn't likely to be listening to them at all, but Murine had a dreadful urge to gloat. She kicked his leg out from under him, and he fell, dying, to the floor. "You're not very efficient," she complained to Shera. "He's taking a long time to die."

"Savor the moment, dear," Shera advised her. "It's not likely that you'll ever see the death of another king in your lifetime." She smiled. "I wanted him to suffer – where's the fun in a fast death?"

"My dear, I do believe you're even more sanguinary than I am."

"I take that as a compliment," Shera said. She glanced down at where Aleksar was still bleeding and struggling.

"You know, I think you may be right – he *is* overdoing it, isn't he? The fun's starting to wear a bit thin." She hefted the dagger again.

Murine held up the sword. "Mine's bigger – allow me." She leaned down and stabbed him through the heart. As they watched, the life went out of his eyes, and his body stopped twitching. His blood continued to leak out, though.

"That's better," Shera agreed. She smiled. "You know, we *do* make a good team, don't we? Perhaps we should extend this partnership?"

Murine raised an eyebrow. "I'll admit you're beautiful, but you're not really my type."

Shera laughed. "That wasn't *quite* what I had in mind." She looked at Murine critically. "Though..." She shook her head. "Let's think about power before sex, shall we? What I was thinking is that there's going to be a bit of a power vacuum now." She nudged the body. "And your cousin and my father are the two most likely to gain an advantage from it. Now, you know how men are – they'll probably just want to start fighting and killing over the position. It's not that I've got anything against killing, of course, but I don't see the advantage to either of us if our relatives hack each other to death."

"Nor I," Murine agreed, intrigued. "I take it that you have a better idea?"

"Well, your cousin and my father are both currently unmarried. If they happened to marry..."

"Ah!" Murine smiled. "I wed your father, and you marry Nephir. Then we'll all be one big, happy family."

"Precisely. You'll be my mother, and I your daughter – won't that be fun?"

"If you *ever* call me *mother*," Murine said, "I will stab you for real."

"Well, maybe *sisters*, then – I never had a sister."

"Fine." Murine nodded. "That makes perfect sense to me. I'm sure we can convince the men that they thought of that plan."

Shera grinned. "Oh, incidentally – not that it's a deal-breaker, you understand – but do you think I'm your cousin's type?"

Murine shrugged. "As far as I know, he hasn't any type. I've never seen him with a woman. Or, for that matter, a man. Or even a sheep."

"Oh. Well, as I say, it's not important." She smiled. "I can always find… volunteers elsewhere."

"And your father and I?" Murine asked.

Shera sighed. "Well, you're a *bit* older than he generally likes."

"I'm only twenty two."

"As I said, a bit older than he likes. He lost interest in me when I was thirteen."

"Ah." Murine shrugged. "Well, as you say, not a deal-breaker. She looked down at the body. "Well, it's time for part two of our plan." She jumped down from the table and crossed to the cell door. She rapped hard on it with the hilt of her sword. "Guard! You'd better come in here – something seems to have happened to the king."

There was a rattling of the lock, and the door was flung open. Two soldiers stood there, their swords drawn. The leader saw the king's body surrounded by blood and then looked at the two women. He started to raise his sword toward Murine.

"I wouldn't do that quite yet," she said, dropping her own weapon. "You'd better think this through."

"You killed the king!" the man growled.

"Technically, yes," she agreed. "But I don't think it would be to any of our interests to admit that."

"What do you mean?"

"Well, first – do you want to admit that you two big, strong men couldn't protect the king against two small, weak and feeble women? That wouldn't go down very well, would it?" She could see that point had hit home, so she pressed on. "Second – now that Aleksar is dead, the most likely candidates to succeed him are *her* father and *my* cousin. Do you think either of them would thank you for accusing us of the murder? I shouldn't think you'll last very long, do you?"

The two guards looked at one another, and a moment later the leader's sword lowered slightly. "But… what else can we do?"

"Well, boys, if you *think* about it for a minute, isn't it very unlikely that we actually killed the king?"

The leader scowled. "Well, we as sure as hell didn't," he growled.

"You might be rewarded by the next king if he thought you did," Shera said.

"Ha! Much more likely we'd be murdered; nobody trusts a soldier who turns on his lord."

"Nor should they," Murine agreed. "So we need a better villain, and what better than a Talent?"

The soldier scowled again. "There isn't one."

"No, you just didn't *see* one," Murine explained. "Doesn't it make so much more sense that this Melayne – who's in a fight with Aleksar – sent as assassin to kill him? A Talent who could turn himself invisible?"

The two men looked at one another. Murine tried to look as if she didn't have a care in the world, but this was the crucial moment in the plan she and Shera had worked out. If these men couldn't agree to this, then the two women would certainly be in very serious trouble of being executed. She couldn't afford to be weak now, and she managed to keep the smile stuck on her face as the men considered the plan.

"We couldn't be blamed for not stopping an invisible assassin, could we?" the leader said, thoughtfully.

"Who could have stopped him?" asked the other man, already half-convinced that was the way it must have happened, despite the evidence.

"Right..." The leader looked at Murine and nodded. "That does sound like a better plan," he agreed.

"Fine," she said, trying not to seem as relieved as she felt. "Why don't you go and get our relatives – they're waiting outside somewhere – and bring them here. It looks like we're going to have to start planning another coronation soon." The two men nodded and hurried off.

Shera joined her as they sauntered out of their jail cell. "Those two are almost endearing in their gullibility," she murmured. "But they are a loose link in the plan – whatever they say now, they know the truth."

"Sister," Murine replied, "do you think either your father or my cousin would allow either of those two idiots to live?"

Shera grinned. "I do believe I'm going to enjoy being related to you."

Chapter 23

Devra couldn't stand it any longer; she'd been agonizing over her decision for far too long as it was. Now Melayne was placing herself in danger again, and she had to act. But she still couldn't make her mind up what she should do. She needed advice, and that wasn't something she'd normally admit. And there was only one person she could turn to...

Corri had finished washing her face. The two of them were sharing a room in Dragonhome together, as they often had in the past. Despite her love for Melayne, there was nobody Devra felt as close to as she did to Corri. They had been inducted into the Farrowholme army together and trained together for months before Melayne had turned up and shown that there was a better way to live. Since then, they had been virtually inseparable. The blonde girl might be a little light-hearted and certainly didn't take things as seriously as Devra did, but she had a good heart, a smart mind and fierce loyalty.

But asking for her advice would mean admitting a few things Devra had hoped nobody else would ever know. Still, if she couldn't trust and believe in Corri, then she might as well just slit her wrists and have done with everything.

"Can I ask your advice on something important?" she finally managed to force herself to say.

Corri looked surprised. "*You* needing advice from *me*?" She grinned. "Normally, you'd be the one *telling* me what I should be doing."

"I know, I know," Devra agreed. "But I really do need advice, and –"

"I'm the only one in the room to turn to," Corri finished, laughing. "Okay, what's on your mind?"

"Poth."

"Oh." Corri grimaced. "Yes, we've noticed that you seem to be having a problem with her. You want me to help you beat her up?" She held up a clenched fist. "I'm ready – she won't see *this* one coming!"

"I don't need help beating her up," Devra growled. "If I thought it would do any good, I'd beat the crap out of her myself. But she's crazy, and I'm not sure even a beating would deter her."

Corri sobered up, and came to sit beside her. "Then what is it?"

"You know she's after Sander, of course – I mean, she doesn't hide it."

"And it's not going to happen, either," Corri said. "You know Sander only has eyes for Melayne – and vice versa."

That was like driving a dagger through Devra's heart, but she tried to ignore the pain. "She's going with Melayne – just the two of them – to confront the Talent army in a short while. I'm terrified that she'll take the opportunity to make certain Melayne won't come back from that meeting. I've tried to convince Melayne, but you know what she's like."

"Yes – she's even more stubborn than you are," Corri agreed. "She's made up her mind to take Poth, and none of us will be able to change that." Then her face fell. "Devra – you're not thinking of *killing* Poth, are you?"

Devra's heart was heavy. "It might be the best solution. I don't *want* to do it – oh, who am I kidding? That bitch irritates me so much, I'd probably enjoy it. But I know it would upset Melayne..." She spread her hands helplessly. "Corri, what am I going to do? Poth tried to enlist me to help her in her mad schemes – she wanted me to find the best way that she could win over Sander."

"What?" Corri's eyes widened. "Wow, she must be crazy." Then a thought occurred to her. "Why did she even *think* you might help her?"

They were getting dangerously close now to the secret that Devra wanted to guard. "That doesn't really matter," she said. "It didn't work, of course. Melayne loves Sander, and I would never help split them up, no matter what. But that leaves Poth with no other option, don't you see? The only possible way she can get what she wants is to have Melayne dead – and she'll have the perfect opportunity this morning. Melayne wants advice from her concerning those invading Talents. All she has to do is to lie, and the other Talents will kill Melayne. Then Poth can get what she wants."

"But Poth admitted she likes Melayne, and doesn't want to hurt her," Corri argued.

"And I'm sure that's perfectly true," Devra agreed. "And if she wasn't a crazy bitch, that might be enough to keep Melayne safe. But she does mad things without thinking them through. Kind of ironic, isn't it, since she can see the future?"

Corri thought a moment. "Actually, that's not true," she said, slowly. "She *can't* see the future – she can only see *possible* futures."

"What's the difference?"

The blonde girl laughed. "You've known me for years now, Devra. You're like my older sister. Tell me the truth, would you ever have expected me to fall in love with a dragonslayer?"

Devra snorted. "Not as such, no. But you're sweet, and beautiful and loving, so I always knew there would be someone out there for you."

"But that's my point," Corri said, enthusiastically. "Even you – who know me and love me best – couldn't have predicted that I'd have fallen for Margone. Let's face it, we didn't even know him until recently. The same is probably true for Poth."

"What? You think she'd fall in love with Margone too?"

"No, you ninny!" Corri laughed. "I mean that Poth saw Sander, and lusted after him. Since then, she's obsessed about him. With her Talent, she's seen all kinds of possibilities of loving him and living with him. She's become so captivated by that one possibility that she's never asked herself the obvious!"

"Maybe I'm just especially thick this morning," Devra growled. "But *what* obvious?"

"Why, she's seen that he would be good to her, and could love her and make her happy. But she's never asked herself if someone else could be better – and more available."

Devra was stunned: that had never occurred to her, either. "Corri, you're a genius! I could kiss you." Then, so happy she couldn't restrain herself, she grabbed her friend and did kiss her. "All I have to do, then, is to use *my* Talent and Find out who she's meant to be with."

Corri laughed. "A simple *thank you* would have been enough," she said. "But I appreciate the gesture."

Then a darker thought struck Devra. "What if I Find she's meant to be with Sander? Then what do we do?"

"Let's not follow that path until it's the only one," Corri advised. "Why don't you go ahead and Find her one true love? Hey, if it works, maybe you could start up your own matchmaking business once this is all over! People could get together with their loves without all the messy emotional turmoil we usually face."

"You forget that I *enjoy* seeing people make fools of themselves," Devra pointed out.

"Yeah, you'd lose all that fun. Oh well, good idea while it lasted. Meanwhile, get busy, huh?"

Devra concentrated, and brought her Talent into play... *Find Poth's one true love...*

The answer stunned her.

She looked up into Corri's eager face. "This... isn't as easy as it seemed," she finally managed to say.

"Couldn't you find her real love?" Her face fell. "It isn't Sander, after all, is it?"

"Yes and no, in that order. But... it's complicated."

"How can it be complicated? Who is it? Maybe I can help out." Corri grabbed her hands. "Tell me!"

Devra shook her head, and pulled her hands free. "Corri, you've done all that you can right now. Trust me, I deeply appreciate it. But... well, this isn't going to be very easy. I'm going to have to think about this – hard." She blinked, and then looked at her friend. "You'd better get ready – Melayne will be leaving shortly, and she'll expect us all to see her off. I'll join you there, I promise. I just need to be alone for a short while."

Then she ran from the room. She had to think this one out without any interference or further advice...

Corri watched her friend rush off, puzzled. Then she shrugged – Devra was always a deep one, never allowing her emotions to surface. She touched her lips, confused. That had been the first time since they'd known one another that she'd seen Devra give vent to any gentle emotion. Usually she was angry, or grimly intent. She had certainly never seemed happy. Yet in that quick kiss, Devra had actually seemed pleased and content for once.

Much as she loved the dark-haired girl, Corri had never quite managed to understand her. There had always been that block, those locked-off gentle emotions that she never allowed to surface. There was always that deeper, secret side to her. Devra always claimed that she didn't have a softer side, but Corri knew that simply wasn't true. Nobody could be such a good friend or leader and not *care*. She simply kept that gentler half buried, for whatever reason.

Mind you, she was so frustrating! To have gotten so close to an answer, and yet for her to refuse to divulge it! The stinker! She couldn't understand why Devra couldn't just say who Poth's intended was. She tried to imagine who it might be, how it could be so difficult to resolve, but nothing came to mind. She was just relieved that it wasn't really Sander...

Then she grinned. Maybe there was another way to approach this, through Poth herself! All she had to do was to talk to Poth and get the girl to consider her other options instead of Sander.

All! Poth didn't want to consider any other options...

Oh well, she'd worry about that part later. Right now, it was almost time for Melayne and Poth to be leaving on their mission. Corri finished brushing her hair and then hurried out to the courtyard.

It was a cool, brisk morning, with a light breeze touching her skin with a slight chill. Most everyone was already there, gathered by the dragons, making ready. Corri hurried to join them.

Melayne spotted her and gave her a quick smile, happy to see her, but she was in the middle of giving out a flurry of last minute instructions to everyone. The dragons were stomping impatiently, ready and eager to take to the air. There was Tura, Melayne's own dragon, her scales glittering greenly in the early morning light. There was Hagon, Margone at his side. He saw her, grinned and waved. She wanted to hurry to him, to hug him before he was aloft, but that could wait a moment. There was Kata, with Sarrow stroking her snout. Sander was standing next to Melayne, but he cast quick glances over at Brek, who seemed to be as impatient as the others.

And there was Poth. The elfin blonde girl was listening to Melayne, her head cocked to one side as if also listening to some private voice. Corri moved across to stand beside her.

"Poth," she said, gently. The other girl seemed to have to gather her thoughts, and then she looked back at Corri.

"Hi."

"Poth," Corri continued, "you're not planning to do anything bad to Melayne, are you?"

Poth shrugged. "I never plan anything. Things just happen."

"Well, *that* had better not happen," Corri warned her. "Anyway, it would be pointless."

"Really?" Poth's eyes widened. "What do you mean?"

"She means," growled Devra from behind Corri, "that Sander isn't the one you're meant to be with. So there's no point in hurting Melayne at all."

Poth scowled. "Of course he's the one I'm meant to be with," she said. "I've Seen it, over and over, over and over, over –"

"We get the picture," Devra said. "But you're just seeing what you *want* to see." Devra laid a hand on Corri's shoulder. "Corri is brighter than all of us put together. She realized that all you're doing is fantasizing. Only, given your Talent, your fantasies seem far, far more real to you than ours do to us."

"No," Poth said. "No, that's not true. I can See the future. I *know* what I see is real."

"Poth," Devra said, far more gently than Corri ever imagined she could ever be, "you *can* see the future, but what you see depends on what you start with. You take one factor and then look along the timeline to see what would happen if it came true. *If.* What you've done is to see Sander and then convince yourself he's *your* future, and then looked at that. Naturally what you saw is that he would be good for you, but that's not because he'd be good *only* to you. It's Sander's nature – whoever he was with, he'd be good to them. He couldn't help it. But that doesn't mean that he'd be the best person for you. Or that you'd be the best person for him."

Corri could see that Poth was listening intently, even though she was shaking her head, trying to disavow what Devra was saying.

Devra was relentless. "I can Find things, Poth. That's my Talent. And I can tell you with absolute certainty that Sander and Melayne belong together. There's no splitting them apart."

"There must be," Poth said, weakly.

"Use your Talent," Devra said. "See if you can See any way to split them up. You can't, because you've already tried. That's why you wanted my help – because you couldn't make your wish come true. And I'll tell you, here and now – neither can I, because they're meant to be together."

"No," Poth moaned, her eyes clenched shut. "No, that can't be true. He's meant to love me, he's *got* to be meant to love me."

"No, he isn't." Devra was very quiet. "Somebody else is."

Poth looked at her, confused. "Who?"

Devra touched her cheek, and then leaned in to kiss her. "Me."

Poth pulled away. She looked almost terrified. "No, it's him, it's got to be him..."

"Use your Talent," Devra urged her. "Look!"

Poth blinked hard, and then she clearly struggled to focus. Slowly the confusion slipped away from her features. She reached out to touch Devra's cheek, and said: "I never imagined..."

None of us did, Corri thought to herself. *Now* she could understand why Devra had been so hesitant about her emotions. She had been in love with Melayne all this time... and in finding Poth's true love, she'd accidentally discovered her own...

Poth leaned in and kissed Devra back. The two of them seemed oblivious to everyone else – which was as it should be. Corri felt happy for her friend.

Melayne raised an eyebrow. "Devra likes girls? Who would have thought it?"

Corri laughed. "Devra likes *anyone*? Who would have thought it?" She was happy. This was a good start to a day that might not end so well...

Chapter 24

Shara was trembling – she couldn't help herself. She'd hardly slept during the night, though Baraktha hadn't faced that problem. After having sex with her, he'd rolled over and gone to sleep, clearly untroubled by thoughts of the morrow. Shara had been unable to do that. Her mind kept playing scenarios over and over – and not one of them ended well.

There were two eventualities, obviously: war and peace. But given Baraktha's nature, the latter didn't look like it was possible. Shara had no idea what this Melayne person was like, but if she was leading the Talents here at Dragonhome, then she was undoubtedly as aggressive and cynical as Baraktha. Putting the two of them together seemed to be a recipe for disaster.

So – war, most likely. In which case, who would win? They had over two hundred Talents on their side, while Melayne couldn't have even a hundred – and probably a lot less than that. But Cavan said she was coming to meet them to talk, and virtually alone. Which didn't make any kind of sense. Except, clearly, she thought that she didn't need an army in order to defeat them.

Did this mean that Melayne was like her? Was she, too, a Death-Caster? Would she be forced to take on someone who might almost be a sister to her? She stared at her own hands in the dim light; she'd drawn the life from far too many people already. Had Melayne done the same? Was she as sick of death as Shara was? Or had all of the killing simply hardened her, as Baraktha had always insisted it should Shara?

She touched her naked stomach, still slightly sensitive from Baraktha's passions. Using her Talent, she reached within herself, and carefully killed all of his sperm. This was no time to be getting pregnant – if any time ever was. This was a handy use for her Talent, one of the few she'd ever found for an ability to murder.

What would happen in the morning? Baraktha had laid his plans for an ambush, certain he'd be able to kill Melayne and behead the resistance of the forces of Dragonhome. But was he being over-confident? Would Malayne just walk into their camp without making plans of her own?

There were stories about this Melayne that some of the Talents had heard. There was no telling how much truth there was in any of them, of course, because tales always grew in the telling. They said she rode a dragon, which was probably true, because she'd heard talk about the last dragonslayers in the world being called together for a grand quest. Nothing had been heard about them since, but there had been sightings of dragons. And Baraktha had Seen that there were indeed dragons back at Dragonhome.

There were other tales saying she protected Talents. Again, Baraktha had Seen other Talents at the castle, so there was at least a kernel of truth there, too. Baraktha insisted that this was less for protecting Talents and more like starting to build her own army. There were stories that she'd cursed the old king and he'd died shortly afterward, so it made sense that she'd be building her own army. Baraktha was convinced that she was planning to take the throne of Farrowholme for herself. That did seem possible.

But the problem was that Shara didn't *know* any of this for certain. It was all filtered through her man's cynical vision. Baraktha was convinced – but *she* wasn't. She wanted to know, to discover the truth for herself, and this meeting would give her that chance.

If Baraktha didn't simply kill Melayne out of hand.

Thoughts like these kept her disturbed all night long. It seemed like forever before the sun began to rise, and Baraktha awoke. Tired and disturbed, Shara prepared their breakfast.

"Are you going to listen to her?" she asked him as he ate.

"What's the point?" He swallowed. "She'll lie, like they all lie, attempting to get an advantage. Better to kill her as quickly as possible, and then strike at the castle." He saw the look on her face and sighed. "You want to hear what she's got to say, don't you?" Shara nodded. He shook his head. "No matter how much I talk to you, no matter how much I show you, you never seem to believe me. You're too good for this world, you know." He stroked her cheer. "Fine – I'll hear what she has to say, okay? *Then* I'll kill her."

"Maybe she's honest."

"And maybe the sun will rise in the west this morning." He glanced up. "No, it's the east again, just like every time." He shook his head. "Then I guess she'll lie to us, like everybody else has."

"I'd still like to hear her."

"And so you shall," he promised her. "Just don't raise your hopes too high. This day will end in blood, and I aim to make sure it's hers."

He made certain his plans had been carried out. He had several dozen men hidden at the edge of the woods, in clear sight of the place Cavan predicted Melayne would be standing. There were two Fire-Casters – though Warra would be with him in the greeting party – two Lifters, ready with rocks to use as missiles, and several men armed simply with bows and spears, in case Melayne had some sort of protection against Talents. In any event, she'd be caught in a trap. And Baraktha would have Shara and Warra with him, ready to strike from close at hand. No matter what her Talent was, she couldn't possibly stop them all.

Shara was sad; it didn't seem to be the right response. Baraktha, understanding her as well as he always did, stroked her arm. "We have to be prepared," he said, gently. "There's far too much at stake here to allow kindness and sympathy to rule us. You see that, don't you?"

Shara nodded, reluctantly. They had to protect their own people.

And then Cavan called: "She's on her way."

"How many with her?" Baraktha called. "And when will she be here?"

"I can't see clearly," Cavan admitted. "Not many, not more than a handful. There are dragons involved, making things hazy. They should be here very shortly." He shook his head. "Those damned dragons."

"No doubt deliberate, so we can't See properly," Baraktha growled. "It's a smart move, I'll grant her that – but it won't help her much."

A moment later, there was a cry from some of the men, and they were pointing at the sky. Shara followed their gaze, and stiffened.

It was a dragon, alright – and bigger than she'd expected. It was flying low, no more than a couple of hundred feet in the air. She could see the beat of the huge wings, and that there was a rider astride the beast. Close by, flying alongside it, were two women, one supporting the other.

There was a murmur in the ranks, and Shara couldn't blame them. The dragon was impressive; the woman astride it more impressive still. To be able to tame and handle such a creature...

The dragon swooped down and landed precisely at the spot Cavan had indicated. The great wings folded, and it sat there, balefully glowering at the assembled horde. The two flying women touched down beside it. The flyer set her passenger free, and then shot off again.

The woman on the dragon slipped down and looked at them. This had to be the fabled Melayne herself. Shara was quite amazed – the woman was younger than she was! Barely twenty, she'd estimate. And the one accompanying her was roughly the same age. Melayne was tall, with a mass of dark hair; her companion smaller, lithe and with blonde hair cropped short.

Confirming her guess, the darker girl stepped forward a pace. "I'm Melayne." She indicated her companion. "This is Poth."

Poth waved her fingers cheerfully. She looked very happy for some reason. "Hi," she said.

Baraktha nodded. "I'm Baraktha, leader of this Talent army." He gestured. "This is my woman, Shara. She wants to hear you talk."

"And you don't," Melayne said, seeming almost amused.

"There's nothing you can say that I haven't heard a thousand times before."

Melayne raised an eyebrow. "You think so? Well, I'd better get straight down to it, then." She half-turned and gestured behind herself. "Starting here are the lands of Dragonhome. My husband is the rightful-born Lord of these lands, and they are under his protection. We will not allow a marauding band of thieves, rapists and killers to endanger the peace. Therefore you have three options. First, you can turn around and go away. Second, you can give me your word that you will obey our laws and enter our lands peacefully." She eyed the army behind him. "If you do that, though, I'm going to have to insist that your men allow any of the girls they've raped to go free. And they are going to have to stand trial for their actions. As are any who participated in the murder and pillaging of those two villages you attacked."

Baraktha laughed. "You said we had three options."

"So I did – but you really won't like the third. If you insist on advancing, I'm afraid we will have to wipe you out. I *really* hope you don't pick the third option; I've never liked violence and I hate it when people force me to use it."

"You seem to have neglected a fourth option," Baraktha said gently.

"No, I don't believe I have."

"*Fourth*," he growled, "we kill the lot of you."

To Shara's surprise, Melayne actually laughed – and she seemed to mean it. "No," the girl finally said, "no, that's not an option."

"Really?" Baraktha was furious – he clearly believed he was being mocked. "Well, in that case –"

"In that case," Melayne said, almost angrily, "don't give the order to attack me. If you do, you'll be signing the death warrants of all of those men in the forest." She saw his expression. "I'm generally a very friendly person," she added. "But don't mistake that for weakness – or stupidity. If *any* of those men attempt to kill me, they will die. Instantly."

Baraktha's eyes narrowed. "What are you – a Death-Caster?"

Melayne laughed again. "No. My Talent is Communications – I can speak with anyone or any beast, and people can only tell me the truth."

"That's not much of a Talent, is it?" He mocked.

"Perhaps not," she agreed, cheerfully. "But it works for me."

Baraktha eyed the blonde girl, who was looking at them all, her head cocked to one side, grinning rather inanely. "And what's your Talent?" he asked her. "Are you some sort of an assassin?"

"Nope," the girl replied. "I have Sight – I can See the future." She nodded at Cavan. "Like him, only better."

"Then neither of you can possibly hurt me," Baraktha said. He raised his hand, giving the signal to the men hidden in the trees. Shara cried out in wordless protest. She was not at all certain that this was the best move to make.

It wasn't.

From the woods came screams, along with snarling and snapping. They lingered just a few seconds, and then there was silence.

"I warned you," Melayne said, coldly. "There was no need for those men to die. Make certain that the very next order that you give is a lot smarter than the last one."

Shara looked at the edge of the trees. There were a dozen wolves standing there, their muzzles red with the blood of men. Clearly this Melayne had some powerful and unexpected allies. She touched Baraktha's arm. "Please – *listen* to her," she urged him.

He shrugged off her hand. "Shara, Warra – *kill her!*"

Chapter 25

"That wasn't smarter," Melayne said sadly.

Warra, his face twisted with sadistic happiness, started to raise his arms to cast his fire. He never finished the gesture. A great dragon head stabbed forward, and dragon jaws crunched. There was a sudden stench of blood and intestines, and Warra fell back in two well-shredded halves.

Baraktha stared in shock, and then spun to Shara. "Kill her, you stupid bitch! Now!"

Shara shook her head. "I've had enough killing," she gasped. "Baraktha, listen to her!"

"You dumb bitch!" Barakthar roared. He reared back and slammed his fist into her, sending her breathless and sprawling on the ground.

Melayne was furious. "Stop that immediately!" Ignoring him, she moved to where the woman had fallen and bent to examine her. There was a livid welt down Shara's cheek and tears flowing that weren't entirely caused by physical pain. "He won't do that again," Melayne promised her.

"Even you!" Baraktha howled. "I always knew that I couldn't trust people – but I had thought that you loved me enough not to betray me."

"I'm *not* betraying you," Shara said, her voice dripping with her pain. "I just want you to see sense finally. Stop only hearing your own voice and *listen* for once!"

He shook his head. "No, you've fooled me for long enough, pretending you loved me, pretending you were on my side. And when push comes to shove – you're as bad as all the rest. You betrayed me."

Melayne started to speak, but Poth put a hand on her shoulder. "You'll never get through to him," she said, sadly. "He's crazier than I am."

"Your friend is right," Shara said, sadly. "He's not basically a bad person – he just thinks that the world is evil, and you have to be harder and harsher than it is just to survive."

"That sounds pretty evil to me," Melayne muttered. "To be willing to destroy anything and anyone who disappoints you? No good person would ever do that." She glanced around at the waiting army, poised to move once Baraktha gave an order. This was a very dangerous situation, and it seemed that Poth was right – for once her power of Communication wasn't too helpful. How do you Communicate with a deranged mind? But she had to try, or there would be even more deaths – possibly even her own. "Baraktha, give it up. Whatever you are planning isn't going to work. Surely you can see that? If you persist in fighting, then many, many more people will die, pointlessly."

"I'll not give up," Baraktha vowed. "I'll never give up. You won't beat me, nobody will." He glared at Shara. "Thank you for reminding me that I can trust no one." He started to raise his arm, ready to order his men to fight.

"If you try to give that order," Melayne warned him, "you will be the first one to die."

He laughed. "Do you think I'm afraid to die?" He shook his head. "I'd welcome death as an alternative to this lousy, deceitful world. But if I die, then I'll have plenty of company." He started to raise his arm again.

"No," Shara said, firmly. "There have been enough deaths. There's been enough pain that we've caused." She staggered to her feet, shaking off Poth's helping hand. She glared at Baraktha. "I've heard those girls screaming as they're raped. I saw the faces of those babies and children you ordered killed. I can't take any more."

"I only did what I had to," he said.

"You may believe that, but it's not true. *None* of that *had* to be done. They were all sacrifices to your perverted view of life. There has to be a better way. Maybe it's Melayne's way, and maybe it's not. But I can't stomach another day of your way – even if you're completely right, and this world is a hell-hole. I'd sooner go down fighting for something I can believe in than something I would hate even if we could accomplish it."

"I had such high hopes for you, Shara," he said, sadly. "I am truly sorry that you're going to have to die alongside these fools."

"And I am more sorry than you could ever know," Shara said, gently. "But this ends – here and now." She reached a hand out toward him.

He suddenly paled. "What are you doing?" he gasped. He clutched at his chest.

"What I should have done before all of this began," Shara said. "Putting you out of your misery." She clenched her fist.

Baraktha's face looked as if it were about to explode. It was red with blood, his eyes bulging. He gasped for breath, and then collapsed, finished.

Melayne touched Shara's shoulder, gently. "I'm sorry it came to this."

Shara turned her tear-streaked face toward Melayne. "I loved him," she said, softly, sadly. "That's why I couldn't do this before. I truly loved him..."

Melayne nodded. "I understand." She remembered her older brother, Kandar, and how he, too, had tried to shape the world in his own image. Sometimes people's ambitions outgrew their morality.

"No, you don't," Shara said. "You couldn't possibly. But I can't blame you." She raised her eyes, looking over the talent army that was shuffling nervously, awaiting their orders. "Well, I suppose I'll have to take care of everything else." She started to raise her arms again.

Poth smacked her across the back of her head with the hilt of her sword. She watched the woman collapse and then shrugged. "She was about to kill everybody," she explained to Melayne. "And people think *I'm* crazy." She cocked her head on one side. "Maybe we should kill her now, while she won't feel a thing. I can See there's a chance she'll carry on right where she left off when she wakes up again."

"Isn't there a chance she won't?" Melayne asked.

"Sure," Poth agreed. She jiggled her hand in the air. "It's kind of fifty-fiftyish."

"Then we'll take a chance on her," Melayne decided. She looked around at the army, and then raised her voice. "Right – your leaders are dead, and I don't know who is next in command – you'll have to sort that out yourselves. But you all have a choice to make, right here, right now. You can continue your dead leader's mad plan to invade Dragonhome and face destruction." She gestured at where Tura was still cleaning bits of flesh from her teeth. "We have dragons – quite a few of them." Greyn materialized beside her, laughing. "We have wolves – more than you'll ever see. And we, too, have Talents. That's option one. Option two is that you give up this insanity. Those of you who raped or killed innocents on your way here will be arrested and will stand trial. The rest of you can make up your own minds – you can either go on your way, away from Dragonhome, or you can join us in trying to build a better world. Those are your choices." She glared at the faces. "So – choose."

Nobody seemed to be quite certain what to do, but after a few moments, they started to break into small knots of people and started muttering between themselves.

"What's going to happen?" Melayne asked Poth quietly. "Fight or reason?"

"Too many variables to be certain," Poth answered. "So many people." She glared at Tura. "So many dragons. But I think they'll jump your way. Nobody really wants to die for nothing, and they don't have much of a purpose anymore." She grinned brightly. "Unlike me. Can I have the afternoon off?"

"I'd ask you why, but I'm afraid you'll tell me," Melayne said. "In detail. If this goes the way we hope, you and Devra can enjoy yourselves to your hearts' content."

Poth clapped her hands happily. "Yes, yes, yes, yes, yes!"

Well, at least there was one person who was happy with the way this day was turning out... She just hoped and prayed that these troops would realize that it was in their best interest to drop their invasion plans... Then there would be a lot more happy people.

Poth gave her one of her odd looks. "You know, I'm glad I didn't kill you."

"I'm rather pleased with that decision myself," Melayne admitted.

"Yes, I always liked you," Poth went on. "But when I was obsessed with Sander... well, even I didn't know what I might do. But that's all over with, and I have Devra now – and I've Seen that we're better together than Sander and I could ever have been. Isn't that strange?"

"Unforeseen," Melayne muttered. She was paying more attention to the mood of the enemy soldiers than to Poth's prattlings.

"Yes, right, exactly!" Poth laughed. "But now, I can't wait to get Devra into bed so we can –"

"I really don't think I need to hear that," Melayne said, hastily. "You just stand there quietly and plan your afternoon, okay?"

"Okay," Poth agreed, a wide grin on her face as she started to do so. Melayne wasn't at all certain that this new Poth was much of an improvement over the old Poth. Still, she was sure Devra would make the odd girl shape up.

A short while later a small delegation made its way to stand in front of Melayne. There were two tough-looking men and a slender, intense woman. The taller of the men spoke up.

"We've discussed the matter amongst ourselves," he

said, "and we've got a few things to say."

"Say away," Melayne replied.

"We've no real desire for a fight," he said. "Mind you, it's not that we don't think we could win it – it's just that we're not certain what the endgame would be if we *did* win. So we're willing to compromise a bit."

"How kind of you," Melayne said, drily. "What did you have in mind?

He looked at his two companions. "We'll agree not to come on Dragonhome lands," he said. "And you let us all go on, peaceful-like."

"Go on *where*?" Melayne asked.

The thin woman glared at her. "I don't see as to how that's any of your concern. We said we'd leave your lands untouched, and we'll keep our word. And that's *all* we'll agree to."

"So, I'm to allow you to go on with your thieving and murdering ways?" Melayne asked. "What do you take me for? And what about freeing those girls and turning the criminals who raped them and killed those children over to me for trial?"

"That won't happen," the man said, flatly.

Melayne raised an eyebrow. "So you're one of them, eh?"

He flushed. "Them's our terms," he snapped. "It's the best you'll get."

"Your best just isn't good enough," she replied. "I told you what your options were, and this is not a negotiation. The criminals get punished and you stop your raiding or else you fight."

"We're not afraid of two girls," the second man said. "Not even with a dragon." Greyn growled. "And a wolf."

Melayne pointed at the scattered body of Warra, and the very dead form on Baraktha. "They weren't frightened either, and you can see what it got them." She glared angrily at the trio. "And I have far, far more than that."

She called out: "Come!"

The rest of the pack started to move out of the shadows, slipping through the ranks of the startled army. Overhead, three shapes that looked merely like circling birds dropped down from the sky, resolving into three dragons – including Hagon the huge, who swooped low over the troops, making them duck.

"You can't scare us," the woman snapped.

"I can't?" Melayne shook her head. "Then it looks as if it will have to be war, doesn't it? Which of you wants to die first?"

The tallest man was obviously a Lifter. A large boulder jerked upward into the air. He clearly aimed to throw it at Melayne. Greyn ripped his throat out. The rock crashed to the ground as fast as the man did. The other man and the woman had been splattered by their companion's blood, and both looked shocked and pale.

Melayne tried to hide her own remorse and self-loathing at what she'd been forced to do. "Do I have a second volunteer?" she asked.

"He was the one who didn't want to turn over the criminals," the woman babbled. "We'll do it, honestly!"

"Good," Melayne said. "And make sure it's everyone – otherwise I will come after you and punish you all. Oh, and I'd advise you to split into small groups when you depart – it'll be easier for you all. If I hear of any more raids on farms or villagers, I will come after you and punish you. And I have *lots* of eyes and ears..." She held out her arms.

From the woods and from the skies they came – birds, squirrels, rabbits, foxes – animals that wouldn't normally come near one another, let alone humans. Slowly, pointedly, they gathered about Melayne.

"Remember," she warned the two delegates. "Eyes and ears – and tongues to tell me all that they know." She clapped her hands, and the animals and birds moved away.

It looked like her point had been made, finally. Subdued, the man and woman fled. She was certain that they would cooperate now.

Poth moved in closer to her. "You can't possibly get that kind of information," she muttered.

"You know that, and I know that," Melayne murmured back. "But *they* think I can. And I didn't actually tell them they'd be followed or spied on..."

Poth laughed in delight. "I like you – you're sneaky."

"Just sneaky enough, I hope," Melayne replied.

Chapter 26

Nephir was furious with Shera. His cousin had left him in a very precarious position with her actions. Not that he could really blame her, he supposed – Aleksar had forced her into it. Be that as it may, here he was without a king to manipulate, and no viable candidate in the offing.

He glanced across the conference table to where Caramin sat. "I don't suppose *you'd* like to declare yourself king?" he asked, hopefully.

Caramin laughed. "No more than you would, my dear Nephir. It seems to be a job with... limited prospects these days." He gave a delicate shudder. "Two kings dead in less than two months? Not inspirational, shall we say?" He shook his head. "Those two women have landed us right in it, haven't they?"

"Yes. It's difficult to be the power behind the throne when the throne is empty. But we can hardly blame Murine and Shera too much, can we? They were in rather a sticky situation, and had to improvise a solution."

Caramin sighed. "True. And I *am* rather fond of my daughter." He eyed Nephir. "Their idea of our intermarrying isn't actually a bad one. It will signal some sort of stability to our allies, and ensure that when we speak together on issues, there won't be any dissent."

"At least openly," agreed Nephir. "The only problem with the idea is that I am rather a confirmed bachelor. It's not that I don't think that Shera isn't pretty, or anything. I'm not even averse to her killing someone from time to time – as long as it isn't me. It's simply that I'm a creature of habit, and I have matters arranged to my liking. A wife is likely to be... disruptive."

Caramin laughed. "There are advantages, you know. My daughter is rather good in bed."

Nephir noticed he didn't add *I hear...* "I'm sure she is," he agreed, judiciously. "It's simply that my tastes don't run in that direction."

Caramin shrugged. "I've a couple of healthy sons, in that case – you can chose – or have both."

"Or in that direction, either," Nephir admitted. "I'm afraid that the thought of sharing myself with *anyone* is... disturbing." Actually, *horrifying* might be closer to the word – the thought of exchanging bodily fluids with *anyone* simply disgusted him. And he had no desire to touch any portion of any other human being's body. Who knew where they had been, and with whom?

"Suit yourself," Caramin said, carelessly. "A marriage in name only, then. Shera will probably appreciate that more, as it'll give her a chance to indulge her own tastes."

"As long as she can be discrete, she can fornicate with horses as far as I'm concerned."

The other lord grinned. "For myself, however, I'm looking forward to a little bed-play with your cousin. She still looks rather young..."

"Enough of that," Nephir said, distastefully. "The women can make the arrangements for the weddings – we have a kingdom to run in the meantime. Might I suggest, since neither of us actually wants the throne, that we declare ourselves joint regents for the time being, until the new king is found? I'm sure we'll have no end of idiots willing to assume that role."

"That certainly sounds like a reasonable plan," Caramin agreed. "Joint regents it is, then." He glanced at the door. "Shall we get the official updates now?"

"Probably the best idea," Nephir agreed. "The country won't rule itself. Who's first?"

"I thought that General Abrin might be best – find out the mood of the army."

"Yes, it would be best to be certain that they'll stand with us," Nephir said. He gave a slight smile. "I have a couple

of my men standing by in case he should prove to be...
disruptive."

"A good idea," Caramin said. He probably had the
same, Nephir knew – it would be hard to over-estimate the
man's planning.

Abrin – another recent promotion, following the death
of his less-than-efficient predecessor – was a graying man
with a sharp eye and precise movements. Clearly career
military, every inch of him reeked of training and discipline.
He snapped to a halt at the head of the table, glanced from one
man to the other and then gave a short salute aimed at the
table precisely between them.

"Thank you for coming," Nephir said. As if the man
had any choice... "You've heard the news about the king, I
trust?"

"Sir," Abrin agreed.

"Killed by a Talent assassin," Caramin said, carefully.

"Doesn't surprise me, sir," Abrin said.

"And why doesn't it surprise you, general?" Nephir
asked, curiously.

"Two reasons, sir. First, I'd put nothing past those
damned Talents. They need to all be exterminated. Second, the
late king refused to act against them when we had the
advantage – short-sighted of him. They were bound to attack
first."

Nephir was starting to like the man – not personally, of
course, but because he was precisely the kind of tool they
needed right now. "I see. And what would you
recommendation be at this moment?"

"To send in the troops, sir. Storm Dragonhome, put
them all to the sword."

Caramin coughed into his hand. "That didn't work too
well the last time it was tried, I hear."

"Different circumstances now, sir," Abrin said. "At this
precise moment, we have an advantage."

"And what would that be?" Nephir asked.

"Their leader has left the castle and taken her dragons with her," Abrin said. "That makes this the perfect opportunity to strike, before she can return."

"And you know she's not there precisely how?" Nephir asked, curiously.

"My Seer informed me a short while ago, sir."

"Seer?" Caramin sat bolt-upright in his chair, all his languor gone. "You have a *Talent* working for you?"

"Of course, sir. More than one."

"Perhaps you could explain why they were not sent to fight in the war?" Caramin asked.

"Tactical reasons, sir," Abrin said stiffly. "First, it's a great help to us if we have instant information – and that is only obtainable by using Seers. Second – we keep the very best here because we don't *want* them at the front. They might ensure that our side actually *wins* the war, and that would never do. The war needs to be continual in order to ensure the deaths of the other Talents."

"I see." Caramin leaned back again. "And your pet Seer informs you that now is your best opportunity to attack?"

"Indeed, sir." The general looked slightly confused for an instant. "I was hoping to obtain the king's approval to attack," he added.

"And you find yourself momentarily kingless," Nephir finished for him. "Not to worry – Lord Caramin and I are the two regents for the moment, and will be ruling in the name of the next king – whoever he will be."

"One of you two gentlemen, I assume?" Abrin said.

"You assume too much," Nephir snapped. "We neither of us have the right to the throne. It belongs by law to the heir of Aleksar – the gods rest his soul – and we aim to do our duty by discovering the rightful heir just as soon as we are able."

"Glad to hear that, sir," Abrin said.

Nephir raised an eyebrow. "Thought this was some sort of a coup, eh? Well, I can't blame you for thinking that.

But it isn't – we mean to ensure that the law is strictly observed." His protests and lies sounded convincing even to himself.

Abrin's rigidity actually waned for a moment. "That's quite a relief, sir."

"But until we find and confirm that person, the kingdom still has to function." Nephir turned to Caramin. "What do you think of the general's suggestion? Should we attack Dragonhome immediately?"

Caramin glanced at the general. "I assume you have some means of getting a message to the troops instantly if we agree to this attack?"

"Indeed, sir. Using more Talents, I'm afraid."

"Well, that can't be helped – at least for the moment." Caramin looked at Nephir. "I'm inclined to agree with the general – after all, we can't allow this damned Talent bitch to kill the king and not retaliate, can we?"

"Indeed we can't," Nephir murmured. "Yes, general, I think you're quite correct. Issue the order for our men to attack Dragonhome immediately. Tear down the walls again and kill everyone inside."

Chapter 27

Devra was confused, which was something of a new state for her. Usually she was quite certain of her actions and simply pushed ahead with whatever she was planning. That had always been her way – no hesitation, no second-guessing herself. Act, and be damned with the consequences!

But now… Now she was dithering around, tense and nervous, her emotions churning around like a whirlpool. One moment she felt elated, the next she was depressed. Her stomach hurt and her thoughts were rushing across her mind like rabbits chased by a fox.

What was *wrong* with her? Well, she knew the answer to *that* at least. She was in love.

Or was she?

She had been in love with Melayne for several years, even knowing how hopeless her feelings were, that Melayne wouldn't be able to reciprocate. She snorted. Reciprocate? Melayne – whose Talent was Communications! – didn't even have a clue how Devra had felt about her. Melayne still didn't suspect how Devra felt – and with a little luck (and Poth keeping her stupid mouth shut) she never would.

And now there was Poth… When Devra had used her Talent to Find the one person Poth should be with, she had been stunned to discover it was herself. She refused to believe it at first, because she didn't even like – let alone love! – the blonde girl. She'd felt a lot more like punching her out than kissing her. Then, despite her strong reservations, she had used her Talent to Find her own true love. After all, just because her ability said that *she* was the person Poth ought to be with, it wasn't a given that Poth was the one *she* should be with. Sometimes there was a mis-match – like with her and Melayne – where one person felt something and the other couldn't.

To her shock – and disgust – she Found that Poth was her match. Not Melayne...

It didn't make sense to her – how could it? She would have been happy to love Melayne unrequited for the rest of her life... Well, no, not *happy*, obviously, but at least content. She could have tolerated not being with the one person she loved if it meant that Melayne was happy. And it was quite clear that Melayne was deeply in love with Sander, to the point where she couldn't even see how other people felt about her. Sander was Melayne's entire world, and that was how love should be. Devra understood and accepted that.

But now... Now, everything was changed. Except not really. She *still* felt love for Melayne, despite everything her Talent insisted to the contrary. And as for Poth...

Well, that was complicated – far more complicated than Devra wanted her life to be. Up until now, Devra had been content to dislike and almost despise the crazy bitch. She had felt contempt for how Poth led her life – living constantly in the future-that-might-be instead of the present. No wonder the blonde girl was so crazy!

Now, though, her perspective was shifting. She kept thinking of seeing Poth naked. Thinking back, she had to admit she was a little aroused... But it was those scars she kept seeing, the burns across her shoulders and back, where the mad Burning God had unwittingly tortured Poth. What must it have been like for the girl to suffer through that? The pain must have been appalling... Was it really any wonder that she'd elected to skip out on the present and live for her dreams of the perfect future?

Of course, being Poth, she'd managed to pick the *wrong* perfect future. She'd seen Sander and fallen in lust with him. She'd Seen how the two of them might be together, and then decided that was the future she wanted.

Only it was the wrong future, just like the one Devra dreamed of with Melayne. The two of them had a lot in common, it seemed, much as the thought rankled.

And now they had the chance at the *right* future. Devra had impulsively kissed Poth this morning before the blonde went off with Melayne. She hadn't needed to do that – she could have simply *told* Poth what she had discovered – but actions always were more impressive than words. And it seemed to have worked – Poth had been confused and shocked at first, but when she had used her own Talent, it was clear that she, too, had Seen that she and Devra were destined to be together. When she'd left this morning, Poth was clearly focusing on a future with Devra, and not one with Sander.

Which meant that Devra had managed to keep Melayne safe again. Poth *probably* wouldn't have hurt her – despite her craziness, Poth had never acted violently toward anyone – but the problem with Poth was that she was quite unpredictable.

Again, there was irony in this – the girl who could See the future was the one everyone else found totally unpredictable...

Now, of course, Devra had to deliver on her promises. And she wasn't absolutely certain that she could. She was meant to be with Poth, she *knew* that. The trouble was that she didn't feel the same about her as she felt about Melayne.

It was a good thing that her own Talent wasn't Sight, because she'd have used it precisely the way that Poth had – only to See herself and Melayne together. As it was, she'd made love to Melayne dozens of times in her imagination – and felt guilty about her thoughts every single time. But she had been unable to wash the desires from her mind, and indulged them constantly.

Hmmm... Maybe she and Poth had more in common than she'd imagined... Love that couldn't be won was like a drug – something in your rational moments you wanted to escape from, but something in your pain and hurt you couldn't avoid returning to.

But now she had something real...

And she wasn't sure she actually wanted it.

Was she just being stupid? Both her Talent and Poth's insisted that they were destined to be together. Why, then, was she struggling against it?

Her feelings about Poth were quite confused. On the one hand, she still loathed the little brat for what she had done. On the other, she couldn't help feeling sorry for what she'd been through. Was it true what people said, that sometimes there was a thin line between love and hate? She'd always thought that a trite and stupid comment – the two emotions were polar opposites! – but now she was experiencing both pretty much simultaneously about Poth.

Devra wanted to hit someone, smash something. Never before in her life had she felt so uncertain, and it was that damned Poth's fault! Why had she complicated what had been such a simple matter? Why did she have to interfere in Devra's love life?

Why?

Devra's thoughts went back to Poth's naked body – not out of desire, exactly, though there was no denying that the other girl was beautiful. And she had the most illuminating smile that was really quite appealing... But instead of her perfect breasts and loins, Devra focused on those scars, the only thing marring that perfect body. Poth had been through so much pain, and it was something she would never be able to forget. Devra felt sorry for the girl's suffering – and *that*, she knew, was a lot closer to love than hate could ever be.

After all she had been through, didn't Poth *deserve* better? Didn't she deserve to be loved, and cherished and cared for? Didn't she need somebody who could ensure she'd never have to suffer pain like that again?

But could she provide that? Devra knew that she wasn't a very compassionate person – that she was quite hard-hearted, in fact. When people suffered, she generally believed that they deserved what they got.

But was that true in Poth's case? Could Devra possibly dismiss her suffering as something she simply deserved?

Devra touched her lips, remembering the kiss. Originally, she had meant it to be nothing more than a ploy to distract Poth from anything she might have been planning to betray Melayne... But when Poth had returned it with passion, well, something had changed.

It had felt quite wonderful, quite perfect. Quite right, like the most natural thing in the world.

Perhaps their Talents were right, and they *did* belong together... Devra had to confess that she knew she'd enjoy more kisses like that. She'd often imagined kissing Melayne, how that might feel, touching lips to lips. Kissing Poth had been a bit like her imagination had suggested, only with extras she'd not imagined. There had been the faint whisper of breath across her cheek as Poth had exhaled during the kiss, like a second, fleeting kiss. And there had been an excitement in her body that she'd not been prepared for, a tingling in her breasts and crotch...

Devra wrenched her mind away from those thoughts. It felt wrong to have lustful thoughts for Poth, as if she were somehow betraying Melayne by doing so. Which made no sense at all, as she and Melayne had never even considered being together. In fact, Melayne had never known how Devra even felt about her...

Maybe Poth wasn't the only crazy person in this relationship?

This was why Devra avoided having relationships with people. It was too hard. She wished that they could all be like she was with Corri – she loved Corri, but like a sister. There were no emotional overlays of attraction, no agonizing over possibilities. Just friendship. Friendship was a wonderful thing, and it felt good knowing that Corri was with her, whatever happened. And she'd defend her friend to the death. There it was – good and simple!

But when you added love to the mixture – that was truly a recipe for disaster.

Why did she have to go and fall in love? And with Melayne, of all people? It was just so *stupid*. And now she was expected to just fall out of love with her, and fall in love with Poth! Just because her Talent told her it was the right thing to do.

She wished she were just the cranky bitch that everyone took her for – somebody who didn't need anyone else, who didn't care about anyone else. Someone who was rock-solid, completely detached from emotions.

Someone other than herself, in other words.

And here she was, alone, raging and doubting herself while Melayne and Poth were off facing the enemy, together. They were risking their lives, and she was just snarling to herself, feeling sorry for herself, and complaining about her life. She fervently wished she were off fighting, because right now giving someone a good, hard punch would make her feel better.

Well, maybe not *better* – but she'd make somebody else hurt to relieve the hurt she was feeling. If she was just *doing* something, instead of being lost in self-doubt...

Resolved on that, at least, she slammed out of her room and headed toward the courtyard. As she did so, she started to become aware that there was a lot of activity going on. People – especially soldiers – seemed to be hurrying about. She grabbed the arm of one man as he passed. "What's going on?"

He gave her an annoyed look. "Haven't you heard? We're under attack." He wrenched free and hurried off.

Attack? Yes! Grinning wildly, she ran to join the others.

Something to do. Someone to hurt.

All was right with the world again.

Chapter 28

Sander had run to the battlements at the first alarm, and looked out across the approach to Dragonhome. All along the expanse of the walls, soldiers were assuming their posts, and those resting were being rousted out. He studied the land beyond the walls – the clearing that led to the woods about half a mile away, and then what he could see of the woods beyond that.

There was movement in the trees as the enemy advanced. The various paths through the trees were filled with soldiers, and several newly-constructed siege towers were trundled forward. Sander could only see a portion of the area, of course, but he knew the same kind of sights must be visible in every direction.

A moment later, Devra was beside him, a wide smile on her face. "At last," she muttered, hand on the pommel of her sheathed sword.

"You're glad to see this?" he asked her. He hadn't known the young woman long, but Melayne trusted her implicitly, which was a good recommendation. Still, she seemed to be rather bloodthirsty.

"I'm in a bad mood," Devra growled. "Punching a few enemies will do me the world of good."

"I'm rather hoping that none of them get close enough to be punched."

"Just a figure of speech – I'll be just as happy to mow them down at a distance." Devra scanned the activity. "So, what's your plan?"

"*My* plan?" Sander shrugged. "I'm not a warrior – I leave that to the professionals. I assume Captain Rause knows what he's doing."

"Never assume *anyone* knows what they're doing," Devra advised him. "This is your home, so you're ultimately in charge."

"I've never fought a battle," Sander said, patiently. "My father trained me to use a sword, but I've never actually used it on anyone."

Devra gave him a glance that appeared to be rather contemptuous, and he flushed. "Well, you picked a heck of a time to have to start," she muttered. She looked around. "Where's this Rause?"

"I don't know – giving the orders, I imagine."

"You imagine a lot." Devra took a deep breath. "Look, I'm sorry, I don't mean to be grumpy and caustic – it's just the way I am. I've had to lead my Talents for a few years now, and I'm not good at sitting back and doing nothing." She glanced out at the advancing men. "It'll be a while before they get close enough to be a problem – why don't we go and find this Captain Rause and see what he has in mind?"

That did make sense, so he nodded. "Right."

"You do know what he looks like, don't you?"

He grinned at her. "That much I do know. Come on." He led the way off the battlements and down to the courtyard. A quick glance showed him that Rause was off to one side, conferring with some of his officers. He and Devra hurried to join him.

Rause glanced up and nodded. "My Lord." He ignored Devra, which Sander could see didn't endear the soldier to her. "I'll be with you in a minute." He finished giving orders to his men, who saluted and scattered. Then he looked at Sander. "What can I do for you, my Lord?"

"We came to see what you think the situation is, captain," Sander said, before Devra could snap something unpleasant out.

"The situation is that we're in trouble," Rause replied. "They've picked their moment well. Your wife took all the dragons off to confront the Talent army, along with a good number of our Talents. They've seized their chance nicely, and they've built new siege towers. It'll take time for them to get them up to the walls, of course, and they'll no doubt make sure we keep our heads down until they do." He bit his lip, thoughtfully. "Dragonhome's been repaired, of course, but the repairs haven't been finished. The east wall is still not up to scratch, and they clearly know this. Let's face it, they've had plenty of time to study the castle in detail while they were waiting. They're focusing their towers in that area, so that's where we'll have to focus our defense. If we had the dragons, then we could just drop rocks on them from the air, like last time. But without dragons..." He shrugged.

"We still have Talents," Devra pointed out. "We have three Lifters, and if they work together, they can hoist and throw some rocks."

"Aye," Rause agreed. "I've seen them practicing, and they'll be a help. But it takes time for them to throw just one rock, and then they have to rest before they can try again. Even if they can take out one tower between them, there'll still be a dozen more left."

"We have Fire Casters," Devra said. "And those towers are wooden."

"Again, helpful, but even they can't take out a dozen towers. We have to face the fact that *some* of those towers were get close, and that means the eastern wall is likely to fall. The enemy is going to breach us there no matter what we do. So that's where we have to concentrate our forces."

Sander could see the man's point. "Are you sure that this isn't just a distraction?" he asked. "You know, to get us to focus there, and then launch the real attack at another point?"

Rause shrugged. "Possible," he agreed. "But they don't need to do it. They know our weakest spot, and they're going for it. But, obviously, we need to defend the entire perimeter. They don't – they can throw all of their forces into a single attack." He looked at Sander. "I'd suggest that you take command of the forces on the south side, my Lord, and allow me to assume command on the eastern wall."

Sander didn't need to be a soldier to get the point. "You want me clear of the worst fighting."

"My Lord, *you* are the Lord of Dragonhome. If you fall, it'll demoralize everyone. I'm just a professional soldier, and if I fall, somebody else will take over."

"And what am I to do?" Devra asked, scowling.

"You'd better take charge of the Talents," Rause told her. "They're not professional soldiers, and they're certainly not trained to follow my orders." Abruptly, he grinned. "But I've seen you handle them, and they do as you tell 'em."

"They'd better," Devra growled. Then even she cracked a smile. "Right, you tell me where you want them, and what you'd like them to do, and I'll make damned sure they do it."

Sanders swallowed and asked the most important question. "What are our chances?"

Rause grunted. "Hard to say. I imagine these troops are well-trained and disciplined, so we have to assume that they can do their jobs well. I'd say we can hold out for at least half a day once the main assault begins – and that will start in about an hour."

"And then?"

"Then, my Lord, they will get inside the castle."

"So you're saying we have no chance?" Sander asked, his mouth dry.

"There are a few thousand men out there. I have almost three hundred." He shrugged. "They're good men, but it's not enough."

Devra glared at him. "You're saying that this is futile, then?"

"What I'd normally say is that we should ask for terms of surrender," Rause replied honestly. "But it's quite clear that they don't want us to surrender – they want to annihilate us. And there's almost nothing we can do to stop them."

"Then there's nothing we can do?"

He shrugged. "Delay 'em a bit."

Sander was appalled; he'd never imagined that the situation could be this bad. "We're doomed?" he asked.

Rause shrugged again. "We'll make 'em pay for every inch they take. But they *will* take us."

"And if we had the dragons?" Devra asked.

"Then *we'd* be the one with the advantage, and we could wipe the lot of 'em out. But we *don't* have them, and they don't know we're in trouble. Somehow, those men out there know this, and they know this is their only chance. They aim to wipe the lot of us out before the dragons get back."

Devra was obviously planning ferociously. "If we can only get a message to Melayne..." she muttered.

"They have us surrounded," Rause pointed out. "Any messenger would be caught immediately. Nobody can sneak past them."

"Corran could," Devra suggested, looking at Sander with a mixture of hope and fear.

Sander shook his head firmly. "He can't even stand yet," he said. "He'd never be able to make it."

"And even if he could," Rause objected. "Even if we *did* somehow get a messenger through the lines, Melayne is two day's march from here. Even the fastest runner couldn't get to her before we'd be overrun."

He was making terrible sense. Sander could see that there wasn't much hope. "Perhaps Melayne will come back soon, anyway?" he said.

"Aye, and perhaps the enemy will all come down with the plague before they reach us," Rause said. "We can't rely on any *perhaps*."

"Besides," Devra said, slowly, "she was planning on disrupting the Talent army and sending it on its way. You know Melayne – she'll stay and see that the job is finished. She won't want any more attacks on the countryside by that army. That's going to take her at least the rest of the day. I'm afraid that the captain is quite right – she's not likely to get back here before dark."

"And by then," Rause said, soberly, 'we'll all be dead…"

Chapter 29

Devra glanced over the battlements and saw that the approaching army was getting closer. Rause had his men deployed mainly to defend the eastern ramparts where the majority of the attack appeared to be centered, but he also had some men spread around the other walls in case this was a feint. Devra was impressed that he clearly knew what he was doing – but had a horrible suspicion that he was correct when he said that it wouldn't ultimately do them much good. It was dismaying to see all of the soldiers arrayed against them.

Still, she had a job to do, and she assembled her small force of Talents in the courtyard. It was hopelessly insufficient, and she wished she'd had the forethought to send for more. And without Melayne and Corri, she felt particularly vulnerable.

And this would have been the perfect time to have Poth around – she could have run strategies past the girl and found out which had the best chance of success. Now she would have to rely on her instincts, and she felt shaky about those.

She had fifteen Talents – three of them Lifters, who were likely to be the most help. Hovin, the Healer – well, he was bound to have his work cut out for him this day, so she couldn't even think about him as one of her troops. There were two Fire-casters, who could be of great help against the siege towers. The other ten were a couple of Invisibles, three Speeders, another Finder like herself – though not as trained, as he was only thirteen – and four Shifters. They'd be pretty good at close-quarters combat, but it was a pitifully small group. She wished she had Corri here to plan with – or even Poth, annoying as she was. But she had to make do with what she had. She sent all but the Lifters off to various points on the east wall, instructing them to help out as much as possible.

Sander came over to see how she was doing. She wished she had better news for him. "The biggest problem we have," she pointed out, "is that these people clearly have their own Talents - obviously at least one Seer, to be able to pick the perfect opportunity to attack. We have to assume this Seer is good, which means that he or she probably already knows what our plans are and is countering them." She sighed.

"That's the conclusion I'd come to also," Sander said. "But we can't give in - they'd just slaughter everyone here." He looked at his gloved hands. "If only my Sight were better, and I didn't have to touch whoever's future I See…"

Devra raised an eyebrow. "Why don't you touch me and see what's going to happen?" she asked. But she already knew the answer to that. "You don't want to see me dead, do you?"

"It's what I'm afraid of," Sander confessed. "Ever since I Saw Cassary's death, years ago, I've been terrified to touch anyone I love - just in case."

Devra managed a grin. "Does that mean you love me?" she asked, cheekily. "You do know I like girls, right?"

To her surprise, he actually blushed. "I don't love you like *that*," he stammered.

"I know," she said. "But it doesn't mean I'm not going to tease you - I have to get *some* fun out of today. I had been hoping to get laid, but I'll take whatever I can…" Then she kicked at a piece of garbage on the ground. "Damn! I'm sounding like I'm already dying. I don't mean to sound so defeatist."

"But I know what you mean," he answered. "What are you planning?"

"To do whatever I can," she growled. She looked at her three Lifters. "Right, let's see what we can do, eh? Come on." She nodded at Sander and led her three men up to the battlements. The attacking soldiers were clearly nearer now. They'd be with firing range shortly…

She concentrated, using her Talent to Find the enemy's weakest spot. Not surprisingly, it was in the assault force on the south wall, not here. Forget that, then – next idea: find the enemy commander.

That was simpler – he was out of sight in the woods to the north, watching his main forces. She gestured in that direction. "Can you men lob a few boulders in that direction?"

The senior Lifter, Parron, scowled. "At what?"

"Their commander is in those woods, about a quarter mile back. Can you drop something large and nasty on his head?"

Parron snorted. "Without knowing exactly where he is?" He shook his head. "It'd be a waste of time – it'd be sheer luck if we hit anything we can't see, and the second he knew what we were up to, he'd move. Give us a target we can see, and that's another matter, lass."

That's what she'd been afraid of, so it didn't really dampen her spirits that much. "Well, we'd better concentrate on attacking the towers, then," she decided. "If I pinpoint their weakest spots, can you throw rocks at them?"

"Now *that* we can do," Parron said, grinning. He eyed the pile of rocks that had been laid in, and were waiting in the courtyard. "Mind you, they're heavy, so I can't guarantee we'll have the energy to throw a lot of them."

"And there's only about twenty missiles," another Lifter said. "Then what do we do?"

"The enemy will undoubtedly provide us with a few rocks from those catapults of theirs," Devra said, drily. "And if they knock some of the walls down, we can use the building stones. I'm not worried about running out of ammunition, unfortunately."

"Aye, lass," Parron said. "It does look a bit... rocky, eh?" He laughed at his own bad joke. "Well, we'll do what we can, while we can."

"Thank you." She found the first Fire Caster next, a scrawny young boy who looked like he hadn't eaten in weeks. Devra eyed him dubiously. "Are you up for this?"

The youth scowled back at her. "Why does everyone assume I'm weak just because I'm skinny?" he complained.

Devra flushed, annoyed. "Well, then, how far can you throw fire?"

"I can hit you from here," the youngster growled.

"That should scare the enemy," Devra replied. "How far out there?" She gestured over the walls.

The boy looked dubious. "How far were you hoping?"

"In my dreams? Those woods."

"In your dreams is right," the boy finally said. "I can *maybe* hit the attacking soldiers in the front line from here, if you want me to try."

Devra shook her head. "Better not – we don't want them to know we have you until you're certain you can hit whatever you're aiming at. And don't worry about the soldiers – with luck our archers will get some of those. You aim for the catapults or siege towers – they're the real menaces right now." She managed to summon up a pretty respectable smile. "Just do your best, kid, okay?"

"Don't call me kid," the boy growled, "unless you want me to set your pants on fire." He waved. "Get out of here – I've got this."

Devra snorted. The kid – *boy!* – had attitude, but Devra liked attitude; she had plenty of it herself. She found the second Fire Caster next. He was a thirtyish man with only one arm, his face scarred from the fights he'd been in. Still, he seemed game, but he estimated his casting ability at about the same distance as the girl. Devra encouraged him the best she could and then left him to it.

So much for her troops… She could only pray that the regular soldiers were in better shape. She glanced over the battlements again, and saw the grim, relentless approach of the enemy army. Neither side had started firing yet, though it couldn't be much longer.

It didn't look good. If Melayne were here with the dragons, they'd have a decent chance, but there was no way to summon her back. Knowing Melayne, she was doing her usual thorough job of laying down the law to the enemy Talents, and making certain that they wouldn't cause any more trouble. It had never occurred to her – or any of the rest of them! – that the enemy might have Seers and know that this would be the perfect opportunity for an attack. Well, it looked like they were going to pay for that oversight.

Devra discovered that the thought of being killed didn't bother her too much. She'd be dying with friends, at least, and there had been points in her life when she had never imagined even having any friends. Since the Seeker had dragged her off to be part of the king's army, she'd been used to getting along on her own. It wasn't until Corri had stumbled in one day that Devra had really had a friend. Not that she had had much to do with it – Corri had simply decided she was going to be Devra's friend, and that was that. There had been no fighting it. And, if she was honest with herself, she'd been very grateful to finally have someone to be close to, to be able to confide things in.

And then Melayne had burst in on them, and turned everyone's life topsy-turvy. She smiled gently at the memory. Melayne was like some sort of primal force – intense and unstoppable. Once she was sure she was in the right, she forged ahead, refusing to compromise or surrender. Somehow, she'd completely broken through Devra's air of tough independence and made her love Melayne. Devra still wasn't sure how that had happened, but there was no denying it – she had fallen in love with Melayne.

She'd managed to hide it, even from Corri. Melayne never had a clue, which was ironic, since her Talent was Communication. She was often the last person to realize things, but with luck she'd never know how Devra *really* felt about her.

And now there was Poth.

She still didn't quite know how *that* had worked out, but she knew that she had confused emotions about that maniac. There were times she could cheerfully kill the Seer, and then times when she just wanted to be alone with her, to explore her...

Well, not much chance of *that* happening now, was there? She was surprised to discover that was the one thing she really regretted about dying. Oh well, she wouldn't miss what she'd never had...

At least she was in good company. It was a shame that Sander and Corran would die, and she knew that it would break Melayne's heart. Maybe Melayne would even have a few moments to grieve for her, too, and that was a slight comfort. As for Poth – well, Poth was pretty crazy already. For her to have found and then lost her love so fast... She'd probably never recover.

"Better make sure I don't die, then," she muttered to herself.

There was a shadow overhead, and, for a brief, wonderful second she thought it was somehow the dragons returning. It didn't last, as the first of the stones from the attacking catapults slammed into the courtyard.

The first shot of the battle had missed, but the catapults would have their range now, and the rocks that followed would be on target...

Battle had been joined.

Chapter 30

Nephir sat at the large table with Caramin at his side. Facing them on the other side of the map was General Abrin, a grim expression on his face. Flanking Albrin – standing, not sitting, of course – were the two Talents he relied on. Nephir had no idea what their names were, and even less interest in knowing. He felt vaguely polluted just being in the same room with them. Abrin, however, had insisted that they were essential, and Nephir and Caramin had acquiesced.

The map, naturally, was of Dragonhome and its environs. The general had set up wooden blocks showing the strength of the troops. The defenders of the castle were painted red, and the attackers blue. The blue lines were strong and thick, the red ones small and weak.

"They have just over two hundred fighting men," Abrin explained. "And thick castle walls. We have more than three thousand troops, plus the siege towers and trebuchets. It's only a matter of time."

"And just how much time do we have?" Caramin asked. Abrin glanced at his Seer, who answered.

"That's difficult to say."

"Say it anyway," Nephir urged, gently.

The man sighed. "The presence of dragons creates interference," he began. "Normally I can see patterns, the most likely being the strongest. At the moment, those patterns are broken, their colors faded..." He saw the annoyed expression on Nephir's face and swallowed. "As far as I can tell, our attack was unexpected and will succeed." He gestured at the map. "The east wall is weakest, and the attack is concentrated there. I foresee it falling in six hours, if nothing changes."

"Nothing had better change," Nephir growled. He glared at the other Talent, the one with Sight. "You – are your abilities as compromised as his?"

This man shook his head. "No, my Lord – there are no dragons at the castle, so I can see quite clearly. The map before you is accurate. They have very few soldiers – we outnumber them something like fifteen to one. We can afford to take losses, and they cannot. The trebuchets have begun their work, and even now they are pounding at the walls."

"Good." Nephir waved his hand. "Both of you, step outside for a few moments. I wish to have private words with Abrin." The Seer raised an eyebrow – the wretch no doubt knew what Nephir wanted to say, and that annoyed him. He didn't want any freak predicting his actions. Nevertheless, both men left and closed the door behind them. Nephir faced the general. "This must be asked," he growled. "How much can we trust those Talents of yours?"

"My lord?"

"Don't play ignorant with me, Abrin," he snapped. "They're *Talents*." He gestured at the map. "The people in this castle are Talents. How do we know these men of yours aren't lying to us and simply telling us what we want to hear?"

"For two reasons, my lord," Abrin said, coldly. "Firstly, these two are *my* men. They have always been loyal, and they understand that the Talents in this castle are traitors and rebels. They have no love for these wretches."

"And the second reason?" Caramin asked lazily.

"I have another Talent who is very useful," Abrin said. "He's a Pain-Caster, and very good at his job. Those two know where they would go next if they fail me in any way."

"*That* is more reassuring," Nephir said, smiling. "Now that is settled, let's have them back again, shall we?"

Abrin was forced to get up and walk to the door to call his Talents back. It never hurt to demonstrate who was in charge. Abrin returned to the table and his men slipped back into their flanking positions behind him.

"What is happening now?" Nephir asked.

The one with Sight shrugged. "Essentially what was happening before, my lord – sieges are not swift."

Caramin sighed, and used his staff to rap loudly on the floor. The outer door was opened and one of the guards peered in. "Get the servants to fetch me a couple of bottles of wine," he ordered. To Nephir, he added: "If we must wait, let's at least make it comfortable. Would you like anything?"

Wonderful – Caramin planned on spending the time getting progressively drunk. Nephir waved the soldier away; he wanted to keep his head clear. One of them, at least, might have some serious decisions to make.

Murine was rather enjoying the company of Shera. She'd never had female friends before – she had always been competing against other women, not allying herself. It felt odd, but oddly enjoyable, to have someone she could actually talk seriously with. She didn't count Nephir; her cousin was far too serious and intense, and looked upon pleasure as something to be denied. More fool him. But Shera understood Murine, and shared many of the same desires and dreams as she did. And now that they were not competing for the same prize, they could sit and talk and enjoy one another's company.

"I have to confess," she said, popping another grape into her mouth, "that I find your company quite – enjoyable."

Shera laughed. "I was thinking much the same thing. It's strange, isn't it? In many ways, we are very like sisters, are we not? I never had any siblings, and I always felt as if I lacked something. And now I have you as a friend." She raised a delicate eyebrow. "Whoever would have imagined it?"

"Not I," Murine confessed. "I, too, am an only child, though I was raised by my uncle after my parents died, and Nephir has been almost like a brother to me."

"Really?" Shera smiled. "Did the two of you ever…?"

Murine snorted. "Not likely! He doesn't even like to *touch* another human being. He's horribly fastidious and dull." She shrugged. "I'm rather sorry you've gotten landed with him as a husband."

"Oh, I wouldn't worry about that," Shera said. "He sounds like quite the perfect man for me – he's not likely to be bothered by my lovers, then, is he?"

Murine shrugged. "As long as they're not *too* conspicuous, he'd probably be very grateful to them. How about your father?"

Shera smiled. "Oh, he enjoys his romps in bed. Apparently he's actually looking forward to bedding you – and I'd have sworn you'd be too old for his tastes." She eyed Murine critically. "But you do *look* young, and having small breasts is an advantage. A word of advice, though – shave yourself thoroughly before bed."

"I'll keep that in mind," Murine answered. "And is he likely to complain about – others?"

"Not if you're discrete. And I trust you won't begrudge him a few girls, either?"

"I'm not the jealous type."

"That's good." For a moment, Shera looked quite fierce. "I may no longer share his bed, but I still love my father. I would not have him hurt in any way."

"To each their own," Murine murmured. "If my father had done to me what your father has done to you, I'd have slit his throat. Quite cheerfully."

Shera glared at her. "My father and I love each other."

"Oh, I'm not judging you, my dear – merely pointing out that though we are alike in many ways, there are some in which we are quite different."

Shera wasn't mollified. "Much as I may like you, if you *ever* do anything to hurt my father in any way, I will kill you. Slowly. Painfully. Do you understand me?"

"Perfectly, my dear," Murine answered. "I'm sure we all feel that way about people we love. I..." Her voice trailed off as something suddenly struck her. "Oh, gods – I knew we were forgetting something."

Shera frowned. "What?"

"You just said it yourself – if anyone hurt your father, you'd kill them."

"So?"

"So – we are going to be wiping out this crazy bitch Talent woman's entire family. How do you think *she'll* react when she returns home? With *dragons*?"

Shera paled. "Perhaps we had better talk with the men."

"That might be a good idea," Murine agreed. "I don't think they've thought this completely through."

The two of them hurried to the war room. There were two guards on duty, who immediately barred their way. "No one is to enter," one of the men declared.

Murine gave him a withering glare. "I have to speak to my cousin."

The guard shook his head. "War is men's business, my lady – nothing for you to bother your pretty little head about."

Murine raised an eyebrow. "If you don't step aside, your *men's business* will be picking up your intestines and attempting to stuff them back inside your slit belly," she snapped. The guard suddenly noticed the knife she'd slid out of her sleeve and held pressed against him.

He went white. "My lady, there's no need –"

"Get out of my way, you moron," she snapped. "I have business with my cousin."

The other guard started to move to intercept her.

"Uh-uh," Shera said, showing a knife of her own. "Let's just stay calm, shall we?"

The door opened, and a furious Nephir stormed out. "What kind of stupidity is going on out here?" he yelled. He caught sight of the two women and rolled his eyes. "I might have known it. What are the two of you doing here? We're trying to conduct a war."

"And we're trying to help," Murine replied. "Only these two idiots were attempting to keep us out."

"They were simply obeying our orders. Now go back to your rooms and wait until we're done here."

"Oh, you'll be done alright," Murine said, slipping the knife back into its wrist sheath.

"What are you babbling about?"

"There's a small something you've forgotten about. But if you're not interested in saving your neck, then we'll just be going…" Murine took Shera's arm and started to turn away.

Nephir let out a sigh of anger. "Oh, very well – come in for a moment and tell us what's on your scheming little minds." He held the door open as the two women moved into the room, and then pointedly slammed it behind them. "Now – start talking, and you'd better make sense."

Murine sniffed. "You might at least fake being polite." Seeing his annoyed expression, she sighed. "Oh, very well. I take it that you've begun the attack on Dragonhome?"

"We're attempting to run it," Caramin said, drily. "It would be easier without interruptions."

"This one you need to hear, father," Shera assured him. "Your wife-to-be is already proving her worth."

"Then *prove* it," Nephir snapped.

"Have you considered what will happen *after* you take the castle and kill everyone in it?" Murine asked.

"Then we attack and slay the traitors who aren't there," Caramin said.

"Traitors who have *dragons*," Murine pointed out. "Traitors who will be very annoyed that you've slaughtered their friends and families. And *where* do you think they will vent their anger?" She gestured around the room. "Here." She saw understanding dawn on the faces of the two lords. "And are you prepared to defend this palace? This city?"

Nephir whirled on the general who was with them. "This Pain-Caster of yours – where is he?"

"In the barracks, my lord."

"Perhaps you'd better bring him here," Nephir suggested. "If that crazy woman brings her dragons here, he's going to have to bring them down with his powers."

One of the two Talents cleared his throat. "My lord, as I explained earlier, our Talents don't work well with dragons. Their own abilities somehow negate ours. I doubt he could affect a dragon."

"Then he can affect their *riders!*" Nephir yelled. "Without humans to direct them, those dragons are nothing but brutes. They'll just fly away."

"There we are, my dears," Caramin said, smoothly. "Problem solved, nothing really to worry about." He patted Murine gently on her backside. "Off you go, and don't bother yourselves anymore."

"Perhaps," Murine suggested, "you should keep us around in case we spot any other flaws in your plans."

"We would have thought of that ourselves," Nephir growled, "if we weren't so focused on the assault. Now, stop distracting us and go away."

Murine was about to protest more, but Shera touched her arm. "They won't listen," she said, softly. "We might as well leave." Murine could see from the men's expressions that she was right. It angered her that they were being dismissed so condescendingly, but this was neither the time nor the place to fight about it. Let the men get on with their war and exclude the women from their confidences. They'd learn their error, sooner or later.

Together, she and Shera swept from the room.

Chapter 31

It took the operators of the catapult three attempts to get their range right. The next boulder crashed squarely into the east wall, embedding itself and sending chunks of stone flying. Devra ducked instinctively as it hit, even though she wasn't close to the impact site. It didn't break through, of course, but it did damage. A few more in roughly the same spot could cause the wall to crumble and allow the enemy access.

She turned to the Lifter, Parron. "Can you somehow catch those rocks before they hit the wall and deflect them some way?"

He snorted. "Can you? Look, I can pick up a rock with my Talent and throw it at them – but catch a heavy, moving object? No. By the time I had some sort of a grip on it, it would have already hit."

"I was afraid of that," Devra admitted. "So there's nothing we can do to stop them chucking rocks at us, then?"

"Nothing directly, no," he said, his tone a little gentler. "I can't throw rocks that far – my Talent is strong, but not that strong. Their catapult is more powerful than I am, I'm afraid. Maybe a Fire-Caster could reach them?"

Devra shook her head. "I've already asked them – like you, their range is limited."

"Then I imagine we're lucky it takes them a while to reload their machines, otherwise they'd have the castle down around our ears in no time at all. And they can't fire once their men get too close to the castle walls."

"True - but by that time, there will probably be no castle walls…"

A few minutes later, another rock came hurtling across and slammed into the wall close by where the first had hit. Again, chunks of the wall flew in all directions.

They couldn't stand a lot of this, and there didn't seem to be a way to stop the machines. A raiding party, maybe – but they'd be cut down by the attacking army the moment they left the diminishing protection of the castle walls.

Then a crazy idea occurred to her.

"Parron, how far can you throw *me*?"

He grinned. "Depends on how mad I was at you." Then he realized what she meant. "You want me to Lift you?"

"Yeah." She watched as tiny men worked at getting the next boulder ready over at the catapult. "Could you get me that far?"

"They'd cut you to ribbons in minutes," he protested.

"Not minutes – I'm tougher than that."

"Hang on." He gazed at her, and Devra felt her feet leaving the stone floor before she settled back down again. "Yes, I could get you out there," he said. "But I won't – it's simply suicide."

"Suicide," she growled, "is sitting here and waiting for them to batter the walls down."

"Lord Sander would never agree."

"Then we don't ask him," Devra said.

Parron looked decidedly worried. "Anyway, what could you manage to do to destroy a catapult all by yourself?"

"My Talent's Finding things – I'd find its weakest point."

He shook his head. "Just because you can Find its weakest point doesn't mean you'd be able to destroy it – its weakest point could still be stronger than you."

"Don't you think I know that?" Devra asked him. "But I can't just sit here and wait for them to bring the walls down."

"All right," Parron said. "Let's somehow assume that you somehow can destroy that catapult – they still have two others they're hauling into range. You can't get all three, so the castle will still be under assault, and you'll be dead. I don't see how that helps anyone, least of all you."

"Do you have a better plan?" she snapped.

He gave her a wonky grin. "Maybe. I'll be back in a few minutes – don't go anywhere." He hurried off.

"And where can I go without you?" she yelled at his vanishing back. As soon as he was gone, she slumped against the wall behind her. She was putting on a brave front, but the thought of being killed didn't exactly thrill her. She knew she was proposing a suicide mission, but she had to do *something*. She knew that it wasn't entirely her responsibility to protect Dragonhome, but she had to do as much as she could. She owed Melayne that much. Those that Melayne loved were here – Sander, and Corran – and it was her duty to protect them if she possibly could. Even if it scared her stupid. But she couldn't let Parron – or anyone else – see her being afraid. She had to keep the fear contained, and only show confidence.

She knew that Talents were limited. Parron had admitted that the catapult she wanted to destroy was stronger than he was – but he was far more flexible than the engine of war. And her Talent of Finding... Well, it had Found her someone to love – Poth - but it couldn't guarantee her the chance that anything would come of that love. She could only hope that if she was killed that it wouldn't hurt Poth over again. The other girl had had enough disappointments in her harsh life.

Then she was surprised that she was even thinking about how Poth would be affected. Maybe she already was a little in love with the crazy girl... It was a shame she'd probably never get the chance to find out.

The attack was continuing as she struggled with her own thoughts. The attackers weren't yet close enough to fire arrows with any hope of hitting anything, but they were close enough for her to hear the men chanting battle cries. Getting their courage worked up, no doubt. They might inevitably win the siege, but a lot of them would die in the process. They needed all the morale-boosters they could get.

Another rock crashed into the wall. This time she didn't duck. It was a worrying thought that maybe she was getting used to it…

Parron reappeared, panting, and he had the younger of the Fire-Casters with him. He grinned at her as he caught his breath. "I've got you a volunteer," he said, finally.

"A volunteer?" Devra scowled at him. "I didn't ask for any dumb volunteers."

"I'll go instead of you," the youth said. "Parron can shoot me out there, and you can tell me where the catapult's weak spot is. Then I can burn it down."

Devra examined the young man critically. "And then you'd get yourself killed," she said. "You don't look like somebody who's ever fought anyone before. You'd probably just stand there and pee in your pants."

"Maybe I would," the Fire-Caster said, defensively. "But I'm willing to go."

Devra realized she was being churlish. "Look, kid – I appreciate the offer, truly I do. You've got to be incredibly brave to volunteer to go to your death to try and save us. I'm sorry if I sound like I'm insulting you, because that's not what I mean. But you've never faced a fight before, and I can't be certain you wouldn't just freeze up out there and get yourself killed for nothing, and achieve nothing. You seem like a good kid, and I wouldn't want that on my conscience."

"I'm not a *kid*," he growled back at her. "From the looks of you, you're only a year or two older than me."

"And I've spent most of those years fighting," she pointed out.

"With your attitude, I'm not surprised," he snapped back.

Devra laughed. "Kid, you're okay. But you still don't go."

"Then how about both of you?" Parron suggested. "I could send you first, then him. But it would drain me, and I don't think I could bring you back straight away."

"Who asked you to bring me back?" Devra snapped. But she considered the idea, and turned to the Fire-Caster. "What's your name? If I'm going to die with somebody, I really think I should know their name."

"Rowin," he replied. "And I have had some military training, you know."

"Every Talent has," Devra said, bitterly. "Mostly just enough to get themselves killed. Okay, grab a sword, say a quick prayer and then let's go."

"Aren't you going to tell anyone?" Parron asked.

"Who? And why?" She shrugged. "If we destroy the catapult, they'll know somebody's out there; if we don't, why make them worry about us?"

He made a face. "So, it'll just be me, worrying that I've sent you to your deaths?"

"Yeah. It'll just be you." She clapped her hand on his shoulder. "Welcome to the wonderful world of warfare."

"Everybody warned me you had an attitude problem."

"Then you should have listened to them." Devra checked her own sword, muttered a quick prayer to the gods she didn't entirely believe in – and who she assumed had a grudge against her if they did – and sighed. "Well, let's get this over with – we have to stop those stones."

Parron nodded. "Hold onto your stomach," he warned her, and then concentrated.

Devra almost squealed when she was lifted off her feet and thrown over the parapet. She'd flown before, when Corri had insisted on taking her up, but this didn't feel at all the same. When she flew with Corri, she was holding (tightly!) onto her best friend, and had implicit confidence in her. Here, she was supported only by the mental powers of a young man she barely knew, and there was nobody comforting to hang onto.

Added to that, she was hurling through the air a couple of hundred feet above an invading army. Several soldiers saw her, and a few of them managed to unleash arrows in her general direction. They came close, but not close enough to hit. Still, it was disquieting to not be able to fight back. She felt scared and helpless, and she didn't like that one bit.

And then she was coming down. Her feet flopped down under her, and she hit the ground fairly heavily, causing her to stumble.

That actually saved her life, as it took her under the swinging ax blade that might otherwise have decapitated her. She slipped her sword from its scabbard and thrust it into the soldier attacking her. With a startled grunt, he dropped his ax and then collapsed after it.

Parron had landed her some twenty feet from the catapult, and the handful of men set to guard it must have had plenty of time to see her coming and to prepare for her touchdown. No sooner had the first man fallen than a second was already on her. She used her Talent to discover his weakest spot, parried his thrust and then stabbed him in the stomach. There was a third, and then a fourth man, and she fought on.

There was a movement behind her, and then Rowin stumbled to the ground on his hands and knees. Not unsurprisingly, he dropped his sword. Devra finished off the fourth attacker and called over her shoulder: "Up and at 'em, kid."

"My name's not *kid*," he growled, finding his feet and his sword. He jumped into the path of the fifth soldier, giving her a few seconds to use her Talent on the catapult. Then she moved into the attack, dropping the defender.

"I could have done that," Rowin protested.

"You're not here to fight, you're here to burn," she reminded him. "The catapult – the part of the frame near the rear left wheel. Blast it, and the whole thing will collapse."

"Right." He paused to focus his abilities, and she moved to protect him.

There were only two more men from the squad left now, and they were being a lot more cautious, having seen their comrades all killed. These two came in together, one from each side. That posed a problem – if she attacked one, then she wouldn't be able to defend herself from the other. Still, she had options... Using her Talent, she Found the answer. She simply waited for their attack, and then dived for the ground.

The two men stumbled into each other, having to pull their blows to avoid killing one another. From her place on the ground, Devra spun about and slashed at their legs. Both men screamed as she sliced through their calf muscles, and they fell down, bleeding. She surged to her feet, and managed to kill them both before they could rise.

Rowin was ready. He stood as if he were about to through a ball, and then whipped his hand forward. Fire grew down his arm, burning and leaping, forming into a globe. It hurled through the air, spitting and sparking, and then crashed into precisely the right spot on the catapult.

The entire left wheel roared into flames. The handlers screamed and backed off as the fire spread to them also. Beside Devra, Rowin collapsed, exhausted from the casting. She moved to protect him, but the soldiers had more important things to worry about for the moment. With a crackling roar, the rear of the catapult collapsed. There was a large rock in the basket, ready to be flung, and that, too, crashed to the ground. Several men were pinned under this; thankfully most of those died instantly, but one man was simply trapped, and then engulfed in flames.

He screamed for almost a minute.

Devra didn't want to watch, but she couldn't help it – this was her doing, after all, and she had to see it through. She didn't exactly regret her actions – these men were attempting to kill everyone in Dragonhome, after all – but she certainly felt no victory in their deaths. Just a numb sense of justice.

She didn't have long to savor her victory. As the catapult burned, the men who had been manning it snatched up their weapons and rushed to attack those who had destroyed it.

Devra nudged the shaking Rowin with her toe. "Heads up, kid – we're in the deep stuff now…"

She braced herself for the attack, wondering how long they could possibly hold out…

Chapter 32

Sander stood on the battlements of his castle, deeply worried. He wasn't certain how old the castle was – hundreds of years, though how many hundreds had been lost to history – but his family had held it for all of that time. It had once been a great house, however a lot of that influence and power had been lost in his grandfather's time, or before. Since his grandfather, the castle had gradually fallen apart. Sander had loved his father, but he had been a weak man, and lost most of whatever money his family had left before he died and passed the castle and lands on to Sander.

Sander had unwittingly contributed to the decay. He had inherited the castle and its secret – the last remaining dragon eggs in the world – and the need to preserve that secrecy had forced him to cut off pretty much all ties with the outside world. The only time he had done anything sociable was his courting and marrying Cassary, his first wife. He had never quite understood what she had ever seen in him, but he had loved her intensely. Unfortunately, she had been ill, and died shortly after giving birth to their son. Her death had plunged him into tormented despair, and he had haunted Dragonhome as surely as any ghost.

And then Melayne had arrived, and turned his world upside down, inside out and every other direction. Melayne was a force to be reckoned with – strong, determined, full of her principles and the courage to do whatever was needed. She had figuratively given him a good shaking up and literally a good talking down. She had made him rethink everything – including his determination never to love again. Against his own nature, he had been forced to step into the light again, to expose himself to the rest of the world.

In many ways, it had been as exhilarating as it was scary. He regretted none of it – except now, its' possible end.

Melayne's brother, Sarrow, had captured Dragonhome, forcing them to flee. He'd worked hard the past few years to rebuild it, and Sander had been pleased to see it growing back to the way it had once been, as he had never before seen it. It was strong, imposing and a declaration that the Lord of Dragonhome was back.

And now... Every stone that slammed into the east wall felt as if it was crashing into his soul. Every chip and rock that flew bore away a little of his life. It hurt him terribly to see the castle he had lived in almost all of his life being battered and assaulted like this.

More than that, even, was the knowledge that there was very little he could do to prevent this attack. He was honest enough with himself to admit that he really needed Melayne here now. Aside from the fact that this would bring the dragons back, he knew that Melayne was a much better leader than he was. Even without the dragons, she'd have had some plan to deal with this attack, and he simply did not.

All he could do was what he was doing – hold out as long as possible and pray that some miracle might happen.

As it happened, one already had. One of the catapults had suddenly gone up in flames. Somehow, obviously, one of Devra's Talents had managed to destroy it. However, that simply meant that there were only two catapults hurling their massive missiles instead of three. Again, it had bought the defenders a little time – but time for what?

He prowled along the parapet angrily, searching for some kind of a plan to save everything and everyone. His son was down below, recovering from his wound, but still too weak to even be able to flee.

As if there was anywhere to flee to. The castle was surrounded by the king's troops. If anyone attempted to leave, they'd be cut down instantly. No, Sander knew, he and the others had to remain inside the castle walls. While the walls still stood...

Another rock slammed into the east wall. With a crash, part of the battlements there collapsed. Luckily, the defenders had abandoned that section, so nobody was killed in the collapse. But it would only be a matter of time until the wall was breached, and the attackers could rush inside.

The handful of Talents that were still here were doing their best. The Fire-Caster was throwing balls of flame at the advancing siege towers, hoping to catch some vital spot and set the engines ablaze. But the men with the towers were wetting the walls of it down, and managing to extinguish the flames before they took hold. The Lifters were throwing rocks at these attackers, but there was a limit to the weight of the rocks they could toss – much, much less than the boulders the catapults could fire.

The advancing soldiers were getting closer – they would be within bow range in a few moments, so the defenders were getting ready to fire. Of course, that meant that the attacking bowmen would also be in position to unleash a barrage of their own – and the attackers had far more bowmen than the defenders...

Sander was frustrated, angry and scared. He was scared of his own death, but, more so, for his son. He had wanted so much for Corran... After Cassary's death, he had rather neglected his son, afraid that he might lose him, too. But Melayne had awakened Corran to joy once more, and – as she always seemed to do! – brought Sander back to his senses and made him realize how much his son needed him. They had all three grown together into a true family.

At least his other children – Cassary and the Nameless Son – were safe in the Far Isles. Perhaps, after all, Darmen and Perria would get to adopt them and raise them as they had planned. Or perhaps Melayne, when she returned, would fly back to them. Knowing Melayne as he did, though, he suspected she'd have other plans.

Melayne...

That was his greatest regret – that he wouldn't be able to hold her and love her again. And that his death would break her heart.

He knew that when she returned to find him and everyone else dead, she would be devastated. And then she would set about avenging them all.

If only there was some way for him to prevent the pain she would suffer – if there was some way he could win this battle... But he knew, realistically, that this was impossible. He didn't have the soldiers, he didn't have the dragons and he didn't have the time.

If he thought it would do any good, he would even consider surrendering the castle. If it would spare everyone dying, he certainly would. But this army wasn't here for that purpose – its aim was to annihilate everyone. If he surrendered, they'd all simply be executed on the spot. So if they had to die, then they would die fighting.

He laughed grimly to himself. Melayne loved her books, and several of them had stories about castles under siege. In the tales, quite frequently, some stroke of genius or some magical miracle saved the defenders. Not for the first time, he wished there was some truth in those stories. But, no – there was only grim reality, and the reality was that they would all die.

And now the arrows started to fly, both from his men and the attackers. A soldier ran up to him carrying a shield, which he offered to Sander.

"My Lord," he said. "Guard against the arrows." Sander nodded, and accepted the shield. The man then unslung his own and held it up against the rain of arrows. Sander followed suit, and within seconds he head the thud and felt the impact of strikes. Other arrows bounced off the stones around him.

There was a pause as the bowmen reloaded, and he took the moment to brush the three arrows off his shield before he had to whip it back into position to protect himself against the next flight.

And so it went on, wave after wave of arrows. Some defenders were hit – some fatally, others merely wounded. Medics under Hovin's direction pulled the wounded into shelter and set about looking after their wounds. Some of those treated were able to return to their positions along the wall, but many could not.

The crashing of rocks against the east wall ceased. Sander risked a look, and saw that the two remaining catapult crews had stood down. The siege towers and the attacking army were too close to Dragonhome's walls now, and the rocks might hit their own men. But the blows they had inflicted had caused enough damage – the parapet had collapsed, and there was a large, crumbling gap in the stonework. It didn't look large enough for the invaders to get in through it, but some were obviously aiming to try. His captain had sent men to guard the gap, but they were coming under heavy fire from the archers, and had to keep their heads down and shields raised. This gave the enemy swordsmen time to advance, and a target to aim for.

As the towers approached the walls, the Fire-Caster had a better view of them, and an easier target. He could throw flames with greater accuracy, and he was having a real effect on the closest tower. The men inside the siege tower couldn't keep up with all of the small fires, and finally one of them kindled the whole thing. Attacking soldiers screamed as flames enveloped the tower, and they fell, burning to death, from the collapsing structure. Other soldiers scattered as the tower crumbled and collapsed, spreading the fire further.

And then several arrows slashed into the Caster. He'd exposed himself too far when attacking, and the bowmen had his range. The young man staggered under the impacts, and collapsed, bleeding, onto the stones. Sander felt regret and anger at the death – and that he didn't even know the brave lad's name...

Sander realized that the young man wasn't the only dead man among the defenders. There were bodies fallen on the battlements; they'd been ignored by rescuers who pulled only the wounded to safety, at the risk of their own lives. How long could any of them keep this up? The fall of arrows seemed to be relentless, but surely the attackers had to run out, sooner or later?

He chanced another quick look before ducking back under cover. There were enemy soldiers in the breach now, clambering over the debris in an attempt to storm the castle. The defending soldiers were in a better position to fight back against these intruders, since the archers couldn't fire through their own men. They were holding their position for the moment, but they seemed to be pitifully few in number.

Well, he was doing no good cowering here... He sprinted down to join these defenders, adding his sword arm to theirs. There was the stench of blood and worse, and fallen bodies with pieces missing. It was a slaughterhouse; Sander couldn't understand how anyone would willingly endure this to fight on behalf of some king or lord they probably would never meet. Surely no amount of money or imagined loyalty was worth this? But he shouldn't complain, else he'd have no men of his own beside him, fighting with him.

The men with him were professionals, far better trained than he was. Oh, he knew theoretically how to use a sword, and had engaged in any number of practice fights during his training. But he had always known that they weren't real, that he and his opponent would salute one another and drink wine together afterward. Here, only one man would survive a fight, and the other would die in agony... It wasn't easy to make that switch in his mind. In the practice ring, there were strict rules for fighting – out here, in the blood and stench, there was only the one rule – win or die.

It felt wrong to take advantage of the attackers as they scrambled – sometimes on hands and knees – through the gap. The men beside him targeted those unbalanced and unable to fight back first, killing them as they tried to regain their feet. True, it was less than chivalrous, but this wasn't about being fair – it was about survival. You took every advantage you could, knowing your opponent would do the same. Sander joined them in killing even the virtually defenseless, because if they regained their feet, they would kill him without a second thought.

The bodies lay where they fell, forming a once-human plug in the defenses. More attackers scrambled over them, treating the dead as no more than an obstacle. And, yesterday, these men probably ate and joked together.

Sander had little time to philosophize – his sword was kept busy striking, guarding, killing. He had no idea how many people he had either hurt or killed; he simply fought on. If anyone stood before him, he cut them down.

There was a pain in his side and he realized that sometime he must have been hit and injured. It burned, but he had no time for that. He tried to ignore the pain as he thrust and maimed and killed. He was awash in blood, and he wondered how much of it was his own, in a sort of detached way, as if the outpouring of his life blood was no longer relevant. He knew he was tiring, and he knew that to stop fighting would be a second's blessed relief and then a swift (if he was lucky) death.

He fought on. And on.

He'd entered into a kind of mindless state, where nothing mattered except that gap in the wall, and the shapes that came at him through it. Tiredly, he battled on, trying to ignore the pain and exhaustion, focused only on those targets to stab and slash and kick aside.

And then he suddenly realized that he no longer held his sword in his hand. He looked at it rather stupidly, wondering what had happened to it. Then he realized that it was still stuck in the chest of the last man he'd killed, and that the man had fallen aside, dragging Sander's weapon with him. Sander blinked, and brushed the hair and sweat from his eyes. He needed another blade, and he looked around. There was one a few feet away, and he crouched to grab it.

A shape loomed over him – a huge man, one-eyed, and with a battle ax held over his head. With a grunted cry, the attacker swung it down at Sander.

Chapter 33

Devra was getting exhausted, and she hurt pretty much all over. She had several small wounds, painful and bloody, but none debilitating – yet. She still had her sword, and was on her feet – though barely in both cases. And still the enemy came at her.

Rowin had surprised her by being a better fighter than she'd expected. The youngster wasn't in her league, but he'd taken her back and covered it still. She could hear him wheezing, and there was pain in his every breath, but he refused to go down. She didn't dare look back to see what kind of a shape he was really in, because there were still a half-dozen attackers coming at her.

They couldn't keep this up for much longer. Rowin was obviously in a good deal of pain, and she was simply ready to fall over. But both of them stubbornly refused to give in.

The next enemy assailant came at her – a burly, rough-looking man with a sword. He had to be twice her weight, and was taller and certainly a lot less tired than she was. He came in fast, swinging his sword down at her. She blocked the blow, but pain lanced all the way up her arm, and her fingers went numb from the pain.

Her sword fell, and she was defenseless. He grinned savagely, and whirled his sword for the killing blow.

So this was it... Devra had barely a second to regret everything she'd be missing, and wonder who might miss her.

Then the man went down, an arrow clear through his throat. For a second, she couldn't even take this in, and she simply stood there, blinking, confused.

"Leave my girl alone, you bully."

Puzzled, she looked around, to see Poth standing just behind her, already notching another arrow to her bow.

"What the hell?" Devra asked, too tired even to be surprised.

Poth flashed her a big grin. "Hey, lover." She fired, and another attacker went down.

Devra couldn't even start to make any sense out of this. A moment later, Corri flew past her, carrying a large branch, which she used to knock further attackers from their feet. Devra looked over her shoulder, and saw that Rowin was as confused as she was. His tunic was soaked with blood, and he swayed on his feet.

"I think we can rest now," she gasped, right before they both fell down.

"Don't worry," Poth assured her. "We've got you covered now." She fired again, and another man went down. She grinned down at Devra. "Bit unfair, really – I can see exactly where they're going to be when the arrows hit them…"

There was a large shadow overhead as the first of the dragons came home…

As the ax swung down at him, Sander's last thought was of Melayne.

And then the man was gone, the last blow undelivered. It took a second for Sander to realize that a dragon's claw had come from nowhere and snatched the man away. He snatched up the sword he needed before looking up.

And there were the dragons! Brek – his own – was the one who had snatched his would-be killer, but the others were there, wheeling and crying out overhead. Two of them carried large rocks, which they dropped on the attackers below them. Hagon the huge simply plowed into the soldiers, throwing them aside and slashing them with his mighty claws.

Sander staggered toward the battlement, and saw that the attack had been completely broken. The catapults were shattered, the siege towers broken and fallen, the troops fleeing. Fire fell from the sky, along with rocks and beasts with slashing claws and tearing mouths.

He had one quick glimpse of Melayne, on the back of Tura. She waved, grinning wildly, and was gone into the fray.

It was all over in seconds, it seemed. The attack was shattered, the enemy routed, and Dragonhome saved.

He sat down on a fallen stone from the rampart, and allowed himself to be exhausted.

Poth stayed close to Devra as she struggled to regain some of her strength and her wits. She wasn't attempting to make any sense out of this yet, but she knew she would, sooner or later. Right now she was simply too glad to be alive to question it much.

Corri had picked up a wicked-looking pike from one of the fallen soldiers, and was now back in the air, using it to hack and slash at the fighters from above. But there were a lot less now, somehow. As the dragons swept across the field, the enemy broke and ran. None of their weapons could be effective against such a force. The attack was well and truly over; the soldiers wouldn't stop running until they reached the capital.

There were no more men to fight now, and Poth dropped her bow. Devra looked at her, and realized she'd never seen a more beautiful sight. She managed to clamber painfully to her feet. "I don't know how this happened," she said, "but I am so glad to see you. I could kiss you."

Poth gave her cheeky grin. "What's stopping you?"

What indeed? She reached out and drew Poth to her, and then kissed her. Poth responded eagerly, and Devra was lost in the pleasure for a while. Then she gently pushed Poth away from her. There was blood on Poth's tunic, and she frowned, afraid the blonde girl was injured. Then she looked down and realized that the blood had come from her. "I'm a bit of a mess?"

"A bit?" Poth laughed. "You're a sight, you know. But

you're alive, and that's all that matters." She gave another of her grins. "As soon as things are cleared up a bit, let's get a bath together, huh? I'll wash your back. And your front. And everywhere else I can think of... And you can do the same to me. Lots."

Devra had to laugh. "Gods, you're a frisky bitch."

"I know, and you should be grateful. Why else do you think we're here?"

Melayne threw herself off of Tura's back and ran to where Sander stood, looking ready to drop. She clutched him tightly, as much to support him as anything. "I was so afraid for you," she whispered to him. "Thank the gods you're alive."

He hugged her back, and kissed her, over and over. "Thank the gods you came in time," he said. "But – how come you came in time?"

Melayne laughed, a rather brittle laugh. "You can thank Poth for that."

"Poth?"

Melayne stroked him, gently. "You know how she is – she was dying to get back and bed Devra, even with all that was going on. So she took a peek at her own future to see how much fun they'd have – and saw that Devra was being attacked. She alerted me, and we flew straight back – thankfully, just in time."

"Thankfully." He hugged her tightly. "I was so afraid I'd never see you again. I was sure you'd never get back, being so busy with the Talent army."

"That's dispersed now," she assured him. "I'll have to go back and check up on things..." She shook her head. "No, I'll send somebody else to do that. I'm staying close to you. If I had lost you..." She clutched him tightly.

Margone stood looking over the devastation that was the battlefield. The siege machines and catapults lay about, broken and burned. Bodies were everywhere, and a stench of blood and entrails clung to the air. Crows had arrived in their hundreds, drawn by the scent and the opportunity to feast on the fallen. He was shaken and appalled by the sight.

Corri landed gently beside him and took his hand. He squeezed back.

"When I was a boy," he said, softly, "I heard stories of fighting and war. My father loved telling the tales of battle and courage, of men who stood against great odds and won fame and glory for themselves." He sighed. "This doesn't look like fame and glory to me."

"It isn't," she agreed. "It's just men who were convinced they were doing the right thing by attempting to kill other men, and dying for that foolish belief. Most of them were our age, or even younger. And I'm sure that they heard the same or similar stories, and dreamed of great victories. And now they're just food for crows and flies and worms."

"It's such a waste."

"It is indeed. And these young men – and women – had families, and friends, and lovers. People who will miss and mourn them. They might even have been people we could have liked ourselves. But they followed the wrong leaders, believed the wrong promises, obeyed the wrong orders. And they lost." She snuggled closer to him. "And, inside Dragonhome, there are more young people dead – people we *did* know and cared about. And they, too, are dead because of this."

"There's no glory in all of this," Margone said, sadly.

"Oh, there's some glory," Corri answered. "Devra and another Talent took out a catapult, and we ready to give their lives for their friends. That took a lot of courage. The men on the walls of Dragonhome – they fought and some died to protect everyone within. But, on the whole – no, there's not a lot of glory in this. Just death and decay."

"And bodies to bury," Margone pointed out.

"That's for another day," Corri said, gently. "Today is a day for being thankful that we're still alive." She looked up at him and he could see the love written on her face. "And you know what that means."

Despite his gloom, he had to smile at her. "Yes – in nine months, there's going to be a lot of babies born…"

She laughed. "You want to see if one of them will be ours?"

"Yes," he said. "Very much – yes."

Hagon surveyed the silent carnage from his perch on the battlements of the castle. Beside him perched his mate, Ganeth. "Humans," he grunted.

"Don't tell me you're not growing close to your own," she snickered.

"There's something rather addictive about them, I'll give you that," he agreed. "And something rather unpleasant and wasteful, too." He nodded at the corpses. "All those bodies, and the humans don't even eat them. What's the point?"

"You *know* humans taste bad," she pointed out. "They probably don't like to eat the bodies any more than we do."

"Then what's the point of them killing one another?" Hagon was genuinely confused. "To fight for a female – *that* I can understand. But to fight for a pile of rocks? It makes no sense."

"If strange dragons tried to take over your home, wouldn't you fight them?"

"Why would dragons want to do that?" he protested. "There are plenty of mountains and rocks to go around."

"But if they did?" she persisted.

"Then of course I would fight them – they would have to be insane, and need to be killed."

"And that is what happened here," Ganeth answered.

"Ah. So the attackers were insane and had to be slaughtered." Now he was starting to understand.

"Something like that, yes," Ganeth agreed.

He looked across the field of bodies. "So – is it now over? Are all the insane humans dead?"

Ganeth sighed. "I rather fear not," she said, sadly.

Hagon shook his head again. "Humans," he repeated.

Nephir heard the cry, and saw the Seer almost collapse. He flicked a glance at Caramin, then demanded: "What's wrong?"

"Dragons," the Seer breathed, supporting himself by clutching at a chair. "Lots of dragons…"

Nephir glared at General Abrin. "What's that fool talking about?"

"I don't know." The general shook the Talent, hard, and then slapped him. "What is it? What's wrong with you?"

The Seer touched his face where he had been hit, and looked up at the general. "Dragons."

"Speak sense, man."

The Seer shook himself free and managed to stand almost upright, though he still looked pained. "I have seen the dragons," he said, as if that explained everything.

"The man's a drooling idiot," Caramin complained. "What is he talking about?"

"More importantly," Nephir replied, "what's happening with our army? Has their assault finally succeeded? Is Dragonhome ours?"

"No," the Seer said, his voice firmer now. "It belongs to the dragons."

Nephir was starting to get a very bad suspicion. "Our men – have they taken the castle? Are the rebels dead?"

"You're not listening to me!" the Seer yelled. "The army is crushed – the dragons have returned."

Crushed? Nephir was stunned. "How? How could they have returned? You told me –"

"That when there are dragons, *nothing* is sure."

"Defeated?" Caramin asked, his voice hollow.

"The dragons have returned," the Seer repeated. "Our army is beaten. The survivors are running, and they won't stop until they get home." He glared from Nephir to Caramin and then at Abrin. "Your plans have failed, disastrously."

"Get out!" Nephir screamed at the Talent. "Get out before I have you executed!" The man fled. He turned to Abrin. "Now what, general?"

Abrin looked as shaken as he felt. "I'll... I'll send riders out to intercept those fleeing cowards... Turn them back..."

"With what aim?" Caramin asked. "They won't attack Dragonhome again while there are dragons there. Their spirit has been broken; they'll be utterly useless to us now. You may as well ignore them."

"To ignore them would send a bad message to the rest of my troops," Abrin said firmly. "It's not for their sake that I'm doing this, but for the morale of the entire army. I cannot allow my troops to be seen as losers and cowards. They *must* be stopped and reformed."

"Well, get out and reform them, then!" Nephir screamed. He'd had quite enough of the fool. Abrin gave a cursory salute and marched out of the room.

Nephir turned to Caramin. "And now what?" he asked. "Our plan has failed - what do we do now?"

"Whatever we can," his companion replied. He seemed to be recovering from his earlier loss of spirit. "We must see to the defenses of the city, for one thing."

Nephir's fury was starting to burn itself out, and he considered these words. "You think this Melayne would attack us? *Here* in the capital?"

"She did warn Juska that she would repay any attack on her - you were there when she did so. And she strikes me as a woman of her word." Caramin looked at him steadily. "Our attack has failed - so, yes, I expect her next move is going to be to retaliate. And she has dragons..."

Chapter 34

Alone in their room, Melayne patched up Sander's wounds. Astonishingly enough, they were all minor – most required little more than washing and salve. One on his left shoulder required a dressing and bandage, but it looked like it would heal fully quite quickly.

She felt overwhelming relief that he was alive. When Poth had warned her of the attack, every second of the flight back she kept imagining the worst... It was such a relief to discover that her horrible imaginings were just that and nothing more.

Touching him – even to simply dress his wounds – made her feel better... and aroused her desire for him again. Glancing down, she could see that he was having the exact same reaction. "Do you think you're up to this?" she asked him, smiling.

"I *know* I am," he answered, grabbing her tunic and pulling it over her head. "I think all of us survivors who can will be having much the same reaction..."

"Glad to be alive," Melayne agreed, helping him to undress her. "Celebrating just living." He reached for her again, and she saw that he still wore his gloves. "Take those damned things off," she growled in mock anger. "I want to feel my husband's touch, not leather." She saw the hesitation and worry in his eyes, and glared at him. "I know you're afraid of what you'll See," she said gently. "But you can't spend the rest of your life terrified of seeing something bad. Just touch me and get it over with."

"But if it's..."

"Then we'll deal with it," Melayne said, firmly. "Take them off."

He looked at her and then sighed, and peeled them off. "You're getting far too used to giving orders."

"Then I promise only one more for now," she said, laughing. She gripped his wrists and pulled his hands against her breasts. "Take me, you beast..."

Devra pulled Poth into the room she shared with Corri. As she'd expected, it was empty.

Poth glanced around. "Are you sure Corri won't be back?"

Devra laughed. "I don't need your Talent to See where she is – in Margone's bed by now, I imagine. We'll be alone."

"Good." Poth reached out and pulled her close for a long, satisfying kiss. "I am *so* glad you're still alive. You were crazier than I am to go fighting without me."

"I should be fighting with you?" Devra asked, mischievously.

"No, you should be loving me." Poth started to strip off her clothing.

"Um..." Devra said, hesitating as she was about to do the same. "Poth? Do you know what we're doing? Because... uh... I've never done this before." She blushed, which made her feel stupid. She was acting so childish... like a girl in love...

Poth laughed. "Neither have I," she confessed. She threw her tunic to the floor.

"But those burns on your back," Devra said. "I thought they were from..."

"Love making?" Poth shook her head. "No. The Burning God didn't *love* anyone, least of all me. He simply burned me when he was angry – and he was angry a lot." She glanced at the two beds in the room. "I'm surprised you and Corri didn't do it. You seem so close."

"She's my *friend*," Devra exclaimed, finding herself blushing again. "Not my lover."

Poth grinned happily. "No, that's *me*." She was naked now. Devra was amazed at how beautiful she suddenly seemed to be. Devra finished undressing too, suddenly very shy. She felt so exposed, so vulnerable, and it made her slightly uncomfortable – and, at the same time, rather frisky.

"I just don't want to disappoint you," she admitted. It wasn't easy for her to say that, but she knew she had to be completely honest with Poth. "I'm not used to making people happy."

Poth looked at her with affection. "If it helps," she said slowly, "I won't be upset if you picture me as Melayne."

"Why should I want to picture you as anyone but you?" Devra asked. To her surprise, she discovered that this was quite true – somehow, somewhen, her desires and fantasies about Melayne had evaporated. Now it was Poth that she wanted. She kissed the blonde girl, and gently stroked her scars. It was up to her to help Poth forget her years of pain and anticipate longer, better years of pleasure.

Poth giggled abruptly, and then said: "You'll do fine, love – after all, with your Talent of Finding, you should be able to discover *exactly* the right places to touch me next..."

Melayne lay on her naked tummy, quite content – at least for the moment. Being with Sander like this *always* made her feel a lot better... and somewhat sensitive. She propped herself up on her elbows and looked at him affectionately. He wore that satisfied grin that he always did afterward. He reached out and stroked her behind, and she playfully swatted his hand away. "Haven't you had enough?"

"Perhaps for now," he conceded, grinning. "But... ten minutes from now?" He shrugged.

She laughed. "If you can manage that again in ten minutes, that's a deal," she replied. More seriously, she asked: "Are you still seeing the future when you touch me?"

He laid his hand gently in the small of her back. "I think you've overloaded my Talent for the moment. Right now, I can't See a thing – except the most beautiful woman in the world."

"Flatterer." But it pleased her, knowing that he honestly meant it. "And what about when you first touched me? What did you See then?"

He laughed. "About five minutes into the future, so I knew that everything was going to be fine – at least for now."

"The future…" Melayne had deliberately not been thinking about that in order to simply focus on the pleasures of the present. But she knew she couldn't put that off for long – she had her duties, and there was much to be done. "I suppose we had better start thinking about that now…"

"Yes." His face lost its smile. "We've survived today, but we have to plan for tomorrow."

"Which means calling a council of war," Melayne said, wishing she didn't have to think about that. "It will involve so many people…"

There was a nervous rap on the door. Melayne blinked and glanced across at it. "Who is it?"

""Cathor, ma'am – the nurse," came the muffled reply.

Nurse?

Sander sat up. "Did we disturb somebody? Those weren't noises of pain, honestly…" Melayne blushed slightly, and slapped him.

"Uh… no, ma'am, uh, sir… Hovin sent me."

Melayne gestured for Sander to pull the covering over them, and then called: "You'd better come in, then."

The door opened, and Cathor hesitantly entered. Seeing their state, she blushed. "I'm sorry, ma'am, but Hovin said I was to notify you immediately."

"That's fine, Cathor," Melayne assured her. "We were quite finished."

"For now," Sander muttered.

Melayne tried to ignore him, but his hand was moving under the covers… He picked the worst times to get playful! "And what are you supposed to notify me about?"

"The patient, ma'am – the one you brought in. He said to tell you that she's waking up."

"Oh, gods!" Melayne exclaimed. She'd quite forgotten! She jumped immediately out of bed and searched around for her gown. Cathor gave a slight gasp, which she ignored – the woman was a nurse, after all.

"What's wrong?" Sander asked, puzzled. "Who's been hurt? One of our friends?"

"No, one of our enemies." Melayne found a robe, and slipped it on, tying it quickly. It would have to do – this was urgent. How could she have forgotten? She looked at Sander. "Don't come anywhere near me until I send for you."

Now he looked concerned. "Why not? What is it?"

"I brought one of the enemy Talents back with us," Melayne said, bundling the nurse swiftly out of the door. "She's a suicidal and possibly homicidal Death-Caster."

Chapter 35

Melayne hurried to the room that held Shara. She'd at least had the presence of mind to have Hovin isolate her, since she had no idea what kind of a state the woman would awaken in. Now she pushed open the door and hurried in. Cathor would have followed her in, but Melayne shook her head and firmly closed the door. She didn't want to expose anyone else to the Death-Caster until she was sure that Shara wouldn't harm anyone.

Except her...

Shara was sitting up, looking around, quite confused. She blinked and managed to focus on Melayne. "Where am I?"

"Dragonhome," Melayne replied. "We brought you here after..."

Shara touched her chin, and winced. "After somebody punched me," she said.

"That was Poth," Melayne said, apologetically. "She's a bit... enthusiastic. She doesn't really think her actions through."

"No, she was right," Shara said. "I'm not sure what I was thinking, but I know I was overflowing with grief." Tears started to trickle down her cheeks. Melayne impulsively hugged the other woman, who seemed startled, and then clung to her, crying openly. Melayne didn't say anything, just held her.

After a few minutes, Shara pushed her away, gently, and then looked around for something to wipe her face and nose. Melayne felt around the pockets of her robe; thankfully, there was a handkerchief, which she handed across. Shara wiped herself off and then blew her nose.

"I'm sorry," she said, her voice wavering.

"There's nothing to be sorry for," Melayne assured her. "You've been through a lot. It can't have been easy for you, doing what you did."

"It wasn't," Shara agreed. "You have to understand, I *love*... loved Baraktha. But... he was wrong. It wasn't his fault, really – he'd had a terrible life, and that colored his views. He was convinced that everyone was out just for themselves. He thought what you offered was an impossible dream. He did some terrible things, and justified them to himself. But... I can't live like that! I can't! There has to be some good in the world, doesn't there?"

"There *is* good in the world," Melayne assured her. "I have some wonderful friends, the best you can imagine. Together, we've been working at building something worthwhile. But I have to be honest – there are those who want to tear down and destroy what we've done."

Shara nodded. "Baraktha would have done that," she admitted. "He would have said that you're idealistic and impractical and needed to face reality."

Melayne snorted. "*That* kind of reality should never have existed in the first place. You have to strive to make reality the way it should be. I just wish it didn't seem to always involve fighting."

Shara looked at her sympathetically. "So what are you doing now?"

Sighing, Melayne shook her head. "Facing Baraktha's kind of reality, I'm sad to say. While I was trying to talk sense into him, the king's soldiers stormed Dragonhome. Thankfully, Poth managed to realize what was going on, and we arrived back in time to save most of our people. Not all of them, though. And the castle's in bad shape again."

"I'm sorry to hear that."

"Not your fault. Anyway, on the bright side, a fair number of your Talent army listened to me, and they decided that they want to join us. My brother is leading them back here." She grinned. "He has the Talent for Persuasion, so he shouldn't have any trouble. We'll be able to find homes for them, after I've talked to them." Seeing Shara's blank look, she explained: "My Talent is Communication. I have to be sure that none of the new Talents committed criminal acts, like raping those poor girls. Those that lost their homes in the attacks are coming here as well, and we'll find homes for them, too."

"And what about me?" Shara asked. "Are you going to use your Talent on me, to make sure I didn't do anything wrong?"

Melayne shook her head. "I don't think that will be necessary – you don't strike me as somebody who'd do evil."

"You're wrong there," Shara said, softly. "I *did* do evil – I didn't stop Baraktha earlier. Even after the first village was destroyed, and the girls taken and raped, I didn't stop him. I let it happen, again and again..." She started crying once more.

"Stop that!" Melayne said firmly. "I know how much it had to hurt you, and I really understand how hard it was to go against somebody you truly loved. Don't blame yourself."

"Who else can I blame?" she asked, bitterly. "I was a moral coward, and I blamed it on love."

"Then *change*," Melayne said to her. "Work to make things better."

"How?" Shara asked. "My Talent is to kill people! You want to tell me how I can use *that* to make people's lives better? Maybe you want to use me as an assassin?"

"Gods, no!" Melayne said, genuinely horrified by the idea. "I don't want anyone else to die, if it can be avoided. It would be wonderful if you never had to kill again."

"Then I repeat: what good am I?"

Melayne smiled. "How about you start off by being a representative for your people?" she suggested. "There's over a hundred of them heading here – not counting those poor girls – and they're going to need somebody to look out for them. I'm nominating you, at least for now. When they get here, they can decide if they agree with that. So, how about you become one of my circle of friends and make sure we don't overlook your people?"

Shara stared at her, too surprised to speak for a few moments. "You think... I mean, you'd *want* me to sit with you? After everything?"

"Only if you promise not to just *sit*," Melayne said firmly. "You can't stay silent – you have to advocate for your people, and help me to discover what's best for everyone. Will you do that?" She held out her hand.

After a moment, Shara took it. "Yes," she agreed, in a wondering voice. "Yes, I promise I'll do my very best."

"Good. I'm glad that's settled." Then she sighed. "And I'm afraid you'll have to start quite soon. We've had a short time to recover from the attack on Dragonhome, but there are people to bury and plans to make. I don't think King Alexsar will stop just because he's lost this battle. And I'm honestly uncertain what I should do about it."

"You'll be calling a council of war?"

"I really wish it could be a council of peace – but that's not Alexsar's way, I'm afraid."

Melayne suddenly heard the nurse's sharp voice in the hallway, and then the door burst open. Poth – dressed only in a *very* short tunic – pushed her way into the room.

"Why didn't you tell me what you were up to?" she yelled at Melayne. "I should have been here to help you, in case this crazy intended to harm you!"

Melayne looked at Shara, and then giggled. Shara, surprisingly, joined in.

"This, I take it, is Poth?" Shara finally managed to ask.

"This is her."

"I see what you mean about impulsive." She stared at Poth, who finally seemed to realize she'd done the wrong thing. "Uh... you're not upset about me punching you, are you" she asked, nervously.

"I probably should be, but I'm not," Shara replied. "You prevented me from doing something I'd never have forgiven myself for. So – thank you." She held out her hand, and Poth shook it.

The blonde girl bent forward and stared at Shara's chin. Melayne could see that she had absolutely nothing on under the tunic. "Wow, that's some bruise I gave you," Poth said, admiringly. "I don't know my own strength." She made a fist and looked at it wonderingly. Then she turned to Melayne. "I'd have Seen what you were up to earlier, only Devra and I were busy." She grinned, widely. "We had such fun when we –"

"I don't think we need to know all of the details, Poth," Melayne said, hastily. She had no doubt Poth would happily have elaborated. "Some things should remain secret between you and Devra."

Poth gave her an odd grin. "Don't worry, some things will."

Melayne turned to Shara. "Poth's just fallen in love," she explained. "And she gets a bit carried away, as I've said."

"Indeed."

Melayne turned to Poth. "Maybe you'd better go and get dressed?" she suggested. "You have a cute backside, but I don't want Devra to think I've been staring at it."

Poth felt her behind, and then rolled her eyes. "Underwear – I *knew* I'd forgotten something." She grinned. "Do you really think I've got a cute behind? I know Sander does, 'cause he looked at it a few times. Clothed!" she added, hastily. "Don't want to cause marital discord."

"Poth, your mouth runs away with you," Melayne said. "Why don't you run after it and get dressed?"

"Right." She grinned again and vanished.

"*Please* don't tell me she's another of your advisors," Shara begged.

"Sorry. But there are times when she actually makes sense."

"Those I must see."

A short while later, Melayne had her core group together around a table in the small dining hall. Sander, of course, was beside her. Devra and Poth were sitting together – and there was actually a smile on Devra's face, which was a rare event; clearly her relationship with Poth was doing her good. Corri and Margone sat together, also looking quite happy. Finally, there was Shara, looking uneasy and a little uncomfortable. Melayne introduced her to everyone, hoping to put her at ease a trifle.

"We've got a lot to do, and a lot to decide," she said. "First – Sander?"

He nodded. "I've looked over the castle, and talked with Captain Rause. We have seventeen dead, mostly soldiers, and over forty injured, some quite badly. Hovin and his team are doing what they can, but he expects at least another ten deaths. As soon as we can, we'll hold an honoring ceremony. The castle – well, the east wall is practically demolished. It took the brunt of the attack. A few stones fell elsewhere and caused minor damage. The question at the moment is whether or not we rebuild – but it isn't our main priority, so it can wait."

"No, there are more important things," Melayne agreed. "Poth, is another attack from Aleksar likely?"

"From him? No – he's dead. Didn't I mention that?" She shrugged. "I guess I got sidetracked when Devra and I –"

"We *know* what sidetracked you," Melayne said, hastily. "But Aleksar is dead?"

"Yes." Poth grinned. "He tried to out-bitch a couple of really lethal ladies of the court, and lost."

"Then who's running the kingdom right now?" Sander asked.

Poth shrugged. "A couple of the nobles. They're looking for another figurehead to hide behind. They're working up their courage to start another fight with us, though."

"Their record so far isn't too impressive," Margone said. "I should think there will be a problem in trying to get a third attack underway."

Poth shook her head. "Never underestimate the stupidity and sheep-like behavior of people," she said. "The futures I can see all tell me they'll have another army on the way in a week or so."

"Then we have a week to stop them," Melayne said. "Well, I didn't think we'd get much time. So we have to decide what we're going to do."

"Do?" Devra leaned forward. "We have *dragons*, Melayne. We go in and level the capital. They can't stop us."

"No, they can't," Melayne agreed, slowly. "But if we do that, a lot of people will get killed."

"*Their* people, not ours."

"Devra, I don't want *anybody* else killed. There's been enough death and injury already."

Margone shook his head. "Melayne, this is war – and you can't fight a war without people getting hurt and killed."

"*Humans* can't," she agreed. "But most of us here aren't merely human – we're *Talents*. And we can do things ordinary people can't. I want to see if we can come up with a way to fight a war that doesn't involve anybody else dying."

"We may be Talents," Devra said, stubbornly, "but there's not that many of us – and there are thousands of people in the capital who want us dead."

"We have more Talents on the way," Melayne pointed out. "Sarrow is leading them here, and they should be with us in two of three days." She looked over at Shara. "You know their abilities – try and think if there is anyone special who might be able to help us out here. We can always bring them in early by dragon."

"I'll try," Shara promised. "But I have to confess that I'm the most powerful in our Talent army, and all I can do is to kill. It doesn't sound like I'll be of much use to you."

"Well, we'll see about that," Melayne said. "But – no, I'd rather you not use your Talent unless it's absolutely necessary. We need another way to do this..."

Abruptly, Poth started to laugh. Everybody looked at her and she stopped. "What? I like Melayne's plan."

"I don't *have* a plan," Melayne pointed out.

"Sure you do," Poth answered. "You're just a bit shy about it because you think it's almost as crazy as I am."

Devra growled. "Poth, I love you, but I promise I will spank your backside if you don't explain yourself."

Poth grinned again. "Oh, right – *that* threat will make me talk. You want to spank me now? It sounds like fun."

Melayne interrupted before things got further out of hand. "Poth, do you mean the idea I had to do the opposite of what they're expecting?"

"That's the one," she said, brightly. Then, to Devra: "We'll talk about spanking my behind later, okay?"

Sander coughed, rather theatrically. "The opposite of what they're expecting?"

"Yes," Melayne said, thoughtfully. Maybe her idea wasn't so silly, after all... "They're bracing themselves and preparing for an attack by dragons – huge, terrifying and overwhelming. And also very lethal. So why don't we do the exact opposite? Small, cuddly and mostly harmless?" She saw the confusion on everyone's face and grinned. She was starting to see why Poth enjoyed making her obscure comments so much – it was fun to confuse people.

So she explained.

Chapter 36

Murine was starting to get rather disturbed by Shera. At first, having made friends with her, she thought she'd found a kindred spirit – and that was true, to an extent. They were equally ambitious, and equally hated being treated as "mere women". Both of them were beautiful and intelligent, capable of devious and cunning thinking. And both were equally unconcerned about other peoples' lives.

But Shera *really* had a problem with her father, and it poisoned everything she thought and did.

The idea that Caramin had slept with his daughter from a very young age had seemed merely creepy and unpleasant at first. Murine was no prude, and didn't really have any opinion either way on what two other people did together. But a father having sex with his own daughter just seemed horribly sick to her – especially given Shera's age when it had happened. She knew that there were men like that, men who only liked young girls, and that someone in Caramin's position could indulge those tastes with pretty much impunity.

She *really* hoped that her marriage to him would be in name only. The thought of being intimate with such a person made her feel sick. But if that was the price of power – well, she would pay it. It would be worth it – just. She could fake passion with him and then feel it for somebody else.

But it was Shera's attitude that she found the most distasteful. Shera didn't feel in any way abused by her father – quite the contrary, in fact. She would have given almost anything to be back in his bed again. It was a sick need in her, to be wanted by Caramin, and *wanted* meant everything to her. Instead of being relieved when Caramin had stopped having sex with her – as any normal person surely would have! – she felt as though she'd been rejected. She'd been judged and found wanting. She desperately craved her old position back.

She was *jealous* that Murine would be getting what she so passionately wanted. That was ironic, because Murine would have gladly let her have it – but couldn't. They would both have to endure their fates in order to get what they ultimately wanted – a seat at the feast of power.

It didn't help matters that she and Shera had been more or less thrown together by Caramin and Nephir. The pair of them knew too much of what was being planned, and the men didn't want them to have a chance to let any of it slip – as if only *women* ever gossiped! So she and Shera were effectively prisoners together as the men matured their plans.

Which, so far, hadn't been too successful. Abrin had stopped the retreat of the units that had fled from Dragonhome, but he'd had to kill a number of them to quell the mutinous troops. He still didn't dare throw them back into any fighting, and couldn't afford to bring them back to the capital for fear they might infect other soldiers with their fears, so they were just holding positions out in the middle of nowhere for the time being.

This Melayne and her ragtag army – augmented by dragons – would soon make its assault on the city, so there were a lot of preparations being made. Huge crossbows, designed to kill dragons, were being constructed and moved into defensive positions around the capital. Troops were digging defensive ditches and training ready for attack. Supplies were being hurried in, preparing for the possibility of a siege.

And she was stuck here, having to listen to Shera's complaints! It was almost enough to make her want to kill the stupid bitch.

"You're lucky, Murine," she said. "You have small breasts – father likes small breasts." She looked down at her own, which were rather ample. Murine wished hers were as full – she'd always disliked being so flat-chested. Shera didn't know how lucky she was.

"Then why not have them cut off?" she asked, sweetly.

"I did consider it," Shera admitted. "But it would leave scars, and father dislikes blemishes even more than he hates breasts." She looked at Murine in concern. "You don't have any scars, do you?"

Only mental ones... "No, dear – my body is as flawless as fine marble." The thought that Shera would have willingly mutilated herself in an effort to win Caramin back was nauseating.

"That's good," Shera said, cheerfully. "Father might have been... upset otherwise."

Murine didn't really care what Caramin liked or disliked – except in as much as she'd have to keep him fairly docile – but she could imagine he would be an unpleasant person if disappointed. Anyone who could do what he had done to his daughter, and then simply toss her aside after she'd outgrown his lusts was clearly a very deranged individual.

The door opened abruptly and her cousin marched in. There was a smile on his face, so Murine knew that one of his twisted little plans must be working out. "Murine – the wedding's off."

"*My* wedding?"

"The same. You won't have to marry Caramin after all."

It was hard to say who was the most relieved – herself or Shera. But... "And how does that come about?" she asked, suspiciously. "Are you trying to push me out?" She wouldn't put it past him – his affection for her was based only on how much use she was to him.

"No, actually, you're getting a promotion. You're not to marry a mere lord any longer."

She glared at him. "You enjoy being cryptic, don't you?"

"Yes indeed," he agreed, laughing. "We've found our next king. It seems that Jaska had a great-nephew named Caradax. The council has decided that he'll be offered the throne."

"By *council*, you mean you and Caramin, I take it?" she said drily.

"Of course – but the others have gone along with it, naturally. Caradax has a small estate a day or so from town, so we've sent messengers to congratulate him on his great good fortune, and to bring him and his family here to court."

This wasn't getting much clearer. "He has a family?"

"Technically. His parents are both dead, and he inherited. He's got siblings, so, naturally, they'll accompany him." He gave one of his sneaky smiles. "Oh, you thought I meant he was *married*. No, my dear, sweet, cousin – he won't be married until after he's crowned. As I said, you're moving up in the world."

Now she understood. "So I'm to be the next queen?"

"That's the spirit – I knew you'd like the news."

Shera pouted. "What about me? Why aren't I to be the next queen?" She glared angrily at Murine. "What's she got that I haven't?"

"Anatomically? Probably nothing. But your father still wants you to marry me to cement our alliance. Do at least *try* to look happy with that news, my betrothed. Or should that be *betrayed*?"

There was still something missing, of course. "And Caramin gets nothing out of this deal?" she asked, suspiciously.

"Did I say that? No, he'll be taking a different bride. Our king-to-be has two sisters, so Caramin will pick one of those once he sees them."

"And this Caradax – how old is he?"

"Eighteen, I believe." Nephir grinned. "Young and virile enough, I should wager, to be able to bed you and satisfy you."

"What does he look like?"

"What possible difference can that make?" her cousin asked. "He's the new king, my dear, so *that* should make him irresistible to you." He shrugged. "Anyway, he's never been to court, so nobody really knows."

"And his sisters?" Shera asked. "The two my father wants his pick of?"

"Twelve and eight, I believe."

"*Eight?*" Shera practically spat the word out. Murine could see that she was insanely jealous. She didn't like the thought of anyone taking her place in her father's bed; Murine had been hard enough for her to swallow, but she'd known that Caramin couldn't have felt much for her.

But if he was getting his victim of choice… This had to be her worst nightmare. She'd *never* get him back with a rival like that…

Good. Let the silly bitch suffer. Murine knew she wasn't herself the most compassionate of people, but even she felt a twinge of sorrow for the poor girl doomed to marry Caramin. Shera, of course, had no such sympathy. And Murine's small slip of conscience was drowned by the relief she felt that she wouldn't have to marry a child molester.

Even becoming queen was a smaller joy than that.

"Does Caradax have any say in all of this?" she asked, in mock innocence.

"Don't be foolish – he'll do as he's told if he wants the crown. And who wouldn't want the crown?"

"You?" she suggested.

Nephir laughed. "I am old and mature enough not to be that foolish. Caradax is young, and no doubt ambitious. Plus, he'll be getting quite a jewel by marrying you. Oh, and I'd advise you against even thinking of killing him – three dead kings in a row might put off future possibilities. Even if he's fat and smells like a pig in mud, you'd better tolerate him and keep him warm and happy in bed."

He didn't say *or else*; he didn't need to.

"I'm sure I'll find him irresistible," she said drily.

"That's the spirit." Nephir turned to Shera, who was sulking. "Do brighten up, my dear – at least *try* and look like marrying me isn't the consolation prize."

"But it is."

"Yes."

She scowled. "And you don't really want me, do you?"

Nephir sighed. "My dear, this is politics, not love. It's not that I don't want *you* – I don't want *anybody*. I find people to be quite unappealing. It's not personal, I assure you. And I honestly don't care if you have affairs every day of our married life – as long as you're discrete about it. As long as you know your place, there's no reason why we can't have a long and happy marriage."

Only her cousin could consider such an arrangement *happy*. If it had been anyone else but Shera, Murine might have felt at least a twinge of sorrow. As it was, she was secretly amused by the whole business.

Shera gave a scream and jumped. For a second, Murine thought the other woman was having a fit of temper, but then she saw a mouse scurry across the floor, and realized that this was what had shocked Shera.

"Come now," she mocked. "Don't tell me you're afraid of an itsy-bitsy mouse? It's probably more scared of you than you are of it."

"I hate mice!" Shera screamed, looking frantically around for something to scramble onto. She finally threw herself onto the table, kicking over glasses and a decanter of wine.

"It won't hurt you," Murine laughed. She looked down at the mouse, which had stopped running and was staring at her. "It's quite harmless."

The mouse dashed forward again, and bit her, hard, on the ankle. Murine screamed and shook it off. It ran behind a tapestry hanging from the wall. Her ankle was bleeding from the small punctures of the bite, and it *hurt*. She snatched a knife from the table, and stalked over to the tapestry.

"I'll kill it!" she snarled, and pulled the wall-hanging aside.

Ten pairs of mouse eyes glared back at her.

She hesitated for a second before raising the knife. As if this was a signal, the mice all rushed forward. They started biting at her ankles, and a couple of them ran up her skirts. She could feel their claws latching onto her skin, and screamed. She twisted and fell, and the mice kept on biting.

She could vaguely see her cousin had drawn his sword, but stood there, unsure what he should do. Attacking mice with a sword clearly seemed futile to him.

"Do something!" she screamed, trying to brush the mice off. Then one was in front of her face, and it lunged for her.

It was going for her eyes! She closed them automatically, and felt tiny teeth sink painfully into her nose. She screamed again, then had a vision of a mouse biting her tongue, and promptly clamped her mouth shut.

Then the mice were gone, and she could open her eyes and prop herself up. She was cut and hurting all over, and blood was trickling off her nose and down her face. She looked around and saw why the mouse had left.

The rats had arrived…

She scrambled to her feet, and moved to where Nephir was standing. Shera was still prostrate on the table, shaking with fear. "We've got to get out of here," she snapped.

Nephir nodded. He eyed the dozen or so rats that were creeping slowly toward them, and then looked at the door. "When I open it, follow me."

"Don't leave me here!" Shera wailed, clutching at him.

Showing his disgust, he shook off her hands. "Pull yourself together and follow me," he ordered. "Or, by the gods, I will leave you behind." He ran for the door.

As soon as he opened it, Murine fled after him. She didn't look back – if Shera didn't follow, then the stupid bitch could face the consequences on her own.

In the corridor outside the room, one of the house cats lay in a patch of sunlight. Several mice ran across it, and the cat didn't even open an eye.

What was going on?

As Nephir hesitated, trying to decide which way to go, Shera crashed into them from behind, screaming and batting at her clothing. Nephir rolled his eyes, but led the way down the passageway.

There was the sound of scampering feet and chittering noises that sounded suspiciously like laughter to her.

All around the palace, she could hear screams, and smashing sounds. Sometimes she glimpsed people running. And there were mice and rats everywhere. The dogs and cats simply lounged about as if nothing unusual were happening, even when the vermin ran across their paws or bodies. She realized that none of them were being attacked – only people.

After an eternity of running, she saw a door ahead that led to the courtyard, and the three of them threw themselves outside, hoping things would be better.

They weren't.

With ear-piercing screams, pigeons, sparrows and other birds hurled themselves down from the sky at anyone they could see. Murine threw up her hands to protect her face, and long, filthy claws raked her arm painfully, drawing more blood.

Then she felt something splatter on her face – something wet and disgusting and smelly. She glanced up as another bird relieved itself on her hair.

She screamed and ran back inside the building.

Confusion was everywhere. People were panicked and ran in all directions to escape the attacks. It was impossible to fight back against their attackers, and nobody seemed to know what to do. Everyone was scratched and battered, and dripping blood and excrement as they ran.

There was a low growl, and Murine turned to stare down the corridor.

A wolf was striding purposefully toward her. Its eyes seemed to burn, and it drooled as it looked at her.

She turned and fled, hardly caring where she was going. She had no idea what had happened to either Shera or Nephir and didn't honestly care. She was so terrified that she was beyond thinking. All she could do was to run, along with the other people in the corridors.

Eventually, there were large doors open in front of her. Exhausted, shaking and bleeding, she staggered into the room. It was a moment or two before she realized it was the throne room, and that it was filling up with people.

The wolves were herding them! She looked around and saw that there was a mix of men and women, servants and courtiers, indiscriminately thrown together. Everyone was cut and bruised, bleeding and messed up. Everyone was scared and exhausted.

Everyone except the woman seated on the throne. She was regal and well-dressed, with a cascade of dark hair framing an attractive face – a face that looked out at everyone with clear contempt.

There were other people gathered about her – all of them untouched by the attacks and quite clearly with her. There were also two wolves seated beside the throne. The woman – barely more than a teenager, she could see – had her hand on the head of one of the wolves, and was scratching it gently. There was a bird perched on the back of the throne behind her.

As Murine caught her breath, the room slowly filled with people, driven in by the wolves and other animals. Eventually the doors slammed shut behind them. Nobody in the room had spoken since they'd been driven here, and all Murine could hear were people breathing and gasping with their pains.

The woman on the throne glared out, and one of the people with her slammed the butt of a spear onto the platform the throne stood on – once, twice, three times.

Everyone turned to stare.

"I am the person you've been trying to kill," the woman said, clearly. "I am Melayne of Dragonhome."

Chapter 37

Melayne looked out at the frightened and battered people assembled in front of her. She wanted to feel sorry for them, but she steeled herself. These were the people who were ultimately responsible for everything that had happened to her and her friends.

It was time they paid for it.

"Is there someone here who will speak for you?" she asked. There were several men in uniform, and one of these was very ornate. "You," she said, gesturing. "Are you there one?"

The man realized he had been singled out. He tried to straighten himself up and look authoritative. "I am General Abrin, yes," he said. "I command the army of Farrowholme."

"Good – that means you're one of the people I want the most." She gestured. "Come forward." He stood up stiffly and managed to march across the room to stand before her. His dignity was somewhat damaged by the rips in his clothing and the blood on his face and hands. "You're the one who ordered the attack on Dragonhome?" She exerted her Talent, ensuring that what he replied would be the truth.

"I was ordered to do so," he said, and then clutched at his throat.

"Yes," she informed him. "You're speaking the truth – you have no choice in the matter. And it's the truth I'm after. Who gave you those orders?"

He struggled not to answer Sweat broke out on his face, and he started to twitch.

Poth leaned in and murmured: "You do know I could point them all out for you, don't you?"

"Yes," she whispered back. "But the rest of them need to see this." Louder, she said to the general: "Come now – *tell me!*"

He had no option. Twisting stiffly, he pointed to two men in the crowd. "Caramin and Nephir," he gasped. Then he collapsed to the floor.

"Caramin and Nephir," Melayne repeated. "If you would care to join me?" She gestured at the space beside the shaking soldier.

Both men tried putting a brave face onto it as they slowly walked forward. The one identified as Caramin called out: "You have no right –"

"Right?" she cried, rising to her feet. "Right? What *right* did you have to attack my home? What right did you have to murder Talents?"

"You're a traitor," Nephir said. "We have every right to punish traitors."

"Well, now you're going to pay for your attempts," she informed them coldly.

"You already murdered our king," Abrin said, glaring up at her. "I suppose you intend to execute us next?"

"I didn't even know your king was dead until a few days ago," Melayne snapped. "And his death was none of my doing."

"One of your Talent assassins murdered him!" Abrin growled.

"I don't have Talent assassins," Melayne snapped. "Who told you I did?" She glared at the other two men. "Let me guess – Caramin and Nephir?"

The soldier paused. "Yes," he admitted.

"Fine. Then let's ask *them*, shall we?"

"You have no right to ask me anything," Caramin snapped.

"Right, you just volunteered." Melayne focused her Talent on him. "Who really killed Aleksar? Tell me..."

She could see him struggling not to speak. He started to turn, to try to run. Beside her, Greyn growled and raised his hackles. If the courtier attempted to flee, the wolf would be on him in seconds. Caramin could see this, and abandoned that idea. He finally ground out: "Murine and Shera…"

Two women in the group gasped, and Melayne gestured at them. Sander walked from her side, the crowd slowly parting to allow him passage. He touched both women gently, and led them, reluctantly, toward the throne. The one named Murine stepped forward. She was covered in small bites, streaked with her own blood, but she still looked rather attractive.

"Yes, so we did it – but you should be *thanking* us."

"Really?"

"Yes – he hated you, and would have attacked you anyway," Murine said.

"And so you killed him just to protect me?" Melayne purred. "How considerate of you."

"He was going to kill us!" Shera burst out. "We killed him to protect ourselves."

"That's more like it," Melayne said. "I'm starting to believe you. And these two men lied about it for their own purposes, to work up popular sentiment against me."

There were low murmurings in the crowd about the room now. Clearly none of them had known the truth before. Abrin looked puzzled, and then annoyed.

"I didn't know any of this," he said slowly.

"Obviously not," Melayne agreed. "They were manipulating everyone with their version of reality."

"You can't do this to us," Nephir blustered. "You and your invading army will soon be stopped by our loyal soldiers."

Melayne laughed. "Invading army?" She gestured about her. Poth, Devra, Corri, Margone, Sander and Shara stood with her. "I don't *have* an invading army. We're it." Greyn gave a throaty growl, and she smiled and scratched his head. "With a few friends, of course. And your army isn't going to come to the rescue – they're far too occupied with all of the fleas and ants and wasps that are attacking them. How else could we have walked in past them?"

Nephir stared at her, uncomprehending. "Seven people? Seven people?"

"And a wolf pack and a falcon. Yes, that's all it's taken to bring you to this position. You're not as strong as you imagined."

Caramin looked out at the hall filled with courtiers and servants. "They can't possibly stop us all," he called out. "We can just rush them and –"

"And *die*," Shara said, flatly, angrily. "I'm a Death-Caster. Which of you wants to be the first to have the life sucked out of them?"

Nobody moved.

"Perhaps I should also mention that we have a number of dragons circling overhead," Melayne said cheerfully. "They're not too happy right now, and they'd probably enjoy any excuse to demolish this whole town."

After a silent pause, Abrin regained his feet. "What is it that you intend to do?" he asked.

"That's better," Melayne said. "Now we're starting to get somewhere. Well, the first thing I'm doing is stopping all attacks on Dragonhome and the Talents. That is non-negotiable. The war stops *now*." She glared out across the crowd. "I warned Jaska of what would happen if he didn't leave us alone, and it's time for me to make good on that promise. You will never harm the Talents again."

She looked at Nephir and Caramin. "These two men lied and schemed to obtain power and keep it. They led the attack on the Talents and they are going to pay for it. For the moment they will be thrown into jail until you can hold a trial for them."

"We? Don't you mean *you*?" Abrin asked.

"They didn't lie to and cheat me," Melayne said. "They should be punished by those they cheated and mistreated."

"I don't understand," Abrin said, slowly. "You've won

the war, it seems. You're now in command."

"I don't want to be in command!" Melayne snapped. "Don't you people understand? All I want – all I've ever wanted – is to be left to live my life in peace. I have two children I haven't seen for months, a home that's been partially demolished, a family that's been attacked, friends you've tried to murder... And for *what*? What has any of this gained any of you?" She stared around the room. "You decide amongst yourselves who you want in charge – I really don't care who you pick, as long as these four aren't it. But you had better understand one thing, and I will make this very clear to you." She stood up and glared at them all. "If *any* of you ever try to come after me or mine again, the next time I will not be so lenient. You may not all have wanted to murder Talents, but by allowing your rulers to do it, you're all guilty in my view. So the next time around choose wisely – or face the consequences.

"I could have destroyed this town. I could have killed every one of you. Instead of turning the rats and birds and insects against you, I could have had your dogs and cats and other pets do it for me. But I didn't want you to fear and hate your own animals, so I spared you that. And I still have dragons... Think about that for a moment."

There was a prolonged silence, and then Abrin stepped forward. "You aim to just leave here?"

"Gods, yes. I told you, I have family I want to get back to. But I want them to be safe. That's the reason for all of this."

Abrin nodded. "I understand. Will you allow me to take charge of the prisoners?"

Melayne studied him. "You seem to me like an honest man, general. I do believe I can trust you." She gestured at Nephir and Caramin. "They're all yours."

"You can't do this to us," Nephir protested. "We're powerful, influential men..."

"And it was all based of lies and manipulation," Melayne said. "It ends now."

"And what about this pair?" Devra asked, gesturing toward Murine and Shera.

"I'll take them as well," Abrin said. "They have a few things to answer for also."

"Wait!" Murine begged. "We can help you, Melayne – I studied you and your history. I know what you're up against. And we can be invaluable to you. We're both nobles, and have strong connections here in Farrowholme."

"I'm not interested," Melayne said, flatly.

"You have a brother and a step-son," Murine said, hastily. "If we arranged weddings between the pair of them and us –"

"You're *really* starting to annoy me," Melayne growled. "They're both *children* still. And I would never presume to tell either of them who they should marry. And if either of them *did* pick either of you, I'd disown them."

"You don't understand –" Shera wailed.

"I understand far too well," Melayne answered, coldly. "You're not getting your hooks into anyone else. Take them away, please, Abrin."

"With pleasure. I believe there's a cell that they're both already accustomed to..." Abrin signaled a handful of his soldiers, who came forward and took charge of the four dispirited prisoners. To Melayne's surprise, the general gave her a formal salute and led them all away.

"Now what?" Devra hissed.

Melayne looked around the room and shook her head sadly. "If you're the best that Farrowholme has to offer, then the gods have pity on us. Alright, go away now and decide amongst yourselves who you want to be in charge." When nobody made a move, Devra yelled: "GO!"

There was a sudden rush for the door. In moments Melayne and her friends were left alone in the throne room, and Melayne was able to allow herself to collapse. "I wouldn't want to do that again," she muttered.

"They're a bunch of mindless sheep," Devra said. "Do you really think they'll make a smart decision about their next king? I wouldn't trust any of them to clean up after a donkey."

"You don't trust anyone, period," Corri said, grinning. Then she clapped her hands together. "Melayne, that was brilliant! I never thought we could just walk right in and stop everything like that. Sometimes I forget how powerful you are."

"I'm not powerful," Melayne protested. "I'm just protecting those that I love." She sighed. "I *really* miss my children – I do so hope I can get back to them soon."

Sander laid his hand on her shoulder. "This *has* to be the end of it now," he said gently. "After this, I promise you, we'll fetch Cassary and the baby to be with us while we rebuild Dragonhome... again."

She laid her hand over his. "To be home," she said, sighing.

Poth started to giggle, and Devra gave her an affection look. Melayne was surprised and pleased by how much her friend seemed to be mellowing. She'd always been afraid that Devra would be alone all her life – more so after Corri and Margone had started their romance. Devra was a wonderful person, but she simply didn't have the ability to make friends – until now. Melayne had been caught completely by surprise, but it appeared that Devra and Poth were actually very good for one another.

"Are you peeking at what we'll be doing again tonight?" Devra asked the blonde girl.

Poth tried to stifle her grin. "Not this time. Though maybe I should..." Then she started giggling again.

"Let her laugh," Melayne said, amused. For some reason this remark made Poth giggle harder. "I know she's improving, but she's not healed yet."

"She will be," Devra vowed. "Even if I have to spank it out of her." That made Poth giggle longer.

Whatever it was, Melayne knew that Poth would explain herself in her own good time. She *was* improving, that much was true. Her craziness had been caused in the first place by her trying to live her life through manipulating events that she Saw thanks to her Talent, splitting her mind into fragments living only for future possibilities. Now, though, she had Devra, and was clearly in love. She no longer needed to try and find a future to make her happy, as she already had one.

And so, thankfully, did Devra.

For the first time in a long time, the future looked promising for all of them. All that mattered now was that the next person to be king should be somebody sensible, someone who wouldn't try to start another war, or oppress the Talents. Or oppress anyone, actually. Once these nobles announced their decision, she would talk to their choice and be absolutely certain that whoever he was, he could be trusted.

And then she could go home! She could see her children again, hold the baby – and think of a name for him! – and play with Cassary again... Gods, how much she missed them both!

She came out of her thoughts to see Shara was gazing sympathetically at her. Melayne gave the poor woman a smile. Here she was thinking about missing her family, and poor Shara had lost the only person she cared about in the world. She realized how lucky she was.

"You're quite amazing, Melayne," Shara said.

"Me?" Melayne gave a small laugh. "I'm just trying to protect those I love."

"Yes. So was Baraktha." There was a moment of pain on Shara's face. "But the two of you couldn't possibly have been more different. You do it without getting cynical, without corrupting your morals." Surprisingly, she actually laughed. "You even fought a war without killing or even badly damaging anyone. I never thought such a thing possible."

"To be honest, neither did I," Melayne admitted. "I was so afraid we'd have to kill people. And – what's worse – there were times when I *wanted* to kill people. When those I love were threatened..."

"But you never gave in to it," Shara said. "I admire you, and – if you'll allow it – I'd like to stay with you."

Melayne grabbed her hands. "Of course I'll allow it!" She stood up and hugged the other woman. "For selfish reasons – I need your help with those Talents that are on their way to join us."

Shara nodded. "It... helps to be able to feel useful again," she confessed.

Devra was prowling up and down. "Who do I have to beat up to get some food around here?" she growled. "I'm starving – I didn't get any breakfast."

Poth laughed again. "That's your own fault," she said. "If you hadn't –"

"And that's all anyone needs to hear about *that*," Devra warned her, blushing.

"I'll see if I can rustle up some food," Margone offered. "I'm rather hungry myself." He glanced at Corri. "I, too, skipped breakfast." Melayne had to admit she was feeling a trifle empty herself, and who knew how long their wait would be?

Devra glanced at Poth. "Is it safe for Margone to go off alone?"

"Oh yes," Poth said. "And the food looks to be quite delicious." She rubbed her hands together. "I have to build my strength up for tonight..."

Margone was gone for less than ten minutes. When he returned, he was grinning widely. "The head cook here's a very nice man," he announced. "Turns out he'd anticipated our being hungry and had set about organizing it. It'll be along shortly."

Melayne was surprised. "I'd have thought he'd have been angry with us for what we did."

Margone laughed. "I wondered about that. Turns out that he – and almost every other servant in the castle – loathed Nephir and Caramin. They're not the nicest of people, treated the servants like they were trash. Pretty much all of the serving staff in the castle are on our side. The cook thinks most of the nobles actually feel that way, too. Caramin, especially, they hate. Seems he's got a thing for little girls – the littler the better. But he was too powerful for anyone to stop him – before you came along. Now he's in jail, and I wouldn't like to be eating what the cooks are planning to feed him. There were lots of them suggesting a certain portion of his own anatomy..."

Devra gripped the hilt of her sword. "I'll be glad to help out," she offered.

Poth laid a calming hand on her shoulder. "There's no need for that, love," she murmured. "He's already dead."

"What?" Melayne sat bolt upright. "How did that happen? Why didn't you warn me?"

"Because you'd have stopped it," Poth said, calmly. "It turned out that one of the lords helping... escort him to the cells was one who had a young daughter that Caramin had victimized. He avenged her."

"Was that what you were giggling about?" Melayne was annoyed with the Seer.

"That? No." She started giggling again. "*That's* still to come."

"And what about the other prisoners?" Melayne asked her, anxiously. "Are they alright?"

Poth shrugged. "Depends on what you mean by *alright*. They're still alive, and will be for a while. Nephir *does* have a black eye and a broken wrist, but that's all. And Murine and Shera are in a cell together. They're going to start punching one another quite soon, but they deserve that."

Melayne would have argued with her further, but at that point the food arrived.

Margone was quite right – it was really rather splendid. There were meat pies, a huge roast, soup, cooked vegetables and cheese, fruits and enough wine to drown everyone. The cook – bowing and introducing himself as Romo – was beaming as his men brought it all in, along with a table and chairs for them.

"You really didn't have to do all of this," Melayne protested.

"We *wanted* to," Romo replied. "We never thought that people like Caramin and Nephir would ever pay for their crimes. Without you, they never would have. Lady Melayne, you have our sincere gratitude."

Devra grinned. "Maybe we should conquer a few more countries…"

Chapter 38

Melayne ate more than she had intended, feeling she'd be insulting the hard-working cooks if she didn't. Devra and Poth enjoyed themselves feeding each other little tidbits of food. Sander ate sparingly, an eye on the main doors all of the time.

"How long do you think we'll have to wait for their decision?" he asked her.

Melayne shrugged. "They're politicians – it could take them weeks to make up their minds."

"Weeks?" Sander scowled. "Do you propose to stay here that long?"

"No," she said. "We'll be out of here before sunset, don't worry. The less I see of this place, the happier I'll be. The only reason we've stayed this long is to give them some sense of urgency. We can always return when they finally make up their minds."

Poth had another attack of the giggles. Melayne was starting to think she was way too happy with Devra. Still, she couldn't deny that the Seer deserved a little happiness. She'd seen the scars her brother had inflicted on the blonde girl and knew she'd been through a lot of undeserved pain in her life. On the other hand, her constant giggling was getting a bit irritating. Not that Devra seemed bothered by it, of course. Oh well… love!

Melayne made sure that Greyn and his pack had their share of the fresh roast, and they settled in the corner to enjoy themselves.

To her surprise, not long after they'd finished eating and the cook's assistants had cleared away the ample leftovers, there was a hesitant knock at the main doors and a small party of men, led by Abrin, entered. It annoyed her somewhat when they all bowed low to her. Well, she *was* sitting on the throne, so she supposed she was asking for that.

"You've made a decision already?" she asked. "To be honest, I thought it would take longer."

Abrin shook his head. "There was only a... short discussion," he explained. "There weren't too many candidates to consider."

Melayne was surprised again – she'd expected any number of people to vie for the empty throne. Maybe there weren't as many greedy and egotistical men in this town as she'd expected.

"Well, as I said, I don't much care who you've selected, as long as he's a reasonable man and is willing to live in peace."

Poth almost fell on the floor, she was laughing so hard. Melayne threw her a glare that only made her laugh more. With a sigh, Melayne beckoned Devra over. "Do you know what's gotten into her?"

Devra's lips were twitching into a smile of their own. "Yes, I'm afraid I do. She told me over the meal. She's not very good with keeping secrets, as you've already noticed."

"Then maybe you'd be kind enough to let me in on the joke?"

Devra shook her head emphatically. "Not me – I'm not going to ruin the punchline."

"Fine," Melayne snapped. "Just try and keep her quiet, will you? Or take her out of the room."

"I couldn't do that," Devra said. "She'd never forgive me if she missed it." Her grin was threatening to spread.

This really was too much! "Do as you please," Melayne growled. "I'm sure you will anyway." She turned back to Abrin. "I'm sorry about that, general. It looks like I brought a jackass with me. Do you think you'll be able to continue?"

Now *his* mouth was twitching! He swallowed and then nodded. "I believe we can make it through this, yes."

"Good." Melayne was losing her patience. "Well, who did you decide would be your king?"

"We aren't having a new king," Abrin said, firmly.

"Oh?" Melayne was surprised again. "A ruling committee, then?"

"No committee as such, no."

"Gods!" Melayne snapped. "Can't *anybody* around here just give a straight answer to a simple question? Abrin, *who* did you chose as your new ruler?"

"You."

Melayne stared at him. He smiled back. The courtiers with him did the same. This time Poth actually *did* fall on the floor laughing.

"You should see your face," Devra said, unable to contain her own merriment.

There was nothing funny about this. Melayne glowered at Abrin. "Didn't you hear what I said earlier?" she demanded. "I *told* you I didn't come here to conquer anyone. I don't want to rule anyone."

"Which was one of the main reasons we chose you," the general replied firmly. "Precisely because you didn't want it."

Melayne couldn't get her head around this. "That makes no sense."

"On the contrary," he insisted. "It's perfectly sensible. The problem we've had in the past is that the worst sort of people wanted to rule – people that in any sane world wouldn't be given the authority to run a bathhouse, let alone a country. They were driven by their ambitions and their greed. *Your* ambition is to live a peaceful, friendly life and to care for your family." He spread his arms wide. "That's what we all want. That's why we chose you."

"I don't want to do it. Chose somebody else."

"No." Abrin crossed his arms. "You *did* tell us to pick anyone we wanted, and that's what we did. You made the rules, not us, and now you'd better live with the consequences of it."

"But I didn't mean you to pick *me!*" she yelled. "I'm not a noble, except by marriage. I'm a farm girl."

"You *were* a farm girl," Abrin said. "Now you're Lady of Dragonhome. And tomorrow, you'll be Queen of all Farrowholme."

Melayne looked at her friends for help. "Sander, please, tell them they're making a dreadful mistake."

Traitor that he was, he simply shrugged. "I can't; I think it's an inspired choice." He smiled at Abrin. "So, does that mean I become a Prince or something?"

"Stop that!" Melayne ordered him, annoyed he wasn't on her side. "Devra, you tell..." And then she realized. "You *knew!*"

Devra grinned. "I told you I wasn't going to ruin the punchline. This is *way* too funny."

"You should see your face," Poth added, having been helped back onto her feet. "I've been seeing it all morning – it's just *too* funny."

"Oh, you're no help!" She turned to her other friends. "Corri, Margone – surely you –" Both shook their heads, looking insufferably pleased. The only one left now was Shara. "Shara, you can see I don't want this, can't you?"

She snorted. "I think we can all see that. Melayne, I've not known you long – just a few days – but I've come to see that there is something very special about you. Somehow, you seem to be the only person blind to it. You have morals that you live by, and dreams you dare to fight for. I had years of living with someone who was cynical and bitter, convinced that the human race is rotten to the core. That's exhausting. But you – you see goodness and kindness, and you inspire people. Look around you!

"There's Margone! He trained as a dragonslayer – now, thanks to you, he has a dragon he cares for. You helped change his life. There's Sander – lost and withdrawn when you found him, and now happy and loved again, all because of you. Devra, Corri, Poth... You've helped them all, accepted them all, loved them all. And – me. I should have been your enemy – anyone else would have killed me the second they had a chance, because I'm a Death-Caster. Instead, you helped me, and took me in.

"Melayne, if they had chosen anyone *but* you, I'd have said they were insane."

Melayne slumped down in the throne. "Isn't there *anybody* who agrees with me?" she pleaded. "Trust me, I'd make a terrible ruler."

"It's because we *do* trust you that we know that's simply not true," Corri said.

Devra stepped forward. "Melayne, you know me – I've never been one to ever shy away from telling you what I think, and I'm certainly not going to start now. What you just said is utter crap. You're the best qualified person I know to be Queen." She drew her sword and went down on one knee. "And I'm going to be the first person to pledge my undying allegiance to you. I vow to serve Queen Melayne to my dying breath."

To her horror, Melayne saw her husband and her friends – and the nobles of Farrowholme, and Abrin – all follow Devra's lead.

This was insane… She couldn't be Queen Melayne; she wasn't even very good at being Lady Melayne…

She glanced down and saw that even Greyn was laughing. The wolf flashed his teeth. "Better straighten up in that throne," he advised her. "You're going to have to get used to it…"

THE BEGINNING

Also in this series from Dragonhome Books:

The Secret of Dragonhome (ISBN # 9780692259504)

Melayne's parents have just been murdered by Sea Raiders, and she and her brother must flee for their lives. But they are Talents, feared by normal humans, so where can they go?

The Slayers of Dragonhome (ISBN # 9780615567082)

Melayne is still in trouble – lots of it. Her brother wants her dead. Sea Raiders are trying to kill her. Her dragons are growing up and want mates. Her husband is missing. And then the dragon slayers arrive in force...

Also by John Peel from Dragonhome Books:

Diadem: Book of Time & Book of Games (ISBN # 9780615726007)

Books 11 and 12 in the series! Shanara decides to reveal her history to Score, Helaine, Pixel and Jenna in her own unique way – by creating a realistic illusion from her memories. But a powerful sorcerer hijacks her spell and transports the five of them back into the real past instead, forcing them to live her troubled story. And if they change anything – anything at all – they might wipe out the future... including themselves...

Outwand (ISBN # 9780615767376)

Andrea Ballard's brother was crippled by a drunk driver, but now, somehow, he is walking again. And strange things have started to stir in the night – creatures that haven't been seen in England for thousands of years... Reality is starting to break down and the end of the world is approaching...

Made in the USA
Middletown, DE
18 February 2018